ONE-TRICK PONY

ONE-TRICK PONY

STAN TRYBULSKI

To order additional copies of this book, contact:
Xlibris Corporation
1-888-795-4274
www.Xlibris.com
Orders@Xlibris.com
61155

The wicked flee when no man pursueth: but the righteous are bold as a lion—Proverbs 28:1

1.

Judge Cynthia Milligan's New York City office was on the southern tip of Manhattan and surveyed the harbor as from the command deck of an aircraft carrier.

It was actually a suite of offices, with rich wood paneling, plush carpeting and leather upholstered furniture that looked expensive and probably was. More like the boardroom of someone rich and powerful. Which she definitely was. I had written her a few days ago at her chambers in the federal courthouse, asking if I could use her as a job reference; she had once been my boss at the Brooklyn district attorney's office. I had received a call back from one of her law clerks, asking if I could meet the judge at the offices of the Milligan Foundation. The offices were on one of the upper floors, a discreet distance from the legal and corporate hoi polloi that occupied some of the less sumptuous space on the lower floors. There was parking underneath the building but I didn't need it; I kept my Boxster parked in the little lot on Chambers Street and walked the eighteen blocks downtown from The Hatchery. That was what we called the shabby, cramped warren of cubicles the City has seen fit to give its attorneys that work for the Department of Education.

When I emerged from the elevator I flipped my ID to a deeply tanned blonde woman seated on the opposite side of a solid glass wall. She looked at the appointment book on her desk, nodded and buzzed me in. She had me sign the log book and asked me to please have a seat; the judge would be with me shortly.

I had dressed my best for the occasion, wearing my one suit from Paul Stuart, a 200-weight summer wool, light gray, white shirt, navy silk tie and cordovan dress shoes that cost me a couple of days pay. If she was going to recommend me to a white shoe law firm that would be dispensing big bucks, I figured I better dress the part.

As I waited I could hear the muffled tapping of a computer keyboard from somewhere behind the paneled walls. A gremlin hard at work. Milligan had been a no-nonsense district attorney, driving her trial assistants like a straw boss. I didn't expect that she was any different as a federal judge, or in whatever capacity she maintained at the foundation set up by her late husband to do good for the world.

I looked at the magazines on the coffee table in front of me: Time, Newsweek, Sports Illustrated, American Lawyer. The usual suspects. No Daily Racing Form. I was about to reach for the Time when a door in the paneled wall opened and another woman emerged. Tall and slender, with olive skin and dark brown eyes, she was dressed in a silk navy blue business blazer and matching skirt. I looked at her shoes. Black pumps built for comfort and style.

"Mr. Doherty?" It wasn't a question.

I stood up.

"I'm Ms Durning, the judge's assistant. Please come with me." She led me back through the door and down a hall to a sitting area with a wall of windows that overlooked Battery Park, the harbor and the Statue of Liberty.

"Please have a seat," she said. "The judge is on a conference call and it'll be a few minutes more. May I prepare you a fresh-brewed cup of coffee? Tea?"

"Water would be fine," I said.

She left and I walked over to the window and looked out. It was a magnificent late spring day; even through the tint in the glass, I could see the sunlight sparkling far below on the tiny harbor waves.

Ms Durning returned with a bottle of Evian and a glass, opened it and poured the contents for me. I thanked her and sipped it while she went out again. In a few moments she returned.

"The judge will see you now," she said.

I followed her along another lushly carpeted corridor until we reached what I knew was the southeast corner of the building. She opened a door and ushered me into Judge Milligan's office. The inner sanctum. Richly appointed with works of art on the walls. I spotted a Derain and a Braque. And all the little doodads scattered around, mementos of a life of collecting by her late, super-rich husband. Behind a desk that was twice the size of my office cubicle, the judge was bent over her computer, typing quickly.

I said, "Judge Milligan?"

She looked up, her gaze resting on my face. "Doherty," she said. "I'm so glad you came; I need to talk to you." She stayed seated; didn't rise; didn't offer her hand. She gestured toward the chair in front of her desk and I sat in it. Other than the laptop computer on her desk and the gold-plated pen pressed between her left thumb and index finger, there was no other sign that I was in an office. No books, no files, only the magnificent vista out over the water.

And it was dead quiet here, not even the sound of her minions plugging away.

Milligan was in her mid-fifties, looked forty, still wearing a full head of the flaming red hair that had been her political trademark for more than a generation. She sat there saying nothing, motionless but for the tapping of her pen on the desk.

A bland look was on her face, devoid of expression, emotion. It was a mask I knew all too well and I focused my attention on her eyes. Jade green orbs that were always full of fire, with life; that twinkled when happy, and sparkled when ready to pounce.

I sat there matching her silence with my own. She kept tapping the pen. The sun filtered through the tinted glass.

"How have you been, Doherty?" she finally said.

"Fine, Your Honor," I said.

"Fine?" She pulled open a desk drawer and took out a piece of paper. My letter to her. "So I guess you really don't need a reference from me?"

"Well, I could be better," I said.

"The Board of Education certainly wasn't a step up from the D.A.'s Office."

"It's the Department of Education now," I said.

"A name change; political window-dressing," she laughed. "You can put perfume on a pig but it's still a pig." I laughed with her.

"I understand that besides the law, you have other interests now."

"Your Honor?"

"Don't be coy with me, Doherty, I don't have time to waste. You think I haven't heard how you solved the Ides of June murders?"

"That was Inspector Parella," I said, "along with the FBI."

"After you handed them the case. And I know just how you did it. You and your partner, Jackson."

She was talking about Hank, aka Henry Lowrie Jackson, a Lumbee Indian from North Carolina who, lucky for me, had my back during a few rough situations.

"He's not my partner, he's my friend," I said.

"Well, Doherty, you've picked up some very useful friends along the way."

I nodded, not saying anything further.

"I'm sure you felt a sense of accomplishment that has been missing for some time from your legal work, if, in fact, it was ever there." She was needling me.

"I helped a woman find the killer of her twin sister, that's all," I said.

"And I understand you met some pretty tough customers along the way."

"That I did."

"Think you could handle another bunch?"

"Why would I?"

"I could give you two hundred and fifty thousand reasons."

I was still watching her eyes. No twinkle of humor when she threw that out.

"That's a lot of reasons, I must admit."

"Are you interested?"

"Very."

Milligan reached over to an antique credenza behind her, picked up a framed photograph and set it on the desk between us. It was a portrait of a girl, late teens or very early twenties. Fresh, beautiful with striking shoulder length red hair and a familiar face.

"Your daughter?"

"Yes. And she's in big trouble." Milligan picked the photo up and looked at it. I waited, saying nothing.

"She's an undergraduate at Columbia. Doing her junior year abroad in Paris. About two weeks ago I was speaking to her over the phone. She was using a fancy cellular with international calling that I had bought her. It was mid-morning here, I remember this so clearly, and I had come off the bench so I could talk to her. She was living in Montparnasse, around the corner from Reid Hall, the university's Paris facility. She was on her way to meet some friends. 'At The Select,' she said. Suddenly I heard a scream. Then the phone went dead. That was the last time I heard Vanessa's voice."

She rubbed her face and looked up at me. "Imagine Doherty, the last time I heard her speak, it was to hear her scream."

I said nothing; I didn't know what to say. Just nodded; seeing a glint appear in her eyes. She handed me the photograph.

"Look at her, Doherty. My precious jewel. Missing. No one has seen or heard of her since."

Her voice was quavering with emotion, matching her eyes. The rest of her face was still outwardly calm.

"Did the university contact the Paris police?"

"Yes." Her voice was firm again.

"And you, for some reason, contacted me."

She nodded slowly. The fire in her eyes was burning brighter now. "I want her found."

I rubbed my chin. "You know there's a good chance—"

She cut me off. "Vanessa didn't run away, Doherty." Milligan reached over to the credenza behind her, unlocked the bottom drawer and took out a Redwel legal file folder. She turned back to me and opened it. "There were witnesses," she said.

"To what?"

"My daughter's kidnapping."

Her voice was still firm but her eyes were watering.

"The Paris police have investigated?"

She nodded somberly.

"And they know who the kidnappers are?"

"Not individually, not by name."

"What then?"

"The *Direction du Surveillance Territoire*, the DST, the French internal security agency believes it's a group called the Mistral Jihad."

"Why would they kidnap Vanessa?"

"It's not well known but it's no secret that the President is considering nominating me to the Supreme Court. His foreign policy is in shambles and he has no domestic agenda left, except to fill an expected vacancy. And his handlers believe the best way to sail the nomination through the Senate is to push a law and order candidate from the other party; and a woman to boot."

"Blackmail then? Vanessa's being held as a hostage?"

"I don't know," Milligan said. "I have to be a realist. She may already be dead."

"Then what do you want me to do? Aren't the French and the FBI and the CIA your best bets?"

I watched as the flicker in her eyes burst into dazzling green fire.

"I want my daughter back, Doherty. Alive, if possible, but I want her back." She handed me the Redwel folder. "Inside are the Paris police reports and enhanced computer renderings of sketches of the suspects who did the actual abduction. Two of them, although the DST says there are a dozen members of the Mistral Jihad; nine men and three women. All their computer images are inside as well."

I took the folder. "There has been nothing in the papers about this."

"That's right," she said. "Not even in France. Only a few people know. But that won't last. What's the chance of keeping something secret for long in Washington or Paris?"

I nodded again. She was right. Once it hit the newspapers all hell would break loose.

"Still, aren't the French best equipped to handle this?"

"Yes, but their methods, while sound, sometimes go beyond the bright lines we have drawn for ourselves in solving crimes. And if it was learned that a sitting federal appeals court judge, a Supreme Court nominee no less, acquiesced in the use of those methods to save her daughter, you can imagine where that nomination will go."

"So you want me to find her, then, and you don't care what methods I use?"

"Not really. Just don't get caught."

"She could be dead," I said.

"Then I want you to hunt the group down and bring them to justice."

"Exactly what do you mean by justice?" My voice was calm but my radar was humming.

"Justice?" Her voice snapped. "For two hundred and fifty thousand dollars and a new career, I expect you to supply the definition."

"You want them alive?"

"I'm not picky, Doherty."

"I'm not a killer," I said. "At least not a killer for hire."

"Use your partner, Jackson, then."

"He's no killer, either." I said this last bit with a straight face, even though both of us knew better. Uncle Sam had swooped down and taken my good buddy under his wing, tenderly and lovingly nurturing Hank over the years into a stone cold field operative, armed with a set of skills few have but many appreciate—from afar.

She stopped tapping the pen and looked at me.

"Where do you want me to start?" I said.

"Paris, where else? That's where she disappeared. That's where they attacked us."

Attacked? She was right. The abduction of a federal judge's child by terrorists had to be considered an attack on the nation.

"Okay, I'm in."

Milligan reached into her desk drawer and handed me a small unsealed white envelope. "I was sure you'd be interested," she said. "Go ahead, open it."

Inside was a check for fifty thousand dollars drawn on a Milligan Foundation account. "When you leave, go down to the 27th floor and see my comptroller, Carlton Andrews. He'll make arrangements for any expense funds that you may need."

"It's going to be costly," I said.

"I'm not a poor widow, Doherty. When will you be ready to leave?"

"I'll have to check my case calendar and clear it with my boss Connie Lacierga."

"Lacierga? Don't worry about her. I carry some weight with the mayor."

And the mayor carries a lot of weight with the schools chancellor. She didn't have to add that.

"You must have a lot of confidence in me," I said.

"I believe you can get the job done."

"There was a time you didn't."

Milligan stared straight at me. "You're a good trial lawyer, Doherty. A tough prosecutor. You never ducked a case, you were always ready for trial. But that's as far as it went."

"You mean there's supposed to be more?"

"Hell yes, and you know it. The D.A.'s a political office; we're a political organization. We have to answer to the people in the end. But you didn't want to answer to anybody. Just try cases. A one-trick pony, that's what you are."

"So why pick me, then?"

"Because for this job, those are the qualities I need. You're tough enough to see this through. You won't run, you won't hide. The cops and the FBI respect you. And so do I."

"You're going to make me cry, Your Honor."

"Not on my dime," she said.

"Okay, money talks; bullshit walks." I stuffed the little envelope in my suit jacket pocket. "I'll find your daughter for you. And I'll find those responsible for her abduction."

"That money would make a nice nest egg for you and Dana McPherson," Milligan said.

She knew about Dana and me?

"I keep tabs on my people," Milligan said. "Dana was one of the few that could have really shone in the D.A.'s office. Talented and she knows how to play the political game."

"I'll be sure to tell her."

Milligan stood up and walked over to me. "You asked if you could use me as a reference." She put her hands on mine. "Doherty, do this for me and don't worry about references. I'll get you a job in any top law firm you want. Partnership track."

I rode the elevator down to the Foundation comptroller's office in silence. Cynthia Milligan's world was clean, almost sterile really; high above the bloody arenas and filthy trenches where the legal warriors fought, clashed. Hers was a world of paper and politics. Full of murmured thoughts and weighty decisions, and then the smooth, syrupy cocktail chit-chat.

Not my world. Never would be. Never could be.

2.

The elevator foyer outside Carlton Andrew's office was the same as Judge Milligan's, five stories above. Plush, with the same solid wall of glass between the foyer and the reception area. I started to hold my photo ID up to the window when the receptionist buzzed me in. She was attired in a brown suede jacket with epaulets over a sheer white silk blouse and chocolate cotton slacks, which ran down long legs and ended at a pair of white pumps with bows. On a table behind her was a large blue leather handbag. All ready to do lunch. As she escorted me back past some cubicles with empty desks, I admired the long, blonde hair cascading around a pair of tinted aviator's glasses. I admired even more the way the chocolate slacks hugged her curves as she walked beside me. I felt like telling her that this old dog could teach her some new tricks. But I kept my mouth shut.

Andrews was facing away from me, busy typing into a computer, tracking numbers on a wide-screen display. When he heard the door open, he turned and got up and came around to shake my hand. Andrews was tall and sinewy with a deep tan, the kind that comes with a series of three-day weekends on a boat. He was dressed in summer poplin with a pinkish bowtie. A real Jivey-Leaguer or maybe Oxbridge.

"My pleasure, Mr. Doherty. Good to see you. Please sit down. Judge Milligan just called to say you were on your way."

That's why the receptionist didn't bother looking at my ID. Milligan certainly wasn't wasting anytime. Mine or hers.

Andrews' hand gripped mine tightly, a surprisingly firm grasp that showed off a gold Rolex when his wrist was extended. His office was more fully furnished than Milligan's, with a club chair and Chesterfield couch, both done in burgundy leather, for visitors. I plopped myself on the couch, taking the end where I could see the Statue of Liberty and Newark Airport out the window. He walked back to his computer and punched the program off. A seascape popped up on the screen.

"My office is on Chambers Street," I said. "I can see the Italian restaurant on Reade Street from my window."

"Do you find it to your liking?"

"What do you think?"

In the distance a plane was lifting off from the airport; its upward trajectory taking it behind the Statue of Liberty.

Andrews looked at me, a thin smile playing on his lips. "I think you think you deserve better."

"Don't we all?"

He laughed. "Can I get you something to drink?"

"It's a little early in the day," I said, inserting a dubious tone into my voice.

"Never too early for a good sherry. I have a nice oloroso; a fine drink to sip and swallow." He pointed to the coffee table where a silver-plated tray held a bottle and some glasses.

I really wanted a Sam Adams or a couple of McSorley's ales but I didn't want to go back to the office with beer breath. At least not before lunch.

Andrews poured the deep brown liquid into two glasses and brought one to me, then took the other one and went back to his desk.

"You know why I'm here then, I take it."

"Of course. And I and the Foundation are rooting for you. When are you starting?"

"I already have."

Andrews smiled. A beautiful capped set of teeth. "Judge Milligan rather thought so."

He pressed a buzzer on the phone bank. "Jacqueline, have you made the airline reservation?"

A few seconds later, the door opened and the receptionist-society matron came in. She was carrying computer printouts which she handed to Andrews.

"Thank you," he said.

We both gave her a smile as she left. She returned mine.

Andrews scanned the papers Jacqueline had handed him. "E-tickets and your hotel reservation. You're leaving tonight on Air France flight 007 from JFK at 7:25. And you'll be staying at the Hotel Lutetia on the Left Bank, not too far from Reid Hall and the Foundation offices."

"Foundation offices?"

"Why, yes. We have an active office in Paris. We do a lot of work with the North African and sub-Saharan youth. God knows, the French don't."

He raised his sherry glass to his lips and sipped some of the liquid. I still left my glass on the table top.

"Tell me a little bit about the Foundation," I said.

"Mr. Milligan made his money—lots of it—trading global commodities. Copper, rubber, petroleum, that sort of thing. Even bought and sold water rights. He truly believed in a global economy and wanted to give back to the rest of the world some—no, much of his wealth."

Andrews sipped some more of his sherry. I still left my glass untouched.

"When Mr. Milligan died, Judge Milligan stepped right in and took over the Foundation's helm."

"No conflict of interest?"

Andrews raised his palms upward. "Heavens, no. The Judge only comes here on lunch hours a couple of times a week and in the evenings when she's finished with her court work."

"I mean no conflicts with any disbursements the Foundation makes?"

Andrews smiled his toothy smile again. "Not at all. Our work is concentrated overseas."

"Charity begins abroad, huh?"

Some of the toothy smile faded. "Mr. Milligan believed—and so does the Judge—that a stable America needs a stable world."

I couldn't disagree.

Andrews sipped some more of his sherry. The gold Rolex on his left wrist gleamed with the movement of his arm as he raised the glass to his lips, and then lowered it. The watch rested just outside the edge of the French cuff of a beautifully tailored silk shirt.

"I imagine she took his death hard."

"It was tragic. Totally unexpected. He went down in the prime of his life. Heart attack. So suddenly like that; no one knew it was coming. But she kept herself together, as much for Vanessa's sake as hers. She's real tough, you know."

I nodded with a smile. "Oh, yes I do. Cynthia and I go way back."

"Really?" Andrews raised his eyebrows, not quite sure whether to believe me.

"Really. We used to trade tequila shots in O'Keefe's every Friday night."

He laughed. A faint, unsure laugh. I kept the smile on my face.

"You're joking, of course," he finally said.

"Ask her," I said. Knowing he wouldn't dare.

I stopped smiling. "Tell me a little about Vanessa," I said.

"Headstrong. Like her mother. A hard worker, though. Dean's list every semester at Columbia. Pre-law, doing a double major in poly sci and French."

"Any boyfriends?"

"Not that I know of. Not that I would know. But it is Columbia, in the heart of New York City." He gestured towards my glass. "You don't care for sherry?"

I picked up the glass and held it to the light and twirled it. "Oloroso, you say?"

"Some of the best."

I downed the sherry in one swallow. "You're right," I said.

Andrews grimaced. "I assume your passport is in order."

"I'll have to go home and get it."

"You won't have much time."

"No. I guess not." I stood up to leave.

Andrews handed me the e-ticket and hotel reservation. "Someone from the Foundation's Paris office will be there to meet you at Charles de Gaulle Airport tomorrow morning. A Ms Avril."

He sat back down again. "Oh, there's one other matter." He opened his desk drawer and took out a white envelope and handed it to me.

"Your bank card. For expenses. And the Judge expects you to use it."

"I always try to live up to her expectations," I said.

Andrews scribbled the bank code on his business card and gave it to me.

I opened up the envelope and put the bank card in my wallet. *Crédit Foncier de Paris*, it read. I silently read off the numbers on the business card Andrews had given me, and then I ripped it up and tossed the shreds in the waste basket.

"I just want you to know," I told him, "I report all my income."

"We would expect nothing else," Andrews said. His eyes told me he thought otherwise.

He walked me to the door. "Do you know Paris, Mr. Doherty?"

"Not as well as I'd like to."

"I could recommend some first-rate restaurants."

"I don't think I'll have the time this trip."

"Well, happy hunting," he said, offering his hand.

I shook it, ready this time for his firm grip.

3.

One p.m. The office was deserted, everyone out for the usual long lunch, but I wasn't taking any chances. So I walked back to one of the small conference rooms to call Dana.

She was home, at my, now our, place in Connecticut, having finally decided to move in with me and play house. Dana was still plugging away as a Regional Counsel for the Department of Ed. This was a heavy time in her region and she was taking a few days off to remind the pedagogical panjandrums how much they needed her.

She fussed but grudgingly agreed to take the train into Manhattan, bringing my carryon suitcase and my passport.

"What about the CZ?" she said. Meaning the little Czech automatic I kept stashed in a secret compartment next to the cellar stairs.

"No can do. Not even stripped down, packed and red-tagged for the airline. Not after 9-11."

Besides, it was almost impossible to bring a handgun into France. At least that's what the French Embassy told me when I called. When they asked for my name, I hung up. This was going to be a problem.

After I finished on the phone with Dana, I called Andrews. Before I ripped his business card up, I had memorized his office number. The private number.

"I'm going to need help acquiring a handgun in Paris."

"You know illegal weapons possession is a very serious crime in France."

"So's getting shot in the head."

He laughed. "I like your sense of humor, Doherty. It so happens that Mr. Milligan maintained a hunting lodge in the Loire Valley. The Judge hasn't been there since her husband died, but I expect that there might be something around in good working order."

"Have them bring it to me at the Lutetia. Not at the airport." I didn't want any of the bomb-sniffing dogs nosing out the ammunition.

"Oh, and a lot of cartridges," I added.

"Will do," Andrews said. "Is that all?"

"Yes, for now, but if I think of anything else, I'll call you."

"Cheerio, then." He sounded slightly peeved.

"Later."

I went back to my desk. The Hatchery was still empty. Files from the desk next to me were spilling over onto mine. Some of them actually had dust on them. Fat Andy, the attorney who was supposed to work there, had been missing in action for a few days and who knew when he'd show up again. I shoved the files back onto the slob's desk and walked over to the window. I looked out at the court buildings on Foley Square. The sun was shining in a blue sky. The park benches in the middle of the square were full of state and federal office workers dining al fresco; a harried attorney or two not wanting to go back to their desks; a motley assortment of miscreants who either had finished with their court appearances or were waiting for the afternoon sessions. A hot dog vendor was doing a brisk business. His shiny metal wagon was parked illegally on Worth Street next to the state office building. No one was giving him a ticket. Maybe if I stayed with the City long enough, I'd earn as much as he does.

I called the house again. No answer. Dana had already packed my bag and left. I shut down my computer and went to the bank and deposited the check Judge Milligan had given me. Now my balance was $50, 684. I tried the bank card for the *Crédit Foncier de Paris* and it spit out five hundred dollars after informing me there would be a buck-fifty charge for the transaction. I put the cash and the receipt in my wallet and walked back to the parking lot to get my Porsche. I didn't bother trying to exchange the dollars into Euros; I would just use the card in Paris to get any money I needed.

I reached the Columbia campus just before one-forty-five, parked on Amsterdam Avenue just outside the main quadrangle and walked over to the dean's office in Hamilton Hall.

I told the secretary up front that I needed to speak to the dean about a student, Vanessa Milligan. She recognized the name off the bat and excused herself and went into a back office. She returned in a moment and asked me to come in; to see Associate Dean Johnson.

Johnson had a tanned and ruddy face, worn by winter and spring sailing in the Caribbean. He kept a comfy office overlooking one of the shaded leafy walks and after I gave him my business card, I eased myself into one of the chairs in front of his desk. While he looked at the card, I looked at the co-eds passing by. Yes, this time of year in New York was pleasant.

"What interest does the Department of Education have in Vanessa Milligan?" Johnson's voice brought my attention back.

"Well, Dean Johnson, I'm actually assisting Judge Milligan, looking into the abduction of her daughter."

Johnson held up his palms. "If it was an abduction," he said.

"Look, I'm not interested in the university's p.r. campaign. If you want to put a positive spin on this, I don't care. But I've read the French police reports, so don't stroke me. Or Judge Milligan."

I had pulled rank big time and Johnson knew it. The yachting tan on his face faded.

"Don't get me wrong," he said. "We regard this as a serious matter. Any missing student is of great concern."

"Good. Then maybe you could give me some background on her."

Johnson asked me to wait a minute and excused himself. When he came back, he was carrying a file folder and there was a young woman with him.

"This is Assistant Dean Vera Racanelli," he said.

I stood and shook hands with her. "Pleasure."

Johnson sat back down at his desk and Racanelli took a chair next to me.

"Dean Racanelli knew Vanessa," he said, opening up the file folder.

I turned to her. "What can you tell me about Ms Milligan?"

Racanelli spun out a mini-dossier of the girl: Vanessa was a serious student but with a good sense of humor. Well-liked by her peers. Dean's List; shoo-in for honors when she graduates. Plans to apply to top law schools. Her acceptance is taken for granted.

"Any boyfriends?"

"That really wouldn't be any of our concern," Racanelli said.

"Nothing untoward, then, in her social life?" I said.

"We try to advise our students, Mr. Doherty. We're not den mothers; they're adults after all." Her tone was a little offish. Johnson threw her a warning look but it didn't seem to faze her.

"But if she had problems, you'd know about it?"

"If she had problems, she wouldn't be making Dean's List every semester," Racanelli said.

Johnson slid the file folder over to me. Inside, on top, was Vanessa Milligan's transcript. For five semesters. All Dean's List grades; each cumulative average being higher than the last.

"She found her groove in academia," Racanelli continued. "Many of our students do, though. But Vanessa was special." She suddenly looked down. "I'm sorry, *is* special."

"How so?"

"She liked to have a good time, hang out on weekends, go to jazz clubs, do different things. But she was very focused; hit the books Sunday through Thursday; maybe even Saturday afternoons.

"I understand she was a political science major."

"Many of our pre-laws are; actually too many. Sometimes I wish they would choose other majors," Johnson said.

"Didn't she also major in French?"

"Yes, as I mentioned, she was special," Racanelli said. "Is there anything else?"

"Her housing in Paris. Was that arranged through Columbia or on her own?"

"Reid Hall, that's our Paris adjunct, has a list of possible rooms but makes no recommendations. It's up to the student," Racanelli said.

"Her Paris address is in the folder," Johnson said.

12, rue Lucien Robert, wherever that was. I wrote it down and thanked them. On the way back to the car, my cell phone buzzed. It was Dana and she was at Grand Central Station.

At two-thirty, I pulled up on Vanderbilt Avenue outside Grand Central. Dana came out of the shadows, pulling my carry-on on its rollers. She looked terrific. She was wearing a deep red jeans jacket over a white cotton turtle neck and khaki slacks. As she walked toward the car, I watched how the khakis hugged her womanly hips. When she reached the Boxster, I opened the door for her.

"I hope you appreciate me," she said as she crammed my carry-on behind the seat.

"Did Tarzan appreciate Jane?"

She smiled at me as she sat down. "You're no Tarzan. And Paris is no jungle."

"That's because you don't have to fight off all the haute-couturiers and the perfumers."

She reached over and gave me a kiss.

"Why the short notice?"

I started the engine and pulled away from the curb. As I drove, I explained about my meeting with Judge Milligan and Vanessa Milligan's supposed abduction.

"And I have to stay up there in the wilderness all by myself?"

"You won't be alone."

"Yeah, right. The cats will be there."

I had three cats: Momma Sweet, Diva and the Little Guy, the youngest who had been named by Dana. She had once hated cats, now she likes them. Well, at least tolerates them to the point of peaceful coexistence in our country abode.

"They're good company and they'll protect you," I said.

She didn't say anything more on the subject.

"What time's your flight?" she said when I stopped for the light on Third Avenue.

"7:45, JFK. Have to be there by five for the security check, though."

"That only gives us a couple of hours," she said.

"For what?"

She reached over and kissed me again, her hand resting on my thigh. This time the kiss was longer and deeper, and when our lips parted she had a wicked grin on her face. "For our goodbyes."

4.

The goodbyes had a few hellos and a couple of see you soons. We had this conversation before, Dana and I, lots of times, but there always seemed to be some new vocabulary added. And hey, both of us loved to talk.

Later, I held her next to me in the coolness of the room, my hand on her cheek, my lips on her shoulder. We were both sated now, and we rested, trying to prolong the moment. I tasted the sweat on her shoulder and licked it, causing her to murmur.

"You won't have to work out tonight," I said.

"Maybe I'll double up my routine."

"Anyone I know?"

She slapped my arm. "Stop. You know what I mean. This was good but an all-over work out is key."

"You mean I missed some parts?"

She nuzzled up against me. "I take it back," she said.

"Take what back?"

"What I said earlier."

"I don't get you."

"Me Jane, you Tarzan."

I pulled her on top of me and let out a bellow.

Thirty minutes later, we were in the Boxster heading for Kennedy Airport. I was driving downtown to the Brooklyn Bridge and Atlantic Avenue, looking to avoid the rush hour melee on the BQE and the LIE. The traffic was still heavy here, making the going too slow, so I zipped around a yellow cab and beat a light turning red.

"Nice driving for an officer of the court," Dana said.

"Hey, I know a judge," I said.

I expanded on my conversation with our former boss. "Maybe going to the Supreme Court."

"Who? Double-shot Cynthia?"

"That was many moons ago," I said. "She's a respected federal judge now, with a billion dollars behind her."

"I guess I have to give the girl a hand."

"You know what she said about me?"

"As long as she didn't call you Tarzan."

I looked at Dana. She was the same youthful woman as the one I met fifteen years ago at the D.A.'s office, when Cynthia Milligan had hired us right out of law school. Smooth skin, hardly any makeup except for her lipstick, most of which she had left all over me in the hotel room.

"Hey, I have only one Jane. And she ain't plain."

"So what did she say?"

"That I was a good trial lawyer. One of the best she had; a real bulldog."

"So why didn't she promote you back then?"

"She said I didn't know how to play the political game; schmooze the unions and the community leaders." I shifted away from the red light. "She called me a one-trick pony. All I could do is try cases."

Dana put her hand on my thigh. "She's wrong, Doherty."

"Maybe."

"No," she said, kissing my ear. "You're not a one-trick pony. You're a stallion and you got lots of tricks."

"Thanks," I said. "Now do you want to hear what she said about you?"

"She talked about me?" Dana sat straight up in her seat. "In what context?"

"Us."

She stared at me.

"She knows about us," I continued. "She said that what she was paying me could help us out a lot in the future."

"So she's worried about our future?"

"She also said you could have gone places in the D.A.'s office, if you hadn't quit. Smart—and political—that's what you are."

"Well, at least she got one of us right."

Dana turned toward me again. This time a slight frown was on her face.

"Who's got your back on this?" she said.

"I'm a lone ranger."

"Can't Hank go with you?"

"He's out of the country," I said. "May not be back for a couple of weeks."

"Well, I guess you know what you're doing."

"Not really, but Milligan gave me a file from the French police, so I have some leads. When I get there, I'll just start poking around."

"Anyone capable of abducting the daughter of a federal judge isn't going to worry too much about killing you."

"I know, but the money's good."

She slapped her hand on the dashboard. "Damn it, Doherty, you act like you're going on vacation."

"I'm sorry," I said, "I didn't mean to make a joke out of this."

We drove in silence now, neither of us speaking. We were on Atlantic Avenue, underneath the Long Island Railroad elevated line. I had the lights timed right and was moving fast, only having to slow once for a group of teenagers crossing from Boys and Girls High School. After they passed, I gunned the engine, shifting gears, and watched the admiring faces in the rear view mirror.

When we reached the airport I pulled in front of the Air France departure area at Terminal 1. We got out and exchanged seats.

"I don't know how long I'll be away."

"Who'll try your cases while you're gone?" Dana's voice was tightening with sadness.

"Milligan said she'd keep Connie off my back."

Dana nodded. "Don't ask me to thank her." Then she started to cry.

I turned away, also caught up in the emotion. "Look at you," I said. "You're going to make a grown man weep."

She cupped my chin, pulling my face back around, and I could see wet streaks below her eyes. "Give her back the money. Let's turn around, go home and you can write Milligan a check in the morning."

"I can't," I said.

"Why not? She'll understand. And if she doesn't, tough."

"I can't," I said again. "I only know how to do what I do. I'm a one-trick pony."

I reached into my wallet and gave her the five hundred I had withdrawn earlier from the ATM.

"Take care of the cats."

"They'll miss you," she sniffed.

"I'll miss them too."

I hauled my carry-on bag out of the back and leaned over and kissed her.

I showed my passport and e-ticket at the Air France desk, as I had been told. The seating was in first-class and there was still plenty of time to go through the security gates. After I put my shoes back on, I walked to the departure gate, showed the passenger agent my boarding pass and passport and went through. It was six-forty-five and soon they would be closing the gate in preparation for taxiing to the runway. I found my seat and opened up the carry-on, taking out my leisure reading. *Down in the Zero* by a guy from Queens, New York named Andrew Vachss. It was work of fiction but it was more real than anything you see on the nightly news.

I didn't start reading though; just sat there looking out the window at the twilight and the ground crews scurrying around. The plane was crowded, every seat taken, even in first-class. So much for worry about the depreciation of the dollar. Then I looked around again. Everyone seemed to be French, returning home after having a great time in New York, spending our debased currency.

I wished I was going on vacation instead of this. And that Dana was with me, although she had made it clear in the past that she didn't care for Paris.

I had left unsaid what I was really going to do in Paris, which wasn't much. The only way I could get to the bottom of this was to make a lot of noise, hoping that the kidnappers would come after me. I would use myself as a stalking horse to attract the predators.

At seven-twenty, we moved away from the gate. At seven-fifty, the plane was in the air, banking over the Rockaways and the outer harbor, climbing up and heading northeast. In ten minutes we'd be almost directly over my house and I wondered if Dana had made it back in time to look up and see the vapor trail as we sped by.

I had two glasses of champagne before the meal, a half-bottle of Cambon La Pelouse Bordeaux with my duck, and then a Poire William to digest it all. I told the flight attendant to skip the coffee and dessert and reclined my seat back and read; letting sleep overtake me. When I awoke, sunlight was creeping in as we approached Brest on the Brittany coast. The attendant was handing out hot towels to refresh us and I could smell the coffee. It wasn't the mud the airlines served in coach.

We landed at Charles de Gaulle Airport in Roissy, one of the outer *banlieues* or suburbs of Paris. It was 6. a.m. local time and I felt refreshed, not tired. Usually at 6 a.m. I'm on my way to work, feeling very unrefreshed. I grabbed my carry-on and followed the signs to passport control and customs, moving fast, staying ahead of the crowd. There was no one on line at the non-Common Market country entry desk and I stepped right up to the booth and handed the officer my passport along with a smiling "Bonjour."

He answered the same minus the smile, took the passport, flipped through it, took some interest in the page-wide visas for the People's Republic of China and Vietnam, then looked up at me. He scanned the passport into a machine, and then looked at me again.

Finally, he shrugged and handed the passport back to me and said, *"Bienvenue à France, monsieur."* I went out into the main corridor and was about to sit when a young black woman, dressed in a blue skirt and jacket over a white blouse approached me.

"Welcome to France, Mr. Doherty." A quick smile appeared on her smooth, soft face and she offered her hand. I took it. Soft and gentle to the touch.

"I'm Sylvie Avril; from the Milligan Foundation," she said. "Do you have any baggage to be claimed?"

"No, just this." I lifted up my carry-on.

"Then shall we go? Please follow me, I have our car waiting outside."

We moved along the corridor and down a long motorized pedestrian tramway and came to the exit doors. There was a pearl gray Mercedes waiting there, its driver standing alongside an open rear door.

"Convenient," I said.

Sylvie smiled. "No sense wasting time or comfort. Judge Milligan insists on the best efforts by everyone."

"Do you know Cynthia, I mean the Judge?"

"She comes to Paris twice a year."

That was something Milligan failed to mention. And I didn't like it.

We sat in the back of the Mercedes and the driver closed the door; then he got in and we drove away.

"Hôtel Lutetia, s'il vous plaît," Sylvie told him. She turned to me and said, "I hope it's to your liking. A really good four-star hotel near shopping, Montparnasse and the Latin Quarter."

"I'm afraid I don't have much time for sightseeing."

"Yes, I know," she said. "It's a pity."

"You understand my assignment?"

She nodded.

"Is there anything you can fill me in on?"

"Let me think about that. After you've checked in at the hotel and rested a bit, we can talk. I'm sure you'd like a hot shower and a short nap."

"That would be just fine," I said.

5.

The Lutetia was a large ornate looking edifice on the *Boulevard Raspail*, not far from the Bon Marché department store. Sylvie signed a slip for the driver and waved the doorman away from my bag. She escorted me up to the registration desk and quickly explained to the clerk that the Milligan Foundation had made a prepaid reservation for me. The junior suite, Sylvie said apologetically to me.

"Judge Milligan admires frugality as much as efficiency."

The junior suite had a queen-size bed, a dining table with two chairs, and a sitting area with a couch and two more chairs, all surrounding a cocktail table. The sitting area faced a slanted window that overlooked the rooftops of Paris and had a nice view of the Eiffel Tower. I had to admit frugality has its virtues. Sylvie thanked the porter; tipping wasn't necessary.

"It's ten o'clock," she said. "Why don't you rest for a couple of hours, and then have lunch. I suggest the brasserie downstairs if you like shellfish, then rest some more or walk around. We could meet at six for drinks and dinner. Is there anything I could do for you in the meantime?"

"I need a cell phone. One that works in Europe and allows me to call the States."

"No problem," she said. "I'll have it for you tonight."

"Oh, and one other thing."

"Yes?"

"While I'm taking a shower, please have room service pick up my suit for cleaning. They have express service, don't they?"

"Of course."

"Thanks," I said and plopped my bag on the settee.

"Should I pick you up here?" she said.

"I may be out for a while. I'll meet you instead. Where do you suggest?"

"Have you heard of the Closerie des Lilas?"

"Heard but not seen."

"*D'accord*; then we'll meet there at seven."

She gave me the address and suggestions on how to get there if I was walking. After Sylvie left, I stripped and padded into the bathroom, turned on the shower and stayed under the hot water for a good fifteen minutes. When I came back out, my suit had been picked up.

I called down to the front desk and asked them to make a reservation for one p.m. at the brasserie and to please wake me at twelve-thirty. Then I slid between the sheets and let myself collapse into a deep sleep mode.

At one-twenty I was seated at a corner table, an array of oysters and other shellfish on a huge raised platter in front of me. Underneath the platter were slices of pumpernickel bread and a hunk of butter. I had a nicely chilled glass of Sancerre in my hand, the rest of the half-bottle refreshing in the ice bucket next to me.

Heaven comes in many forms, Doherty.

A dozen Belons is only of them.

But it's a damn good one.

Relaxed and refreshed, I was heading back to my room when the clerk at the concierge desk beckoned me.

"There is a package for you, Monsieur Doherty," he said, handing me a small box wrapped in brown paper. Heavy.

I took it, thanked him and went back up to my suite. I sat on the sofa and opened up the package, yanking out tufts of the *Le Monde* newspaper in order to find what was inside the box. My fingers bumped a hunk of metal. It was the gun. At least it was a gun. A .22 caliber match pistol, single action, with a beautifully crafted walnut grip. I picked it up, hefted it and turned it over. Where the safety catch was, a small key stuck out of a hole. I played with it and found that if I pressed it in, the magazine was released. Further complicating matters, I had to turn the key to change the mechanism from safe to fire.

What the hell did Andrews think I was going to do with this? Try out for the Olympic pentathlon team? There were two additional ammunition magazines in the box and I took them out and put them in my carry-on bag. I stuck the pistol in my waist band. It was better than nothing, I figured. And it was comfortable. I took it back out and went over to the bed and lay down again and closed my eyes.

When I awoke, it was six. On my way out I picked up a map of Paris in the lobby and stuck it in my trousers' pocket, right next to the target pistol. I walked down the *rue de Sèvres* to the *rue des Saints-Pères* and then hung a right on the *Boulevard St. Germain*, passing the Café de

Flore and the Deux Magots and then the ancient church of St. Germain des Prés. The boulevard was crowded with students, the academic year now ending. I wondered if Vanessa ever spent time down here. I made a mental note to find some free time; one day, maybe two, for myself and come back.

I pushed up the *rue de Rennes* to the St. Sulpice church and then walked through the Luxembourg Gardens, filled with young couples holding hands, and the elderly, well, looking elderly. Walking up the *Boulevard St. Michel*, I came to a plaque on a wall that memorialized where some Sorbonne students had been killed in the August, 1944 uprising against the Germans. What would they have given for the match pistol jammed into my waistband? So be grateful for small gifts, Doherty.

My journey buoyed me, although I didn't know why. Maybe it was the different sights. Common sense told me that danger should be nagging in the back of my mind. But it wasn't. At least not on this early June evening in Paris.

At the intersection of the *Boulevard St. Michel*, the *Avenue de L'Observatoire* and the *Boulevard Montparnasse* stood the Closerie des Lilas, on the right, with a statue of Maréchal Ney standing guard. I remembered him as the valiant general left in charge of the disastrous French retreat from Moscow while the great Napoleon beat it back to Paris. And while Napoleon lies entombed in fancy marble in the Invalides, Ney stands here outside the Closerie des Lilas, still in a fighting stance. He must have seen thousands of patrons entering and leaving over the decades. How many ever saw him?

The restaurant was surrounded by hedges which enclosed an outdoor dining area. I walked inside the building and told the maitre d' that I was to meet a Madame Avril. He escorted me up a short flight of stairs to a comfy dining area where Sylvie was seated on a leather banquette along the wall. Next to her was a man. Both of them were sipping champagne. Cozy. I wondered if I was the odd man out.

That same broad smile broke across her face as I approached and I felt I was wrong.

"Mr. Doherty," she said, "allow me to present Jean-Claude Pasquier."

The man rose and offered his hand. We shook and I sat down next to Sylvie.

"Join us for champagne?" Jean-Claude said.

The waiter approached.

"I'll have a pastis," I told him.

"Two more champagnes," Pasquier said.

When the waiter left, Sylvie said, "Jean-Claude is an investigative judge. He specializes in terrorist cases. In fact, he is an expert."

Pasquier raised his hand, demurring. "I wouldn't say expert; just experienced."

The waiter brought us our drinks. I mixed water into the pastis, watching it cloud up and then added some more. Pasquier lifted his champagne glass. "Welcome to France."

I sipped the pastis while Sylvie and Pasquier drank some of their champagne. Pasquier was tall and thin, with an angular face under a mat of dark, close-cropped hair. He was wearing a navy-blue suit, expensively tailored; its cut accentuating his leanness, making him look much younger than what I guessed was his early fifties. His skin was smooth and his mouth assured; seemingly relaxed except for his eyes which were alert, always moving back and forth around the dining room. Despite this calm façade, I could feel an uneasy tension about him.

Sylvie was dressed differently then she had been earlier, now wearing a black jacket with gold piping and a gold brocade belt, black pants and a cream silk top. Dressy but not formal. She reached into a large clutch purse that was next to her on the banquette and pulled out an envelope. She smiled as she slid it across the table to me.

"I didn't forget," she said. "Your phone."

I nodded and picked up the envelope and took out the cell phone. It was a Vodaphone model. I'd figure out how to use it later.

I turned to Pasquier. "I'm somewhat familiar with the French criminal justice system from law school but would you bring me up to date on what your actual function is?"

"Let's have the waiter do his job first," he said. He flicked his head slightly and the waiter came over. Sylvie ordered salmon; Pasquier and I had the steak tartare and frites; he had insisted I try it; it was the speciality of the house. He selected a bottle of Burgundy, a Clos de Santenay that would go well with all our dishes.

I complimented him on his choice.

"You know French wine, Mr. Doherty?"

My turn to be modest. "Some. I tend more to Bordeaux and Châteauneuf-du-Pape." I drank some more of the pastis.

"What do you know about this group Mistral Jihad?" I said.

Pasquier said, "We have pretty firm intelligence on all the militant groups in France. Let me explain that under the French criminal code, unlike in the U.S., we have extraordinary leeway in investigating and building terrorist cases."

"For example?"

"Well, for one, terrorist suspects don't have the right to an attorney while they're being interrogated. In fact, we can and do grill them for up to four days before they see their lawyer."

I nodded. "What else?"

"And their attorney consultations are limited to thirty minutes."

"That must go over big with the bar association."

Pasquier laughed.

"And we can hold suspects for up to four years without bringing them to trial."

Now that was a goody. I looked at Sylvie as Pasquier talked. Her face was a blank and I wondered what she was thinking about all of this.

"We also use wiretap information at trial as well as confessions gathered abroad."

"No matter what the means." Sylvie interjected herself into the conversation.

I looked at Pasquier.

He raised his eyebrows. "Yes, it is true, some countries have rather primitive questioning techniques. Brutal but effective."

"Who decides when a wiretap is installed?" I said. "For example, when I was in the D.A.'s office, I had to go before a judge and make a probable cause showing, and the tap would be limited to thirty days."

"I decide," Pasquier said. "I'm the judge. The investigation head and the preliminary court all rolled into one."

"So have you investigated the Mistral Jihad?"

"The group that supposedly abducted the Milligan girl?"

"Supposedly?"

"Mr. Doherty, we're not even sure the Mistral Jihad exists as a stand-alone organization. We know of a dozen individuals under code names, *noms de guerre*, that we haven't broken."

"Who are they?"

"Youths. Native European, maybe an Arab or two, that's all we can discern from the computer enhanced identities that were developed by the DST's Sub-Directoire of Police Techniques and Science."

"What do they do?"

"Bank robberies, mainly. Some kidnappings."

"So maybe money, not politics is their primary objective."

Pasquier smiled. "With terrorist orgs, they are the same. Underground movements require a constant infusion of funds."

"As far as I know there has been no ransom demand for Vanessa Milligan," I said.

"We are still officially treating it as an abduction. For the sake of good relations between our countries." Pasquier did have a sense of humor, I had to give him that.

"But your investigation is low-key, isn't it?"

"We have an active investigation," he said.

"But not pro-active."

Pasquier didn't protest. "Mistral Jihad is one of several organizations we are trying to roll up. I can tell you some others are involved in schemes to blow up the Eiffel Tower or the American Embassy; or manufacturing deadly chemicals."

"Did you find anything of investigative value in her studio?"

He shook his head. "Not a hint of what happened. Feel free to look around yourself but we've packed everything up and shipped it back to New York."

"For God's sake, why?" I set down my wine glass just a little too hard, sloshing some drops onto my wrist.

"It was Judge Milligan's request. We saw no reason not to accommodate her."

"So the Mistral Jihad is low priority, and the DST and the police judiciary manpower is used elsewhere. I understand, but I need to find Vanessa Milligan." And those responsible for her abduction, I said to myself.

Pasquier poured some of the wine into our glasses. "Feel free," he said with a smile. "But remember, here in France we have very strict firearms regulations."

I nodded and smiled back.

6.

The waiter returned with our steak tartare, mixing the ground sirloin in front of us, then bringing Sylvie's salmon and the piping hot frites.

Pasquier was right. About the food, anyway.

The pearl gray Mercedes taxi was waiting outside the restaurant when we left, but I turned down the ride and walked up the *Boulevard Montparnasse* in the cool evening. It was just after nine o'clock and the sidewalks were busy, the serious diners now arriving at the area's restaurants. I hadn't made plans for the next day and the jet lag hadn't hit me yet. So I was in no hurry and I followed the lights.

The Mercedes sped by, Sylvie waved at me and I waved back. Right behind the Mercedes was a black Citroën with two beefy men in the front. Pasquier apparently didn't travel alone. Investigative Judge for terrorist cases. I couldn't blame him.

I decided to make a quick detour and crossed the *Boulevard* to take a look at Vanessa Milligan's building on the *rue Lucien Robert*. It was a short dog-legged street with trim apartment buildings and small quiet restaurants. On the outside of Number 12, I saw Vanessa's name on a buzzer. I didn't bother to waste time checking out the apartment, only wondering why Cynthia had her daughter's belongings removed so quickly.

When I reached the *Carrefour Vavin*, where the *Boulevard Raspail* slices the *Montparnasse* on a diagonal, I stopped. The statue of Balzac by Rodin loomed on my right. Its stone base was surrounded by a clutter of motorcycles parked in the tiny space separating the lanes of the *Raspail*. Modernity's insult to the past.

Up ahead on the opposite corner was the Rotonde, its sidewalk terrace packed with patrons having a night cap while people-watching. I crossed the *Boulevard Raspail* and walked by the café, giving the tables a quick side-sweep with my eyes.

My watch said 10:30. Back home it was three-thirty. I imagined Dana out by the pool with the cats, working on her tan. I looked at the Dôme across the street and the Coupole further down. Both brasseries were also crowded. I continued walking, going past the Select and when I reached the Église Notre Dame des Champs, I turned down the *rue Stanislas*. At the end of that street was the *rue Notre Dame des Champs*. I turned again and walked back up to the *rue de Chevreuse*. There, at number six, behind a large locked wooden door, was Reid Hall. Where Vanessa Milligan had been enrolled. I'd come back in the morning and look around.

Still too early to turn in, I walked back to the Rotonde and spotted an empty table three rows from the street. Squeezing in, I sat and watched the passersby until the waiter noticed me. I ordered a large *picon bière*, not knowing what it was, only that it was the priciest brew on the little menu in front of me. After all, I was quenching my thirst on Judge Milligan's dime. The waiter nodded appreciably and rushed off, picking up empty glasses and taking refill orders on the way inside to the bar.

I watched the women walking by. Some with men, others in pairs or threes. They all seemed so young.

It's you that's getting old, Doherty.

Dana should be here with me, I told myself. And would be except that she didn't care for Paris and this job was too dangerous and someone needed to take care of the cats while I was gone.

I was still feeling sorry for myself when the waiter brought my *picon bière*. It turned out *picon* was an orange bitter that was mixed in with the beer and damned good and strong. I drank it faster than I probably should have and signaled with a wave to the waiter to bring me another.

The whole corner was like a brightly lit arena, no, a stage where the actors and the audience all sit and walk and drink and pose together. Across the Boulevard, the competing theaters of the Dôme and the Coupole were just as active. I sat there and drank my *picon bière*, more slowly this time, and promised myself that someday I'd come back with Dana; first convincing her that she'd love it, then proving it to her.

I was mulling over whether to order a third *picon* when the jet lag slammed into me. My body started to sag and I decided to pack it in and go back to the hotel.

I walked down the *Boulevard Raspail*. As opposed to the brightly lit *Montparnasse*, it was dark here, the leaves shading the street lamps, throwing shadowy spiders on the pavement. It felt damp and I wondered if rain was coming.

My bladder was aching from the wine and the *picon bières*. Where in the hell were the public urinals, the *pissotières* of Paris that I had heard so much about? I really needed to take a leak and the shadows were inviting. But I knew better. I could see the headlines: Department of Education attorney arrested for indecent exposure in Paris. That would go over big with the Schools Chancellor, the mayor and Judge Milligan. And with the loaded target pistol in my pocket, I'd be going to the slammer, what Pasquier called the *placard*, for a long time. Luckily, I could see the lights of the Lutetia a few blocks ahead and I stepped up my pace.

Inside the lobby, I scooted across the black and white tiled floor to the men's room next to the bar. Relieved, I headed back to the elevator, grabbing a copy of the International Herald Tribune on the way.

Gray light filled the windows and I could hear the soft patter of drizzling rain. I turned over in the bed, knocking the Trib to the floor. I had fallen sleep last night while trying to read the paper. I looked at my watch. 9:30. Too late to go for a morning run.

I picked up the phone and called the Milligan Foundation office and asked for Mademoiselle Avril. When Sylvie answered, I told her what I needed. After I hung up, I showered and shaved and brushed my teeth and went out for some coffee, grabbing today's Trib and *Le Monde* in the lobby.

Outside, the rain was cold, so I threw the hood to my windbreaker over my head and broke into a trot up the Boulevard. When I reached the *rue de Vaugirard*, I turned and slowed back down to a brisk walk, fitting in with the crowd. I crossed the *Boulevard Montparnasse* and walked up the *Avenue du Maine*, going past the railroad terminal, where I found a café whose aroma of coffee dragooned me inside.

I sat there reading the Trib, thinking about Vanessa Milligan, trying to sort things through, realized I didn't even have enough to start puzzling anything out, and turned to the sports pages. The World Cup soccer tournament was on. Over here, they called it football.

I was in a locals' café; workers and maybe travelers from the Gare Montparnasse frequented it. I didn't see anyone else in the place that looked like a tourist, let alone an American; certainly there were no *journaux étranges* lying about to read. The *Avenue du Maine* angled through the glassed in terrace and I could sit there for the rest of the morning just reading and scoping the scene. But I had work to do.

So, after two double *café crèmes* I was off again.

I walked over to the *rue de Chevreuse* and Reid Hall and saw that the big wooden door was open. I stepped inside, and in halting French, told the concierge—a man—I thought all concierges in Paris were nosy women—that I wanted to speak to someone from the office.

Inside the office, I explained to the lady at the desk that I was inquiring about Vanessa Milligan, that I was working for Judge Milligan and showed her my ID. Her English was much better than my French so I let her lead the conversation. Yes, it was terrible, she was sure Vanessa would turn up safe; and no, I couldn't post a notice on the bulletin board, it was for students only and besides, it would needlessly upset everyone.

I had expected as much and had Sylvie already working on Plan B. So I thanked the lady and left.

I walked back to the Lutetia, taking a longer roundabout route down the *rue d'Assas*, past the botanical gardens of the University of Paris's Science Faculty. The street was crowded with students, the school year still had another couple of weeks.

Pasquier had said he would make available the investigative file on the Mistral Jihad, at least as much of it as wouldn't compromise the DST's sources and methods. When I got back to the hotel, the package was waiting for me in an official *Police Judiciare* envelope. There was also a large envelope from the Milligan Foundation; Sylvie was efficient to be sure.

I took the envelopes back to my room. I opened up the package from Pasquier first. There were duplicates of all the police reports and the two computer images that Cynthia Milligan had given me, along with ten more images that Milligan didn't have. There were also witness statements and reports about rumored Mistral Jihad activity, much of which was in Marseille, in the south of France, not Paris.

I noticed that these computer enhanced images had names on the bottom of each. What Pasquier had called the guerrilla members' *noms de guerre*. Aliases, he said. These were given, however, by the DST, not the terrorists. Still it was more than I had yesterday. I read over the material again, making sure I hadn't missed anything; more importantly, that the French police hadn't missed anything. Nothing popped up.

I sat on the couch, facing the Eiffel Tower through the slanted window and reread the reports a third time.

Solid. For an initial investigation. I gave them that. I knew they weren't going to do much more; Pasquier had as much said so. They had bigger fish to fry; anthrax, ricin, nitrate bombs.

I opened up the package Sylvie had sent me. Inside were two dozen flyers printed in French, with a photo of Vanessa Milligan displayed prominently. The flyers said she was missing and asked that anyone who had information to contact me. The bottoms of the flyers were cut into strips, each with my name and the hotel address and phone number.

I lay down on the top of the bed and closed my eyes, taking some deep breaths to relax. The Lutetia had a physical fitness center and I would use it. But after lunch. Lunch? What time was it? My watch said 11:45. Time enough to walk back to the *Carrefour Vavin* and post the flyers before eating. I hadn't expected cooperation from Reid Hall or the French authorities so I had already sketched my first step out. I was going to do what I did when Mitchum, my little boy cat, ran away last year. I would ask the community for help in finding Vanessa. I just hoped for more success than I had with my little furry rascal, who never returned.

After taping up a dozen of the posters, I went to the Rotonde for lunch. The rain had stopped and the waiters were serving on the terrace, which was half-deserted. I ordered the cold roast beef platter with frites and a half-bottle of Chinon rouge and settled in. What else was I going to but wait? I spent the next hour and a half eating and finishing off the wine, while watching the Gallic pulchritude saunter by; with plenty of African and Asian femininity mixed in to sweeten the scene. Funny thing though, as I watched them pass by, they were all Gallic in attitude. But it didn't make them bad people. I polished off the wine and ordered a *vielle prune*, hoping the strong spirits would perk me up before I nodded off. The liqueur did wonders for my sinus passages and I felt good enough to wander around and check the flyers.

No bites yet. I went back to my room and lay down and flipped on the television. The World Cup preview was on, France would be playing Spain in a few days. I turned the set off and picked up the Vachss novel and read until the alcohol cleared from my head. Then I went down to the physical fitness center and worked out for long time.

The next morning I roamed the streets around the *Carrefour Vavin*, checking my flyers. One on the *rue de la Grande Chaumière* had been torn down. I taped up another one. Then I took the Metro down to the Musée d'Orsay. It was early and the entrance line was still forming so I got on queue near the front. I had been standing there for about thirty minutes while tourists lined up behind me, snaking all around the block. A little later, an official came out of the museum, carrying a bullhorn, and announced that due to an industrial action the museum would be closed.

"What's an industrial action?" a man behind me drawled in English.

"A strike," I said and walked away.

I followed the quais along the Seine, looking at the stalls run by the booksellers, the *bouquinistes*, and at about noon found myself staring at the Eiffel Tower from the Pont d'Alma. Sightseeing, in spite of myself.

I set up a routine for the next few days. In the mornings, I'd jog up to *Vavin*, check my flyers, have some coffee and a croissant, then back to the hotel and spend the mornings waiting for someone to call. I bought a *carnet*—a ten trip Metro ticket—and spent the afternoons traversing Paris, trying to get a sense of what it was like living here as a student. I went to the Père LaChaise Cemetery and La Villette, the Marmottan with its fabulous Monet collection, the Musée Rodin, and of course, the Louvre. I lucked out; no industrial action that day. Every afternoon I'd check the hotel desk for messages. Nothing. I spent the evenings going to restaurants, using the Milligan Foundation bank card; half-expecting to hear from Andrews, the Ivy-League bean counter. But no one complained about my lifestyle. The monthly statement probably hadn't come in yet.

After a week I was ready to go to Plan C. But first, I'd have to come up with one. I wasn't going to pack it in; I had plenty of reasons to keep going. Like Cynthia Milligan said: two hundred and fifty thousand of them.

The next day I was headed to the hotel bar—the Ernest—after a workout when the man at the front desk signaled to me that I had a telephone call: I could use the courtesy phone in the lobby.

"Hello."

"Is this Mr. Doherty?" A man's voice; I couldn't place the accent.

"Yes, who's speaking?"

"Just listen. I have information you want. Go to the waterfall at the Parc Belleville tomorrow at noon."

"How will I know you?"

"I'll know you."

The phone went dead. I walked back to the front desk.

"Do you know who called?"

"No, but he called a little while earlier, I recognized the same voice."

I thanked him and went up to my room and showered and changed into some loose trousers and my windbreaker. The target pistol was tucked in my waistband, the windbreaker covering it. I put my jogging shoes back on; I wasn't going out anywhere special for lunch.

I walked over to St. Sulpice and caught the Number 4 Metro train to the Châtelet station and changed to the Number 11.

I got off at the Pyrénées station and walked past some cafes and stores, the customers and employees all wearing North African faces. Turning up the *rue Piat*, I went about fifty yards before I suddenly stopped. This was the way they would expect me to come tomorrow. I pulled out my little map and found that if I went back to the Pyrénées Metro stop and walked down the *rue des Pyrénées*, I could reach the back end of the *rue des Envierges* and approach the Parc Belleville that way.

At the head of the *rue des Envierges* there was a semicircular viewing area that looked down on the park below and had vistas that spread over the city of Paris and beyond. It was deserted here, except for a couple of Japanese tourists snapping pictures.

I stood at the wall, looking at Paris; the Sacre Cœur to my right, the Eiffel Tower to my center and the Pantheon to my left. This is what the Mistral Jihad figured I'd be doing tomorrow at the rendezvous, scoping the magnificent view when someone came up from behind and rammed the blade into my back, or maybe cut me down with a hail of bullets from a parked car.

A panoramic view of Paris. And then lights out.

I compared the streets and the paths with the map, wanting to know where everything was when I returned tomorrow. Following the sloping path through the park, I reached the waterfall below the wall. There were lots of bushes and shrubs here for concealment and I could see myself ambushed in a crossfire. Or maybe someone would just walk up to me with a smile and pump a couple of rounds into my skull.

They knew me; I didn't know them.

Memo to the file upstairs: Bring the extra ammunition clips tomorrow.

I checked the other paths out; one had a tiny vineyard growing alongside. How long would that last in the Big Apple?

I left the park by the *Passage Plantin*, descending sharply to the *rue des Cascades* and wandered the narrow streets until I arrived back at the *rue des Pyrénées*. When I reached the back of the *rue des Envierges*, I walked that street again, this time on the other side, looking at all the alleys and doorways.

I found a restaurant near the park and went in and sat in the coolness of the shadows.

At this time of day, the bartender was doubling as the waiter and when he brought the menu to me, I ordered a small *pichet* of Brouilly. The *plat du jour* was an endive salad with Roquefort cheese; ray with capers and a fromage blanc in honey for dessert. Worked for me.

While I was waiting for the food, I looked around the place. What was it once like, this resto? This street? This *quartier*? Piaf, Chevalier singing on the sidewalk for coins while some old drunk played the *orgue de barbarie*, that old crank-driven street organ you only saw in vintage post cards, along with the jugglers and mimes busting their asses for a loaf of bread and couple of bottles of cheap wine.

Almost like being a lawyer for the City of New York. I could really relate.

I dug into the food, relishing the fish, the Beaujolais from Brouilly actually going quite well with it.

You're eating some terrific meals for a condemned man, Doherty.

Stop it. I'll get them first.

But what good would that do? I'd whittle down their ranks but others would come after me; better armed, better prepared.

But isn't that what you want?

Yes, dammit. But not if I kill them all, where would that leave me? With no Vanessa Milligan; no damsel in distress rescued.

I looked at the map again; the exits to the park. I had to make sure I didn't get all of them. At least one had to escape and I would pick up the chase from a distance.

But this is their city, Doherty, not yours. What makes you think you can follow their trail?

I was polishing off the fromage blanc with honey when the answer came to me.

You're a bastard, Doherty, I told myself.

Yes, I am, I agreed.

7.

I was back at the hotel by five and priming myself for tomorrow's meet with my unidentified caller. Okay, so they knew me. I was sure I had been watched when I checked the flyers I had posted. Maybe more than once. They might have even photographed me. But I had their computer images, so I knew them too.

If it was the Mistral Jihad that called.

But also there were twelve of them and only one of me.

Better get cracking, Doherty, you've got work to do.

I decided that first I had better call Dana, make amends for not reaching out to her for the past six days. She was miffed, I could sense it, and wouldn't call me.

On the third ring, the phone picked up.

"Dana?"

"Doherty! Thank heavens you called. I was worrying myself sick."

"Not so worried that you'd call."

"Hell, no." Tension was lurking in her voice.

"I still love you, anyway."

"Are you safe?" The tension was now replaced by another, softer tone.

"Of course." Was I?

There was a pause on the other end.

"What's the matter?" I said.

"Nothing," Dana said. "I just put the cats up on the bed so they could hear your voice. Go on and talk to them."

I said hi to each of them and told them I missed them and that Daddy would be back. I could hear Dana laughing in the background.

"They're purring and rolling around," she said.

"I have a way with cats."

"And women. So stay away from the Parisian bunnies, I mean it."

"They don't want to stay from me."

"You tell them that your girlfriend trains with Naomi Campbell. I'll beat their asses."

"Is that what you are, my girlfriend?"

"Of course," she said.

"It's just that we've know each other for fifteen years and this is the first time you've said it." Her words had really struck me hard.

"Oh, Doherty, I'm your girlfriend, your baby, anything you want me to be."

I was starting to choke up. "I just want you to be there when I get home."

"I will, I will. I love you, Doherty."

"I love you; that's another first."

"Stop it; you're making me cry."

I promised I'd call again tomorrow night.

"I wish Hank was there with you."

So did I.

"Tell him where I am if he calls."

We left it at that.

I went over to the sofa in the sitting area and studied the DST computer images. Had I seen any of them around the *Carrefour Vavin* or the *Parc de Belleville*? I realized that I hadn't been looking, never checking my surveillance, waiting instead for them to contact me.

Be more proactive, Doherty. At least more vigilant.

Thanks for the tip, bro.

I studied each image for several minutes, set the photo face down, recited the features to myself; and then picked the image back up. When I got it right, I went on to the next one. When I got that one right, I recited the pair in my mind; then did the third and fourth; then recited the four and compared them to the face down images. It was almost seven when I had worked my way through the dirty dozen. I was starving now, I suddenly realized. But not for restaurant food. I had been eating out for a week and I was sick of it. What to do?

What would you do in New York, I asked myself.

Take out, of course.

No Chinese restaurant in the neighborhood. There were a bunch of them on the *rue du Maine*, just off of the avenue with the same name, but I didn't feel like walking all the way up there. I could go to one of the *traiteurs*, the Parisian delis. But why waste the bank card the Milligan Foundation has so generously provided me? I was looking out the window at the Eiffel Tower, swigging a bottle of Evian, when that little bad boy appeared in my ear.

"La Grande Épicerie," little bad boy Doherty whispered. "You can pick up a nice bottle of wine too."

What a great idea I said to little bad boy.

I stuffed the pistol in my waistband and put one of the extra clips in my pocket and slipped my windbreaker on.

I walked over to *rue de Sèvres*. There were two motorcycles parked on the sidewalk by the Sèvres-Babylone Metro station just across from the hotel. I passed them and continued down the street to the Bon Marché department store and went around to the *rue du Bac* where La Grande Épicerie was; a Zabar's, a Daniel Boulud's and a Zachy's, all rolled into one.

The food was divided into islands scattered around the main floor. I picked up a *ficelle*, the long, thin baguette, nice and warm, and went over to the sausage island. The lady behind the counter suggested a *terrine provençale* and *Galantine aux champignons*, which was a loaf of some meats with mushrooms. Then I selected a cheese—I told the clerk that I was planning to drink a nice red wine with my meal and he cut off a thin wedge of a *Livarot* from Normandy. I took that, and to be on the safe side, opted to also buy something familiar, a *bleu d'Auvergne*. Finally, a couple of raspberry tarts for dessert.

Moving on to the wine cellar, which was really on the main floor, I was surrounded by walls of wines. I showed the clerk what I had bought for food and asked what Bordeaux could he suggest. He walked along one of the walls and came back with a *Pichon Comtesse '98* and a small bottle of Sauterne, already slightly chilled. For the *bleu d'Auvergne*, he said. I handed him the bank card. He rang up the wine and wished me a good evening.

"If Dana was here, it would be better," I said.

The clerk looked puzzled.

"Forget it. *Au revoir*."

I was on my way back to the Lutetia, approaching the entrance to the Bon Marché, thinking of the sausage and the cheese and the fresh bread and wine, when I heard a car door open behind me, on the right.

There was still plenty of light out and shoppers were entering and leaving the department store. This was a no-parking zone, I guess making it easier for taxis to pull up, and the only vehicle I had passed was a dark blue Peugeot van. And when I passed, there had been no one in the cab.

Someone had come out of the back of the van. A beat-up van, at that.

I had the shopping bag with the *ficelle* and the dessert wine and the cheese and sausage and tartes in my left hand, and the *Pichon-Comtesse* in my right. This must be a Frenchman's version of being caught with your pants down.

Still holding the bottle of wine, I moved my right hand over to the left side of my waistband, keeping it just under the edge of the windbreaker; my index finger touching the butt of the gun.

How in the hell was I going to draw my weapon and fire without dropping the bottle?

I looked up ahead, my eyes sweeping the street.

Smile, blonde hair, flashing dark eyes, wisps of raven strands underneath the blonde. Blonde hair and dark eyes? Strange genetics in Paris.

Genetics of death, Doherty.

As the eyes passed me, I ducked through the entrance of the Bon Marché, almost bowling over two matronly women who were carrying large shopping bags.

"*Excusez-moi*," I muttered as I ducked around a large gray stone sculpture of a woman on a pedestal that was in the middle of the lobby. As I scooted past, I read the name, "*La Pourvoyeuse*." There was a floor to ceiling glass display case on my right and I slipped quickly behind it, squatting underneath a large Gucci sign. A clerk behind the counter looked down at me but she said nothing, only arching her eyebrows.

I peeped up to see Blondie coming through the door, two men right behind her. No mistake now, I recognized them from the DST computer photos: code names ALI and FRITZ. Just to throw everyone off base, ALI was a tall, curly blonde Nordic type while FRITZ was thin, olive-skinned with close-cropped dark hair.

Blondie looked around, and then moved forward, ALI and FRITZ behind her. She signaled them with a shake of her head to fan out and the two men moved away. No weapons were visible but I knew they had them; knew I had to get out of here. There was another entrance to the store on the corner of the *rue Velpeau*; I had seen it on my way to buy the food. But there was no way I could reach it without being spotted. Yet, I couldn't stay here squatting up against the case; it wouldn't be long before they saw me. I scuttled along the floor, moving in and out of the aisles until I found myself in the midst of the perfume counters, near some white leather chairs.

I had lost sight of them for a few moments but now FRITZ emerged into view, riding the escalator to the second floor. There was a balcony up there that overlooked the perfume area below and if he walked along it, there was no way he could miss seeing me here, with my baguette and bottles of wine and food, with Dior and Guerlain as my backdrops.

Would the bottles smash when he pumped a couple of rounds into me? Would the French cry for me, lying there, life ebbing away in a pool of blood? Or would they shed tears for the broken bottle of *Pichon Comtesse* instead?

You've got to do something, Doherty.

What? Run for the other door and take it in the back?

FRITZ was at the second floor landing now and I watched through the glass perfume case as he moved toward the gallery, his lean torso slipping by a bottle of Chanel Mademoiselle.

Nice present for Dana, I thought. Would she wear it at my funeral? No, she's wearing Issey Miyake this month.

FRITZ was on the gallery now, edging slowly along the railing, his right hand hovering near his open denim jacket. He wasn't looking straight down, his eyes were focused further out. Still it was only a matter of seconds before he came even with the Hermes display, and then he would pass it. His eyes would be facing my aisle and the sitting duck called Doherty.

He nods his head, eyes still focused out beyond me. Someone—Blondie?—has signaled him. I look behind me and see a face ducking behind the counter at the end of the aisle.

My hand moves for my pistol just as FRITZ comes into sight above; his right hand now underneath his jacket. My eyes blink as he yanks out an automatic and extends it forward, starting to draw a bead on me, and the crack of the pistol sounds so sweet as I fire up at him, hitting him once, then again.

FRITZ bends slowly over the railing, his gun hand still extended, waving slightly. I see the golden yellow flash from the muzzle and a fiery jolt slams across the side of my head. I shut my eyes and roll as it goes off again and hear the shattering of glass below my left hand and wetness all along my side.

When I opened my eyes I could see FRITZ plunging over the balcony and, after a heartbeat, smashing into the perfume case beside me.

My head was on fire, throbbing as if a church bell clapper was striking my skull from both the inside and out. Between the thudding jolts of pain I could hear screaming and shouting, and the slaps of terrified feet on the floor as the crowd stampeded for the doors.

I started crawling down the aisles, my knees crunching over tiny bits of shattered glass. The shards and slivers of the bottles of wine. FRITZ, that bastard, had broken my *Pichon Comtesse* with his second shot. But I still had the Sauterne intact. Suddenly, I stopped crawling, realizing that I was heading toward Blondie's last position and ALI.

ALI? Where in the hell was he?

I reversed course and crawled the other way, underneath the gallery. I was in the Dior makeup area and I turned and propped myself up in a sitting position in an alcove where customers could sit while a saleslady applied samples to their faces.

The hoo-wa, hoo-wa of police sirens in the distance struck my ears. They couldn't be far, the hoo-wa was sounding clearly through the throbbing in my head.

ALI would have to make his move quickly or abandon the kill. Just let him do it before I pass out.

He did. And I didn't.

First, Blondie's face popped again around the case at the end of the aisle.

I didn't fire.

She ducked back, and then ALI's bulk loomed in her place. He advanced crab-like, scuttling slowly toward me, his automatic out, pointing at my face. I knew that as soon as he got close enough to ensure a kill shot, he would let loose.

I still didn't fire.

Now he was in range.

I fired.

Nothing.

I pulled the extra clip out of my pocket and tried to eject the clip that was in the gun.

No good. The key was gone, somewhere scattered on the floor; I couldn't see. Wiped away the blood in my eyes. Tried to work the ejector slide again. Still no go.

ALI saw me, saw what I was trying to do and rushed me. He wasn't sure my pistol was empty and went for it. As he swung his leg up to kick the gun out of my hand, I blocked his boot and upended him, slamming his head back against one of the glass cases.

I was on him, grappling now, and I gouged his eyes with my left hand while my right pulled out my ball point pen.

Click.

While he turned his face away from my jabbing fingers, I drove the pen into his throat, ramming it as hard as I could. His blood spurted up, spraying me and he went limp, eyes dilating and his throat only making a soft, bubbly, gurgling sound.

"Didn't your mother ever tell you the pen is mightier than the sword, fucko?" I gasped.

But just barely, Doherty.

Anyway, it didn't really matter, he was beyond hearing now.

I grabbed his gun and held it, waiting for Blondie.

She never showed.

Another date standing you up, Doherty.

Hoo-wa of the sirens close now; echoing loudly in my ears.

Red lights flashing, reflecting off the glass cases.

"Drop the gun," a voice yelled. It was in French but I saw the uniform and the weapon pointed at my chest and the two-handed shooting stance and I didn't need an interpreter.

I let the gun fall to the floor next to me.

"Lie down," he ordered.

I held up my passport. "American," I said. I threw it across the floor to him. "Call Judge Pasquier."

"Lie down," he said again, picking up my passport.

"Jean-Claude Pasquier, he'll explain." My teeth were chattering.

"Get on the floor, prone." He was back in his shooting stance.

"I can't," I said, touching my forehead, a smear of blood coming off on my hand. "I'm shot."

Blackness surrounded me and closed in, a buzzing noise started up and grew louder, then faded away and then there was nothing.

8.

"Monsieur Doherty." I felt a hand gently shaking my shoulder.

I opened my eyes. The left one, at least. Something was keeping the right one shut. Touching my temple, I felt a bandage taped to my head.

The voice was Pasquier's. He was sitting beside me in the back of a police car. A uniformed officer standing outside handed him something; I couldn't tell what, red lights from other police vehicles and an ambulance were flashing in my face.

Pasquier held the object up in front of my open eye. It was my target pistol.

"Do you recognize this?"

I nodded.

"Is it yours?"

I shook my head.

"Whose, then?"

I closed my eyes for a moment. "There was a blonde. She fingered me for ALI and FRITZ. When I tried to run, she pulled out the pistol but I grabbed it out of her hand." I opened my eyes back up.

Pasquier was giving me the fish eye.

"Where is she? Did you shoot her?"

"No, I already had disarmed her. Besides, I didn't have time; they were behind me so I ran into the Bon Marché."

I was feeling a little sick and I leaned over but the blood rushing to my head jolted me with pain and I sat straight back up.

"Take it easy," Pasquier said. "You've been shot. Try to focus on the events. They followed you inside and you killed them?"

I shrugged. "They tried to kill me first."

"And you're lucky they didn't."

"I guess I am." I touched my forehead again, wincing from the pain. "Who put the bandage on?"

"The police surgeon." Pasquier pointed to a man with horn-rimmed glasses and a dark suit who was closing a medical bag. He was talking with another bespectacled man in a business suit. "That's the *médecin légiste*, what you Americans call a medical examiner." Pasquier motioned for the police surgeon to come over to the car.

The doctor leaned inside, lifted up my left eyelid and flicked on a penlight. He felt my pulse, then opened up the bag and took out some pills. He gave them to Pasquier, saying something in French to the magistrate. I wasn't listening, trying not to upchuck all over the back seat.

Pasquier turned to me. "The bullet grazed your skull. You'll be all right. Maybe a headache for a few days and a slight scar below the hairline." He handed me the pills. "The doctor says to take the blue ones for the pain every four hours; the round ones every six hours for infection."

"Infection?" I touched my forehead again.

"Yes," Pasquier said. He pointed down and my good eye followed. My jeans were ripped and my knees were bandaged, the white gauze spotted with flecks of blood.

"You were pretty well cut up from the glass on the floor."

"My wine," I said. "FRITZ shot the bottle." I grimaced. "It was *Pichon-Comtesse 1998*. A really good Bordeaux."

"Yes, I know," Pasquier said. He held up a sodden label. "I saved this for you."

I took it from him. "Thanks."

A uniformed officer came over to the car and Pasquier handed him my target pistol.

"The police will check all of the guns with the manufacturers; try and trace their ownership. Maybe that will give us some clues about the Mistral Jihad."

I nodded again. And when they trace the target pistol back to the Milligan hunting lodge in the Loire, they'll be back for me. With handcuffs.

Pasquier pointed toward the entrance of the Bon Marché. Two ambulance attendants were removing ALI and FRITZ, entombed now in heavy-duty body bags. The leak-proof kind.

"I guess we don't have to worry about them," he said.

I shrugged again.

The uniformed officer returned.

"*On piquait son pinard*," Pasquier said to him. The officer wrote it down in a memo book.

"What?" I said.

"I told him they were stealing your wine." Pasquier smiled.

"I've got to get back to my hotel." I tried to ease myself out of the back seat of the car but felt unsteady and gave up.

"We'll drive you back," Pasquier said.

Pasquier and the uniformed officer helped me upstairs and I wasn't complaining.

"Remember," he said before leaving, "illegal possession of a firearm is a very serious crime in France." He slapped the pills the police surgeon had given him into my hand.

"I'll take two and call you in the morning," I said.

He laughed. "Do us both a favor. Take three and stay in bed all day."

After Pasquier left, I went to the minifridge and took out a small bottle of cognac and downed it. It didn't make the headache go away but I felt better and opened another.

Well, even though the authorities would trace the gun, they couldn't prove I possessed the pistol illegally; but they could still put me on a plane and ship me back to New York *toute de suite*. I only had a few days to flush out the Mistral Jihad and to get Vanessa Milligan back home.

I washed down the antibiotics with the second cognac and a water chaser. My head was throbbing and my knees burned, but I flushed the painkillers down the toilet. I'd need a clear head for tomorrow's rendezvous.

The next morning, daylight smacked me right in the face. I rolled off the bed gingerly and went into the bathroom. My head bandage was loose and dried blood caked the dressing on my knees. I went back and called room service and ordered a large pot of coffee and the morning papers; then returned to the bathroom and washed and changed the bandage.

While I drank my coffee, I read through the papers. Nothing about the shootout in the Bon Marché. Bad for tourism and why scare the local *citoyens*?

I put on another pair of jeans and a light wool sweater, sliding the jeans gently over my bandaged knees. Then I poured another cup of coffee and sifted through the DST computer photos of the suspected Mistral Jihad members. I culled out ALI's and FRITZ's profiles and drew diagonal lines though their faces. Then I folded the prints and put them in an envelope and addressed it to Judge Milligan at the Milligan Foundation in New York. She'd know what the diagonal lines meant, and that I wasn't just loafing on the leafy banks of the Seine, soaking up culture.

I left the envelope at the front desk to mail and hobbled over to the Metro station. I didn't know if I was being surveilled or by whom. Mistral Jihad? I wouldn't put it past them to make a second try, although they'd probably do it at the meet. The DST? Yeah, why not trail me? Use me as a stalking horse to flush the bad guys out. Wasn't that what I was doing?

The Number 4 train took me to the Denfert-Rochereau station. I got off and got on the bus to Orly Airport. Anyone following me on the train would have to do the same. After the bus had gone three blocks, I demanded to be let off. No one else got off behind me and I hailed a taxi and took it to the Milligan Foundation offices on the *Boulevard St. Germain*.

Yesterday, I had called Sylvie from the restaurant on the *Butte de Belleville* and explained today's activities, well at least the safer parts, and told her what I needed.

She was waiting outside the Foundation offices, holding a large shopping bag. I paid my driver and hobbled over and kissed her on the cheek.

"What happened to you?" she said, touching the bandage on my forehead.

"I ran into some angry shoppers at the Bon Marché."

"I hope it was worth it."

Sylvie waved her hand and the pearl-gray Mercedes pulled alongside the curb.

It was comfortable in the back and I relaxed while Sylvie emptied the contents of the shopping bag onto the seat.

My sheep's clothing. A dark wool jacket and black beret, both worn. I closed my eyes while she adjusted the beret so that it covered the head bandage.

"*Bien! T'as une nouvelle dégaine,*" she said. "You have a new look. Now, you are a real Parisian."

"Does that mean I get the beautiful woman?"

"Maybe."

9.

The driver let us off on the *rue des Couronnes* below the park. We walked, me hobbling, up the path past the park's little vineyard, to a spot right below the semicircular viewing area at the end of the *rue des Envierges*. The driver was to park the car on the *rue Bisson*, below the waterfall. Paths led downhill to the entrance there and if my dates decided to make a quick exit that way, Sylvie and I could follow them in the Mercedes. It wasn't much of a plan, but it was better than nothing.

There she was. Blondie. Up above in the viewing area, facing the street, her back to us, waiting for me to appear. Others were probably below us, hiding in the bushes near the waterfall, watching for her signal.

When they jumped out, it wouldn't be to say 'boo.'

It would be *au revoir*, Doherty.

I didn't recognize her at first. Blondie was no longer blonde, her hair now black and covered by a cap, sunglasses covering her dark eyes. She was giving me some new looks. More than the Knicks offense ever gets. Which wasn't much.

Sylvie and I sat on a bench, holding hands, my arms around her while Blondie patrolled above, casually moving from post to post. Every once in a while, I leaned over and nuzzled Sylvie's ear and kissed her on the cheek. The views of Paris from here were gorgeous and Sylvie was soft and warm next to me. I could really get to like countersurveillance work. But I had Blondie up above and Dana back home. That was enough to worry about.

At one o'clock, Sylvie and I went over to a grassy spot and reclined in the sun next to each other. We could see Blondie up above and the waterfall and the bushes below. I was sure my intended assassins were hiding down there but I couldn't see them; not even a rustle of bushes to catch my attention. I looked up at the buildings on the *rue des Envierges*, where I had eaten lunch yesterday in the cool shadows of the old café. Only a hundred yards from us, but another universe away.

From time to time, couples or small groups of tourists would stroll down the path from the viewing area to the *Maison de l'Air* and take pictures. Blondie eyed them quickly, double checking to see if I was among them, probably also worried I wouldn't come alone after last night.

At two, she was growing impatient, nervous. She looked out across the wall and down at the shrubs near the waterfall. I held Sylvie close to me, kissing her face and watching Blondie over her shoulder.

Suddenly, Sylvie was kissing me back.

Blondie lit a cigarette, puffed it furiously a few times, and then stomped it out. She disappeared from view and then suddenly emerged on the foot path, walking right past us, ignoring the kiss Sylvie was planting on my lips.

Helluva a time to give up, Blondie.

After she passed the waterfall and disappeared down the path, I helped Sylvie to her feet.

"Let's follow her," I said.

"Was I good?" she said.

"Hell, yeah." I wiped my cheek and lips, making sure there was no lipstick left on my face.

I unfolded my little map and spread it out on the grass. I studied all the downslope approaches to the park again, reminding myself that each was also an exit. I didn't come to Paris to play act this deal.

See Paris and Die, starring Doherty and an unknown cast of about a dozen. Not with Milligan's fifty thousand in my bank account; two hundred thousand more to be collected; Dana McPherson warming my bed, and three cats who depended on me.

No, I had too much to live for.

We spotted Blondie again, alone on the other side of the *rue Bisson*, walking uphill toward the *rue de Belleville*. She wasn't checking her surveillance and she was on foot. I was lucky this time.

These blocks were residential and the sidewalks not very crowded, but the *rue de Belleville* would be teeming with shoppers. I told Sylvie to take the car and go back to the office. I would track Blondie on foot and call her later.

She was moving fast now, my target was. Moving with purpose, walking as if she was heading in a known direction even as she zig-zagged through the streets. Not even looking back to see if anyone was tailing her.

Amateur.

Hey, what are you, Doherty?

Yeah, but I'm getting paid 250 large.

What did Jean-Claude say about these kids? Two-fifty large was a day at the casino, maybe only an afternoon.

We were walking along the *Canal St. Martin* together, Blondie and yours truly. Not together, together; I was still keeping about fifty yards behind. The foot traffic was light this time of day and there was no reason to close the gap between us. No way I was going to lose her.

On the *Quai de Valmy* now, my head throbbing from the exertion, my knees starting to bleed again from rubbing against my jeans. I was sorry I had thrown away the painkiller. Tired, and more sorry because I told Sylvie to take the car back to her office.

You can't do everything alone. Doherty.

Do I have a choice?

Blondie stopped at a small building and punched numbers into a keypad by the door; and then ducked inside.

I set up an observation post by the canal. Staying in the shade, fighting off nausea brought on by the exertion of last night's work-out in the Bon Marché. The OP was good because while the trees blocked me from being seen from the building windows, I had a good view of the front door; ready to pick up Blondie or one of the others when they came out.

If they came out.

I stayed there in the shade, waiting, leaning against a tree by the canal. What the hell else was I going to do? Blondie had led me somewhere up the Mistral Jihad food chain. I had to wait and see who would bite.

But what was this location? A safe house? The apartment where they were holding Vanessa Milligan?

If they were holding Vanessa Milligan, you mean.

I was more thirsty than tired now and when my watch ticked 4:00, I walked down the street to a small café and ordered a Perrier and kept watch on the building.

Since Blondie, over the past two hours, no one had come in or out.

Where were the others? Inside? Elsewhere?

I was half-way through my Perrier, pretending it was a Stella Artois, when the building door opened and Blondie popped out. She was walking straight toward me and passed by without batting an eyelash. I threw a five-Euro note on the table and followed her.

I was exposed now, my cover thin, and with no concealment. And no choice. I had to follow her; I had no other lead.

Luckily, she only went a few blocks, stopping at a bank on the *Place du Colonel Fabien* where she used the ATM machine.

Colonel Fabien. The long dead warhorse of the Communist *résistance*. What would he think of my feeble attempts at clandestine activity? Not much, I guessed.

Blondie held out her hand and snatched up the money when the ATM spit it out. I noted the time. 4:09 p.m. Then she stuffed the cash into her handbag and started back towards me. She had a pretty nice swing to her hips, controlled but sensuous; she was definitely made for better things than the bullshit she was caught up in now.

As she came closer to me, I faced away and started walking. I was pretty sure she was heading back to her safehouse and I set a fast pace, moving ahead of her, stopping to look into the window of a small shop just before her building.

I watched the reflection of her passing in the glass, her blonde head of hair slicing through the leafy trees behind me. She tapped the security code again on the entrance key pad and from my vantage point I could see the movements of her fingers. 4-6-1-7-A.

Blondie disappeared inside and I rushed up to the building and punched in the numbers and when the door lock clicked open, slid inside. I could hear Blondie's footsteps on the stairs, and then a door open and close. Two flights above, I figured from the sound. I went back to my OP by the canal, trying to puzzle out what my next step would be.

I had some choices but none of them seemed very good. I could go back and punch the code again, slip inside and wait in the third-floor hallway and hope to rush them when the door opened. But that would be a stupid play for a thousand reasons; not the least of which was I had no weapon. Besides, I didn't know who was inside. There might be too many of them. Or none at all. And if Vanessa wasn't there, I would have blown my only lead. And if she was there, she'd still be there tomorrow. They couldn't risk moving her around.

So that left me with only one decent choice: go to dinner and get a good night's sleep and resume my surveillance in the morning. The Mistral Jihad had made their first breach of operational security and it had been a biggie. I would need a clear head and a recovered physical condition to maximize it.

I took the Metro at the Oberkampf and rode to the *Place d'Italie*. There, I moved through the crowd and changed to the Number 6, heading back to Denfert-Rochereau where I caught the Number 4 to Sèvres-Babylone. Emerging from the station, I tossed the beret in a trash receptacle and crossed the street, walking towards the Lutetia. But instead of going inside, I went around the corner and into the brasserie. It was early and there were few patrons inside, so I had no problem being seated.

The young lady at the front escorted me back to a quiet, glass enclosed section of small tables and three-sided green leather banquettes below mirrored walls. I ordered a glass of Loire sauvignon blanc and a mixed platter of oysters: creuses de Bretagne number 2; fines de claire d'Oléron, and the large claires de Marennes. I didn't know what the claires de Marennes were, except they were the most expensive oysters on the menu and the Milligan Foundation was springing for the meal. I followed with a crab meat and avocado entrée.

While I waited for my sea food, I looked around. The whole room was filled with bright stainless steel and glass. Outside, on the street, people were hurrying home from work. The oysters soon came and I polished them off, sipping my sauvignon blanc. When the crab meat and avocado appeared on my table, I plunged in, pushing aside the mesclun greens. I wasn't from the West Coast.

I skipped dessert and went back into the hotel, using the inside entrance from the brasserie. I was thinking about how nice a long hot bath and a deep sleep in the queen size bed would feel. As I passed the Ernest Bar, I looked in. I could hear some blues on the sound system. Gut bucket rhythm and wailing. So I went inside and sat down on one of the soft leather chairs at the bar and ordered an ice-cold bottle of 1664. The whole room was art deco, the walls and ceiling paneled in a light brown wood with darker trim, and art deco lamps were ensconced in the wall paneling. The bar was lacquered black wood with a brass top, not zinc as I had imagined at first, and with a brass railing extending out for imbibers to rest their arms. There were also some low tables surrounded by comfy chairs. A few oldies sat at these. Otherwise, I was alone. Except for Sebastian, the barman who didn't raise an eyebrow when I ordered a Belvedere chaser.

I had been decompressing for about ten minutes, listening to Howling Wolf, wondering what the *aristos* sitting around the low tables thought of him. The 1664 hit the spot and I hadn't yet sipped my vodka when I was joined at the bar by another patron. A young man with dark brown hair and deep set eyes, which he averted when I glanced his way. Not much taller than me, he was leaner, almost thin. Sebastian went over to him and they spoke. I could barely hear him. Soft British accent, too low for me to make out the words. Sebastian smiled and poured him a glass of Taittinger Rosé.

Just another thirsty customer.

Except that he was dressed in jeans and a wool pullover sweater. And it was a very warm evening. And he kept the corners of his eyes on me through the glass behind the bar. And kept his right hand near his waistband where I was sure he was packing something very ugly.

He probably wasn't alone. After last night, I had expected another try. Since they thought I didn't show at the *Parc de Belleville*, it made sense they would try and take me down at the hotel. And if there was no reasonable way they could get past the hotel security to get up to my room, then the optimal killing ground was the lobby area.

As soon as that thought emerged, I took it back. But only for a second.

I was wrong. Serious players would have found a way to get to me in my room. When I walked in the door. Taking a shower. Dead asleep. They would make the last option a reality.

That these guys had to make the hit down here told me they were amateurs. Dangerous amateurs but still not pros.

When we had talked over dinner the other day in the Closerie des Lilas, Pasquier mentioned that the DST had posed the theory that the Mistral Jihad was merely a cover name for another terrorist org; a tactic to confuse the authorities as to who they really were and who might be behind them.

Looking at my watcher sitting down the bar, I concluded differently. They were who they were. Nothing more. But just who in the hell were they? And where in the hell were the others?

The Ernest Bar was flanked by two corridors. The one at the end my watcher had entered through was lined with displays from all the smart shops of the Sixth Arrondissement: Alain Figuret shirts and ties; Crockett and Jones shoes; Longe Parfum, Lancel handbags, etcetera, along with a Welte mignon antique player piano.

At the other end of the bar was the corridor leading back to the brasserie and also to the elevators in the lobby. When I had come in I noticed the unisex restrooms were there.

Since the lean boy in the sweater had entered the bar from the other end, his partner must be lurking somewhere near the corridor to the brasserie. No way was I going to get past them to go upstairs. If they were brazen enough to try and gun me down in the Bon Marché, they would have no problem with doing a hit right here.

I had to make a move soon. Before the other man figured that the reason his partner was dallying in the bar was me. Then he would come looking, alert, and while I tried to disarm one, the other would finish me off.

So if we were going to war, let me choose the battleground. I got up and walked toward the restrooms, feeling my watcher's eyes on the back of my neck. When I reached the corridor, I looked around. No one.

The rest room door opened to a washing and grooming area with a large basin surrounded by a marble countertop, and a rectangular mirror above. There were two hand towel dispensers on the wall. The roller type that gave you linen to dry your hands.

The facilities were in two small cabins. One men's, one women's. Neither was in use I quickly found out. There was no lock on the front door but there were interior latches for the cabins.

I closed the door to the men's cabin and slipped into the women's, leaving the door unlatched. I took off my jacket and wrapped it around my left arm in case he decided to use a knife, and waited, keeping my right hand on the door knob. Outside, I could still hear Howling Wolf.

It wasn't long before the outer door opened. Softly, oh so softly, but luckily the women's cabin was closest and I could hear the tiny creak. If I had been squatting on the other throne, I never would have heard it.

I counted imaginary footsteps crossing the white tiled floor. Four. No one turned the handle of the women's cabin. My watcher or the other must be by the men's cabin door.

I waited, my right hand still on the women's cabin latch. Silence outside. No movement. Nothing. A minute passed. Maybe only fifteen seconds but it felt like a minute. Then the soft grinding of a handle being turned and the swift click of the latch being opened.

10.

"Hey," I yelled as I shoved the cabin door wide open, knocking the man back against the wall. It wasn't my watcher but another, his partner. Also quick and lean and younger than I was. I had to do this fast, knowing he would wear me down in a long struggle. I had guessed right, he had a knife out and when he came back off the wall he had it in position for a downward kill stroke.

I raised my left arm, letting the jacket absorb the stab, feeling the blade slice through the wool. At the same time, I rammed the knuckles of my right hand deep into his throat, crushing his larynx and Adam's apple. He started to sink with a gurgle and I caught him and shoved him into the men's cabin. He was a goner, bouncing off the toilet, dead before he hit the floor.

I picked up the knife where he dropped it and gave him a quick frisk. No wallet, no ID, but he was packing a Beretta—U.S. military type. That bothered me and I promised to mention it to my good buddy in the FBI when I got back to the States.

I left him there and closed the cabin door and went over to the wash basin. There was a cabinet underneath and I shoved the gun way in the back, behind some rolls of clean linen towels. Then I turned the hot water faucet on and pumped lots of soap into the basin. When it was half-full, I turned the faucet off and waited, my eyes watching the restroom door in the mirror, my left hand holding the knife in front of me. It was a switchblade, not the kind that would cough up misdemeanor weapons possession pleas back in Brooklyn. This one was long-bladed and solidly built, meant for use, not show.

I waited but I didn't have to wait long.

I could see the surprise on my watcher's face as he came through the door. His thoughts were obvious: The target was washing his hands. Where is my partner?

His fluster lasted only last a moment and as he started to move for his weapon under his sweater, I turned and flung a scoop of hot soapy water into his face, momentarily blinding him. Reflexively, he tried to wipe it away but stopped when he felt the point of the knife jabbing into the underside of his chin.

"Keep your hands up and don't make a sound," I said, probing his chin with the knifepoint. He knew a hand sweep would be useless, even if he managed to move my knife arm, his throat would be slit in the process.

I reached up under his sweater and pulled out his piece. Another Beretta. I liked this even less. I held it down along my pants leg and glared at him.

"My French isn't very good so you better speak English. Do you understand?"

He threw me a blank look.

"*Verstehen sie?*"

Still nothing.

"*Comprenez-vous?*" At least I could speak that much French.

"*Nique ta mère.*"

I knew what the "ta mère" meant and figured out the rest.

I slapped the side of his face with the gun.

"I'll *nique ta gueule* if you wise off again. Understand?

This time, he nodded, his left eye closing rapidly from the slap of the gun metal.

"Okay, now I'm going to ask you a few questions." I prodded his jaw with the knife for added effect. "And I want answers."

His eyes darted around.

"Never mind about your buddy. Unless you want to join him." I slapped his face again with the pistol. This time his left eye closed all the way.

He was getting the message. Reading what I had written on his face. And he didn't like it, but knew he had no choice.

"Where is she?" I asked.

He shook his head.

"Look, I'm not fucking around with you. Where is she, the Milligan girl?"

His one good eye spat hate at me. "*Nique ta mère,*" he said again.

I slapped him one more time with the gun.

"I'm going to start on your right eye next."

He said nothing.

"Or your nose."

Silence.

"Or maybe, if you piss me off some more, I'll just do you." Jabbed him with the knife again.

The look of hate was still in his one open eye.

"I get paid whether you live or die," I told him.

"Go fuck yourself." English this time.

"So you do understand me," I said. "Good, now let's talk."

"I have nothing to say," he said, the pain adding a sharp edge to his voice. "Go ahead, hit me again. All you fucking Americans think you are tough guys."

"Okay." I slapped his eye once more with the pistol, this time causing the swelling to burst open and sending a trickle of blood down his face.

Suddenly energized, he made a move for the knife in my left hand, but my knee slammed into his groin as he caught my wrist. He collapsed with a shudder and I swiped his skull with the Beretta on his way down.

I stepped over him and went out into the corridor and called Jean-Claude on my cell phone.

"They made another try."

"Where?"

"At the Lutetia."

"How many?"

"Two. One's gone, the other's yours."

"Gone? You mean escaped?"

"No, departed. In the American sense."

"Are you okay?"

"Yes, just a little woozy from the exertion."

"We'll be right there."

"Your package is in the rest room by the Ernest Bar."

I went back to my seat and finished the 1664 and downed the Belvedere. When Sebastian asked if I wanted another, I shrugged. Why not? I had put in a hard day's work.

Pasquier and the two DST heavies arrived about ten minutes later. He was still dressed for work, sporting a dark blue lightweight wool suit; the jacket cut to his body, but leaving just a little give under the left breast and armpit for the pistol he was carrying. In the U.S., we laughed at the pistol-packin' judiciary but Sylvie had explained that here in the République Franceslamique, Jean-Claude had a large price on his head.

I stayed at the bar while the DST men checked out the restrooms, then waved Pasquier in. The pair were wearing sailing parkas over automatics on their hips and the leather-covered sappers in their back pockets. They were dressed for work, too.

I sipped my beer and waited. After a few moments, Pasquier came back out.

"Let's go for a walk," he said.

I followed him out the lobby and up the *Boulevard Raspail*. We stopped by a parked motorcycle on the corner. Pasquier took a pack of cigarettes, ignoring my disgust.

"How's your head?"

"Still throbbing like a college marching band," I said.

"You're a very lucky man."

"How so?"

"I like you. So I'm not going to press charges."

I stared at him. "For what?"

Pasquier laughed. "This is France. We can always find something. Assault, attempted murder, littering a rest room. But in the spirit of international cooperation, I won't." He lit up a cigarette and drew deeply, exhaling the smoke slowly.

"Goddammit, they assaulted me. With weapons. A gun and a knife."

"And now one of them is dead; the other seriously wounded. And there is no gun."

I slapped my forehead. "Jean-Claude, I am so sorry." I reached into my pocket, took out the Beretta and handed it to him. "See, I had no choice."

"They could have killed you," he said.

"But they didn't."

"They will try again."

I shrugged. "Maybe. Probably." I was trying to sound casual but I was shaking inside, adrenalin still pumping.

We were behind the hotel now, near the service alley, and we watched as the DST officers first dragged out the dead man, and then his partner, still unconscious but handcuffed and fettered.

"Are you taking him to the hospital?"

"If he cooperates," Pasquier said. "But I need details from you first."

I gave him a rundown of the incident, starting from my dinner in the brasserie. He didn't need to know about the aborted rendezvous in the *Parc de Belleville* and the Mistral Jihad safehouse on the *Quai de Valmy*.

68

He made some quick notes on a pad of paper, and then motioned for one of the DST officers to come over.

"Vincent, bag this," he said, handing over the Beretta, "then come back and escort Monsieur Doherty up to his room."

The kid took the gun, gingerly holding it between a pair of nicotine stained fingers, and gave me a curt nod as he left. I was pressing my fingers on the bandage covering the side of my forehead. I could feel the veins throbbing underneath and a wave of nausea started to roll over me. I didn't nod back.

Jean-Claude grabbed my elbow as I tottered.

"Easy, *mon ami*. We'll get you upstairs right away. Should I send the doctor?"

I shook my head.

"Well, before I leave I must warn you that we may not be able to keep these antics out of the news."

"So?"

"You will draw the attention of the politicians and editorial writers, and I'm afraid they will cause trouble. For both of us."

"Does that mean you're keeping me on a leash?"

"Not at all," he said. "You're doing all right. A public service. And if you happen to get killed? Well, that's an embarrassment for your government, not ours."

I nodded. Vincent had returned and was waiting.

"Well, good night," I said.

Jean-Claude held my arm. "One more thing, Monsieur Doherty."

"What's that?"

"If you so much as harm one hair of an innocent French citizen, I'll have you locked away in the *placard* until you are bald and all your teeth have fallen out.

I laughed. I could do a year standing on my head.

11.

I ran the bath water and while it was filling the tub, I took out the set of DST composites and found the two belonging to my restroom companions. SAMIR and SHELLEY read their assigned *noms de guerre*. SHELLEY was the dead one. SAMIR was now undergoing special medical treatment by the DST. After drawing diagonal lines across their faces, I put the two photos in an envelope and addressed it to Judge Milligan just as I had this morning. Then I stripped and slipped gingerly into the tub, taking my cell phone with me.

I let the heat work into me for a few minutes, and then I hit the name on the phone, listening to the buzzing on the other end.

"Hi, sweetheart," I said.

"Do you know who you're calling?" Dana said.

"How many sweethearts do you think I have?"

"You better only have one," she laughed.

"That's more like it," I said.

"Where are you?"

"In the middle of a tub of hot water."

"No, I mean, where?"

"In the hotel. I'll be in Paris for a few more days."

"When are you coming home?"

"Not for a while, honey," I said. "I've been very busy."

"Yeah, drinking wine and chasing skirts."

"There's only one skirt I chase and I've already caught it."

"Talk, talk, talk."

"Listen, Dana," I said. "I need for you to reach out to Hank. Right away. Tell him where I am and that I need his help really badly. Now."

"Will Sonny know where he is?"

Sonny Ha-Ha was a gangster friend of ours. Sometimes he did some work for Hank's people. While the CIA hadn't used anyone with a criminal record for years, the taboo never ran to subcontractors or subsubcontractors like Hank's firm. But still, Hank always kept Sonny at arm's length.

"No," I said. "Call Arthur Browne at the TechnoDyne Corporation in Reston, Virginia. Look in my address book. It's on the night table; the number's there. Tell him that you're calling for me and ask him to contact Hank and have him call you back. Okay?"

"Yes, of course. I'm glad you're finally using some sense."

"When Hank phones, tell him to fly into Charles de Gaulle and to call me on the cell phone." I read the number again to her, making sure she got it right. "Remind Hank that his presence here is crucial."

"Okay. But what is the TechnoDyne Corporation?"

"An engineering firm," I said.

"Hank is an engineer?" she said.

"A social engineer."

She didn't say anything for a moment.

"It's lonely here without you," the words finally came out.

"When this is all over, you could join me here in Paris."

"You know I hate Paris."

"No one hates Paris."

"You know what I mean."

"I'll make you love the place."

"How?"

"You know how."

"Promises, promises." Dana was laughing again.

"So will you come?"

Silence once more.

"I'll think about," she said finally. "Maybe if I miss you enough."

"Okay, then. I'll call back in twenty-four hours for word about Hank."

"I'll be here. So will the cats."

"Give them my love."

"What about me?"

"I'm saving that for Paris."

"Goodbye, Doherty." The connection went dead and I put the phone on the floor. After setting the timer on the Jacuzzi for fifteen minutes, I pressed the start button, and closing my eyes, I sank back down into the tub.

The rapping on the door jolted me awake. It was the breakfast I had ordered the night before. I slipped on the hotel bathrobe and let the man in. After he left, I hung the do not disturb sign outside on the door.

Then I sat down to a plate of eggs, sausages, bread and *confiture*, and a large pot of coffee. While I ate, I watched the news on CNN. More bombings in Iraq. Fifty-two civilians this time. More U.S. troops killed. I flicked the set off and opened up the Trib. More of the same. The war against terror's going great. They, our government, says so. Must be true.

I looked out the window. Low clouds covered the top of the Eiffel Tower. Rain was coming to be sure. I threw on some clothes and took the envelope down to the lobby to be put in the morning's outgoing mail. On my way back, I jotted down some telephone numbers from the display cases. Then I went to the restrooms behind the Ernest Bar.

No one else was inside. Who would be using it this time of morning? I knelt down and reached into the cabinet under the wash basin and felt around the stack of linen towels until my fingers caught a solid object.

It was still there. The Beretta I had hidden the night before. I tucked it into the waistband of my trousers and took the elevator back to my room.

It was almost nine o'clock here in Paris; a few ticks shy of three a.m. in New York, but I decided to give that bean counter Carlton Andrews a call anyway. I wanted to leave the info I had about the ATM on his voice mail. On the third ring, he picked up.

"Still at the office?" I said.

"Who is this?"

"Doherty."

"Oh, no, I'm home. I have my office calls forwarded here at night."

"You must be really dedicated."

"Cynthia is not a stingy boss." Sleep was still in his voice.

I ran down Blondie's description to him and gave him the bank name and location and the time she used her bank card to make a withdrawal at the ATM.

Andrews said he'd see what he could come up with. The tone of his voice convinced me that I'd be hearing back from him soon.

After he clicked off, I pulled out my list of clothiers and haberdashers and started ordering a new wardrobe; giving them the number of the Crédit Foncier bank card and instructing them to deliver the clothes to my room at the Lutetia. Then I split for the OP.

The sun was bright and the air clear, at least above the carbon monoxide fumes of the Boulevard, and it bothered me that I had to take the Metro. But it was too far to walk and I had to run some counter surveillance measures to make sure that I, the watcher, didn't wind up being watched.

I wasn't so worried about the Mistral Jihad clowns; four of those amateurs were out of the picture, and only eight to go. Though I wasn't sure how easily I could do Blondie and the other females if, when the time came.

You're too squeamish for this, Doherty.

That's why I need Hank. Anyway, those are problems down the line. Right now, I'm worried that Pasquier sicced some DST bird dogs on my tail, even though he said he wouldn't. Besides, they reported to the Interior Ministry and could be getting their orders elsewhere.

So, the Metro it was; the best way to disrupt foot or mixed foot and vehicle surveillance. I tried not to be too obvious, not playing any tricks to expose them if they were there. I changed trains, doubling back, sauntering casually from one end of the station to the other, mixing in with the crowd. I took my time and it was after ten before I was under the shade trees of the *Canal St. Martin*.

Back here, even if anyone stuck their head out the window all the way, I couldn't be seen. Blondie would have to come out the front door, cross the street and walk into the park along the canal before she could pick me up.

An hour passed and my feet were becoming sore from standing still, but I didn't want to move out from under my cover. The two large cups of *café crème* were starting to bloat and irritate my bladder. C'mon Blondie, show yourself.

She must have heard my plea. About twenty minutes later she came out and crossed over to the *Quai de Jemappes* and walked toward the *Place du Colonel Fabien*. Probably going to make another bank withdrawal. I decided to follow her instead of waiting and it was a good thing I did. A damned good thing. Instead of going to the bank, she went down into the Metro station. I followed and watched her push through the turnstile.

Then I made an about face and marched right back to her building. I punched the code—4717A—and slipped into the foyer. It was dark and quiet. Not turning on the lights for the stairway, I went up to the third floor where I had last heard Blondie's footsteps and the slamming door.

Just below the third-floor landing, I took my piece out from under my jacket and held it down by my right side. Then I made my move up into the hallway.

There were two apartments on the floor; the one nearest me faced a courtyard in the back of the building; the other one looked out onto the *Quai de Valmy* and the Canal. I edged close to the first door, breathing slowly, deeply, and waited. Nothing from inside. I pressed my ear to the door, which was heavy wood, trying to pick up sounds of movement. Still nothing; then what were distant cries of a baby, an infant, from way in the back. Then yelps of another child.

Not Blondie's pad.

I moved to the next door, Beretta still down by my thigh. Flattening myself along the wall, I did the ear to the wood trick again. For a full minute. There was only silence. I rapped my knuckles on the door. No one spoke. No movement; not a peep.

I twisted the door knob. Locked. I looked at the lock, framed in the light from the window. I wasn't going to be able to pick this. I didn't have the tools, besides, even if I did, I'd still be at it, sweating and cursing, when someone, maybe the Mistral Jihad, caught me. And if I lived, my only lead would be blown.

But there was something I was good at. Had been since my college days when we would break into the campus pub after hours for a few free brewskis. I took out my American Express card; I never leave home without it; besides I didn't want to use the Milligan Foundation bank card and damage my gravy train. I was having a lot of fun and they were paying for it.

After about five minutes of edging and sliding the card in the door crack by the lock, I was able to slip it behind the tongue of the mechanism and ease it back into the groove. When the knob turned, I pushed inside, assuming a firing stance. When I saw I was alone, I closed the door softly behind me and gave the place a quick once over.

The living room was neater than an army recruit's barracks before inspection. That's because no one seemed to be living here. There was no furniture except for a small table with a two day old copy of *L'Équipe*, the Paris sports newspaper, lying on it. No chairs, no couch, no television. I went to the window and looked out. I was right; you couldn't see my OP from up here. I went back to the little table and looked at the *L'Équipe*. Five stories about the World Cup tournament on the front page; nothing else.

I checked the bedroom next. There was actually a bed. But no bedding. No other furniture, either. I opened up the closet, first stepping to the side in case someone was in there waiting to clip me. It was empty of clothes but there was a suitcase on the floor. A large carry-on, good quality. I hefted it, rattled it around. Empty.

Going over to the window, I looked down at the street. No Blondie. But I couldn't stay too long. I didn't know if she'd be gone an hour or twenty-four. Or who else might show up, armed and dangerous.

I moved to the kitchen. It too was unused; not even a drop of water in the sink. I went through the cupboards: no dishes, cups or glasses. No food. I looked under the sink. Not one cleaning rag or sponge.

The refrigerator was running but empty.

I was getting a little pissed off now. What kind of safehouse was this?

I went through the bathroom next. No soap or towels. I needed to use the facilities but I was afraid the sound of the toilet flushing might be heard by someone next door or downstairs.

I checked the bedroom again; this time looking under the bed and tossing the mattress. Nothing stashed there. They hadn't been holding Vanessa Milligan here; that much I figured out. I went back into the closet and felt along the top shelf. I came away with dirty fingers. I pushed aside the suitcase in order to stand on my tiptoes and get a better look. When I did, I saw that the section of the floorboards where the carry-on had rested was lighter toned than the rest of the planking.

Kneeling down, I felt around until I came to one board whose groove was wider than the others. It took a little effort, but I pried it up with my fingers, than the one next to it, and the one next to that. I reached down inside and felt around, pulling out an automatic, than another, and another until I had a half-dozen of them on the floor next to me.

I reached further into the space and felt a package. I pulled it out and looked at a brick of brown putty-like material sealed tightly in heavy plastic. I shoved it back where I found it, then looked at the pistols beside me on the floor. All Berettas; nine mm, U.S. Army issue. I picked them up and looked at the serial numbers. They ran in sequence and I wrote the first and last down in my little note pad. I'd have to make a call about this.

After returning everything the way it was, I looked out the window again. Still all clear. I left the way I came. Softly and in the dark. This time I took some worries with me. Whatever those clowns were up to, it was more than kidnapping. That wasn't play dough they were hiding under the floorboards.

And the apartment wasn't a Mistral Jihad safehouse.

It was an armory.

12.

I was leaning up against the railing of the Canal St. Martin, after relieving myself at the café on the corner and rehydrating myself with a Stella Artois. It was a fair exchange, I decided.

The shade from the trees gave good concealment and Blondie never saw me as she came striding back to the apartment. She wore a change of clothes; an aqua tank top had replaced the sweater she had left with and she was wearing a pair of fancy Nikes instead of flats. If she had a weapon, I tried to guess where she was concealing it. When I tired of speculating about that, I moved my guesstimation to other areas. I stayed at the OP, watching the front door to the building. I had no hits so at about three I packed it in and went back to the hotel.

I used room service and ordered a *pâté de foie gras au Loupiac* and a half-bottle of Sauterne.

While I was waiting for my food, I put in a call to my old friend Sharpe, the Assistant Special Agent in Charge of the FBI's New York City office.

When the phone on the other end picked up, I could hear the brusque, formal West Indian accented voice of his gate-keeper.

"ASAC Sharpe, please," I said.

"Who is calling?" she said.

"This is Doherty."

"You know he is a very busy man, Mr. Doherty."

I kicked off my shoes and leaned back on the bed. "I don't want an appointment," I said. "I just need to speak to him for a moment."

"Is it important?"

"Very." I was holding up my note pad in my hand.

"Just a minute." The phone went dead as she put me on hold, and then it clicked back on.

"Sharpe here. What is it?"

"It's me, Doherty. I'll be brief. Any stolen military weapon cases?"

"We always have those. Every time some bugger goes AWOL or just home on leave, he or she seems to take something with them."

I read the serial numbers off to him and gave him my phone number in case he was interested enough to call me back.

"Where are you?" he said.

"Paris. Gay Paree."

"The Department of Ed must have increased their budget this year."

"This trip is not on them."

He laughed. "Don't tell me any more. I'm sure I don't want to hear it."

"Just get back to me then on what you turn up."

Sharpe thanked me and hung up.

The waiter brought the foie gras and the Sauterne. I sat there eating it and sipping the wine while flicking through the TV channels, trying to watch Law and Order dubbed in French. Sam Waterston was never so good. And Jesse Martin was *très* smooth. Those guys were always shooting on location right outside my office on Chambers Street and I promised myself that I would drop them a word about their Parisian accents when I got back to the Big Apple.

After the program was over I ran the bath water and called Dana at home. No answer. Of course not, Doherty, she has to go to work too. I tried her office and reached only her voice mail.

"It's me," I said. "I love you. And I'd love to hear your real voice."

I was luxuriating in the tub, sipping the last of the Sauterne, when she called back.

My message had reached Hank, Dana said, but she had no word yet as to his arrival time. I told her all over again how much I loved her and coaxed her into whispering the same into the phone. I ended the conversation less worried then when I started. But only a little. I was tired and went to bed, the television still on, and dreamt of Semtex and fireworks and body parts flying.

The next morning I still hadn't heard from Hank. I really needed him to be here in Paris.

I knew a lot about Hank. Full name: Henry Lowrie Jackson, after one of his forebears, a Lumbee Indian who stood up to the white man in nineteenth-century North Carolina, fighting them to a standstill.

Hank and I went way back. He was my work out partner when he was in town and he had helped me out big time on the Ides of June murders when that grimy little mobster Jimmy Murphy had put a contract on my head. A former Army Ranger, Hank had also served in Korea like me, and was fluent in that language as well as Arabic, French, Spanish and

German. He had always had a book in one hand and did the New York Times crossword puzzle in his head. Smartest high school graduate I ever knew.

He was the only other living human to have free reign of my wine cellar, my *cave*. My three cats all loved him, especially Diva, the flirt, who always skipped her Naomi Campbell routine when he was around. Good looking, smooth and quiet; women dropped at his feet. Literally. But he was a one-woman man. One at a time, that is. His current squeeze was a hometown girl as brainy as he is. Yet, the only time marriage seemed to be on his mind was when he joked about being the best man as Dana and I tied the knot.

Now, he worked for TechnoDyne, one of the hundred of defense-related firms that made northern Virginia a paradise for the ex-military. Whatever he did for them, he spent a lot of time in the Big Apple. But I never asked what and he never offered to tell.

Watching my back on this case was asking him for a big favor. Here in Paris, I hadn't bothered with cover for status. My strategy had been to be open about who I was and what I was about. I laid all my cards on the table for the DST and Pasquier, as well as the Mistral Jihad. They all knew why I was in Paris and what I wanted.

Hank was another matter, though. His showing up on the set would raise questions and moreover his people would be extremely annoyed if his name and photo were added to the DST's huge computerized data bank. So even though we were friends, business was business and I was prepared to make it worth his while.

I was mulling over all this at my OP under the shade trees by the *Canal St. Martin*, waiting for Blondie to emerge. It was a long wait. Too freaking long. She never appeared; no one went in or out of the building except for an old man who left and returned ten minutes later with a *baguette* under his arm, and an hour later, a *maman* with *deux enfants* went for a stroll. Blondie never showed her face and with my bladder swollen and the sky overcast now, the clouds low, I decided to pack it in before the rains came.

If Hank were here, we could man the OP almost around the clock; run SDR's—surveillance detection routes—making sure the watcher, I, wasn't now being watched. But I was alone, and the surviving Mistral Jihad members, eight of them, knew I had some capability to commit damage. Maybe they'd already split? I didn't know.

I needed Hank. Where the hell was he?

When I returned to my suite, the expensive new clothes I ordered had arrived.

There was a gray silk suit, a navy tie with gold diamonds, another lighter blue tie with silver stripes; a dark blue light wool blazer; a hounds tooth checkered sports jacket; two pairs of trousers, one gray; the other tan; four silk shirts, and a pair of cordovan shoes. I smiled at the thought of Carlton Andrews' face when the bill hit his desk.

I set all the boxes in the closet and went to bed and rested for a couple of hours, lulling myself to sleep considering what I would do with the money I was earning.

Then I went down to the brasserie and ate, and went back to bed, and thought some more about it.

The next morning Blondie obliged me. I had been at the OP for less than an hour when she sauntered into the front door of her building. Twenty minutes later she breezed back out. I followed her to the Colonel Fabien Metro stop. When she went down into the station, I followed.

I was wearing some of my new duds and had enough of a different look that I could stay in the same *voiture* as her without being spotted. We rode all the way to the end of the Number 2 line at the Nation terminus. She led me through the maze of passages until she got on the Number 6 train. At Bercy, she got off and changed to the 14, and we rode two more stops to the *Bibliothèque National*.

I hadn't taken Blondie for a library rat. Had she been alerted and was running an SDR on me? But she hadn't tried to lose me. I followed her up the street to the *Bibliothèque National*, that glass and steel monstrosity that houses much of France's literary treasures. I stopped and started again, checking my surveillance, praying she wasn't leading me into a trap.

When she reached the entrance to the large library, she didn't go inside; instead sat on one of the stone seats outside. They had metal detectors inside the building and she was probably packing some firepower, so whomever she was going to meet, they would meet her here.

I took up a position across the street, near a small café, buying a Badoit mineral water and standing in the shade, sipping it, trying to look cool in my silk navy blue ribbed shirt and gray trousers. I kept the shirt untucked, hanging over my waist line and the Beretta I was carrying.

Blondie didn't move off of her stone seat and I stayed put where I was. After a couple of hours, I sat at one of the café tables and ordered an expresso. I was stirring in the lumps of sugar when my cell phone buzzed. I pressed the button and held it to my ear, my eyes still on Blondie.

"Lafayette, we are here."

"Who's we?"

"Me, myself and I."

I told Hank where I was and to get here *toute de suite*; I was tired and had to tap a kidney. If Blondie made a move, I had Hank's number in my cell phone and could call him back with new directions.

But she didn't move. Just sat there.

About an hour later, a sleek Mercedes taxi passed me and went down the block, stopping at the corner of the *rue Fernand-Braudel*.

Hank's lanky silhouette emerged from the back seat. He was toting a long gym bag with an easy going, smooth walk. Inside, he was lean, mean and full of spleen. Just what I needed but the opposition didn't need to know it. I wanted to surprise them.

"You owe me two bills and a deuce for the flight and the taxi," he said with a smile as he sat down across from me.

"What about the rest?"

"Uncle takes care of that."

I checked out his duds. He was wearing a plum silk shirt and tan trousers and designer shades.

"At least you didn't show up in cammies," I said.

"I had time for a quick change at Rhein-Main."

"You packin'?"

"In the R.F.? Not with their gun laws and my status."

"Just what is your status?"

"Single and alive. And I mean to keep it that way."

"I can take care of you. You're comfortable with a Beretta, right?"

He shrugged. "I prefer my Sig-Sauer but sure, the Beretta was my active duty piece."

He stopped talking to me when the waiter came by. Hank ordered an Orangina and after the man left, he looked at me quizzically.

"How'd you get the gun in-country?"

I smiled. "It was a present from someone I bumped into the men's room."

"Mighty generous of him."

"Yeah, he was all choked up with emotion."

"So what's the play?" Hank said.

The waiter brought Hank's Orangina and I was silent until he left; then I told Hank I was leading a teen-age rescue effort for the Milligan Foundation.

I nodded across the street at Blondie.

"Who's she?" Hank said.

I explained and asked him to keep an eye on her for a couple of minutes while I used the facilities. When I came back, she was still there. Hank was popping a pill with his Orangina.

"What's that? Your vitamins?" I said.

"Yeah. Anti-malaria plus iron."

"For Paris?"

"Nah. Looks like Musharraf will never get his act together and let us do our job and go get OBL. So the firm told me to get ready for my next gig."

"Where's the set?" I said.

"No can tell, you know that," he said.

He swallowed the pill with a large gulp.

"Milligan Foundation must pay well," he said.

"No can tell, you know that," I said.

"What's my cut?"

When I told him one large a day, he didn't bat an eyelash. And the thou was over and above what he was collecting from the G through TechnoDyne. I reached into my pocket and pulled out five hundred Euros and slid the money across the table to him.

"Go to the Lutetia and get a room and get some rest. Pay rack rate, if you have to."

He nodded. "What about you?"

"I'll stay here for a while. Watch Blondie, then go back to the hotel if nothing's happening. Come up to my room around six and we'll strategize."

After he left, I went back to work. At four p.m. I quit and caught a cab on the *Quai François Mauriac* and rode back to the hotel.

I popped open a 1664 when I got to my room, and then hung up all the clothes I had bought. After that I took a long hot shower, using up two containers of body gel. I had dressed in my new maroon silk shirt and tan silk slacks and was watching CNN when there was a rap on door.

I flicked the TV on mute and went to the door, holding the Beretta at my side.

"*Oui?*" I was really mastering the French language now.

"It's me," Hank said.

I let him in, silently thanking him for the look of appreciation he gave my outfit.

"Had anything to eat?" I said.

"Man, I'm starved," he said. "Only had peanuts and coffee on the flight. You go ahead and choose the menu, counselor."

"I'll order up and we'll talk over dinner." I handed him a cold 1664 from the fridge. "Here, start on this."

While Hank sipped the beer, I called room service and ordered a bottle of Taittinger rosé champagne. It was the *vin ordinaire* of the Lutetia. Then for good measure, I added a bottle of Lynch-Bages 2000. I told them we wanted the drinks now.

"It's important to prioritize," I whispered to Hank.

"That it is," he said.

Then I ordered a *foie gras façon torché en lobe et son pain chaud*; two *côtes de bœuf*, grilled *à point*. I skipped the cheese and ordered a chocolate mousse and a strawberry soup in red wine for our desserts. Hank had his choice. I could eat either. Or both. I said to bring the food in forty minutes.

"Sylvie, huh? Sounds like my type."

"She is, Hank, she is, but she works for our client, so leave her alone."

"Boring."

"I'll tell you what. If you can seduce Blondie into giving up Vanessa Milligan's location, I'll give you an introduction."

"Well, I'll just have to give it the old college try." He poured some more of the champagne into our flutes.

"You never went to college," I said.

"That's why I can read, write and speak six languages."

I had no answer.

The food was quite satisfying and while I wheeled the table out into the corridor, Hank poured the rest of the Bordeaux.

"So what's the plan?" he said when I returned.

"Follow Blondie."

"And hope she'll lead us to Dagwood?"

"That's it in a nutshell."

Hank sipped the Bordeaux. "Foot surveillance or vehicle?"

I thought about that for a minute.

"You have your cell phone, right?"

He nodded.

"I'm thinkin' combined." I ran down the exact location of the Mistral Jihad armory and the Metro stations around it.

"I know the area," Hank said. "But for what we're doing, progressive surveillance is best. Back to the *Bibliothèque National* tomorrow. We'll pick her up from there."

It sounded good. I took the Beretta out of my pocket and tossed it to Hank. He caught it and looked the piece over, turning it around in his hand. Then he got up off the couch and went over to the desk and picked up a pen and went into the bathroom. When he returned, the nub of the pen was wrapped in tissue paper.

After removing the clip and unloading the chamber, he probed the gun barrel with the pen, then pulled it out. The tissue paper was streaked with brown.

"Pretty dusty, huh?" I said.

"Not dust, sand."

"Sand?"

"Yeah, this pistol's been in the desert and hasn't been cleaned."

"Pretty sloppy of our opposition," I said.

"And dangerous," Hank said.

"Dangerous?"

"Real dangerous. Your friend, the one you bumped into in the restroom, he could have blown his hand off if he tried to use it."

13.

We kept up a progressive surveillance for four days. It didn't progress. When Blondie left the *Bibliothèque National*, she only went back to the armory. We had no idea where she ate or slept. Only that it wasn't on the *Quai de Valmy*. I was paying Hank big bucks and we were getting nowhere. Just tired, bored and stupid.

"They don't want to die like the others," Hank said between sips of Stella Artois while we drank and mused at the Café Fabien. "They made two runs at you and wound up with three dead and one at the tender mercies of the DST, probably wishing by now he was dead. They can't afford to lose any more cadres."

"So why is Blondie so nonchalant that she doesn't even check her surveillance?"

"Something to be considered," Hank said.

"Maybe they're still surveilling us, so they know we're watching and that's why she's acting all cool and just going to the library."

Hank shrugged. "To what end, counselor?"

I ignored the dig. I was an attorney, a former prosecutor, and Hank always called me 'counselor' when he was unsure how sound my reasoning was. I let him get away with it, something I never let any smart-ass detective do.

"In other words, she really doesn't know we're on to her," I continued. "She hasn't even bothered to alter her route." My voice started to trail off, even I was sounding dubious now.

"Maybe they're just waiting for you to give up," he said. "Then they'll come out of hiding."

"To do what? They haven't even made a ransom demand for Vanessa," I said.

"Those guns and the *plastique* aren't your ordinary kidnapping tools."

"So you think they've got something else planned?"

"Probably more than one thing but they're waiting for you to leave the set."

"That bothers me, good buddy," I said. "I don't like the idea of them having access to that stuff."

"Me neither."

"So let's be a little proactive."

"I thought we were," he said.

"I mean, let's step up the action," I said.

"You won't get an argument from me."

"Let's try and spook Blondie. Let her know I'm onto to her, that she's under surveillance, and so's the Mistral Jihad armory. Maybe she'll bolt. And if she bolts, maybe she'll lead us to the others and Vanessa Milligan."

"Roger. And she won't know there's two of us. She'll only be doing surveillance detection routes for you."

"And while she's running the SDR's, you'll pick up her trail and stay on her."

"Like white on rice."

Hank swigged some more of the beer then poured the rest of the bottle into his glass. Next to him, resting on the table was his book du jour.

I picked it up. "*L'Absolue Perfection du Crime*," I read out loud with what I hoped was a reasonable French accent. The Absolute Perfection of Crime.

"A novel by Tanguy Viel," Hank said.

"What's it about?" I said.

"A casino heist."

"I think I saw that movie."

"Not the way this is written."

I nodded and took a long, easy swallow of my Stella.

"I have to admit you really amaze me."

"Why do you say that? I know I amaze most people but I'm curious as to why I amaze you."

"No college. Not even an undergraduate degree and you have this tremendous knowledge. Real intellectual knowledge, not just street smarts. I know about the Korean I was there too but where in the heck did you pick up such facility with French?"

"Doherty, you've know me what, fifteen years?"

"About that long, I guess."

"And we've never lied to each other, right."

"No darling," I laughed.

"Funny guy." He sat his beer back down on the table. "Think about it. Did I ever say I didn't go to college?"

I thought about it. I took another swig of beer, even longer this time, and thought some more. Hank was always easy going but very closed mouthed about himself.

"No, I guess you didn't but you never talked about it either."

"I don't talk about a lot of things."

"If I had asked you, would you have told me?"

"Maybe."

"So why are you fessing up now?"

Hank shrugged. "This game is moving into a new phase. A real dangerous phase."

"I thought you were used to danger."

"I am. What about you?"

"We've been through gun battles before."

"This is different," he said. His voice was firmer, icy frozen now. "This is their turf. And they don't mind dying."

He had moved off the subject, trying to deflect my question but I sensed it was only half-hearted. So I asked again, this time more directly.

"Tell me then, where did you go to school? Pembroke State?"

"You think Pembroke because I'm a Lumbee from Carolina? Just a copper-skinned Tarheel happy to stay close to home?"

"No, but you have a girl there. Seemed logical that you might have."

"Might have is right. Except I scored very, very high on my English SAT. They didn't get too many Native Americans with those kinds of scores at Princeton."

"Princeton? You mean you went to school with Don Rumsfeld and Jim Baker?"

Hank laughed. "The geriatric brigade? Those old fogies were more than a few classes ahead of me. They didn't study ancient history; they lived it."

I laughed too. "And a few brains behind." I drank some more beer. "So how is it you wound up in this kind of work? I mean instead of Harvard Law, or investment banking or the State Department or mingling with the Agency white-collar crowd?"

"Prinecton's a mighty expensive place. They were generous with financial aid, but even so, I had to work all four years tending bar, and ROTC chipped in some chump change. After graduation it was off to

Fort Huachuca in Arizona for six months of intelligence training. Then Korea."

"I thought you were in the Rangers?"

He set down his beer. "Enough about me. We've got plans to make and I need a new piece. I can't clean this Beretta properly."

After we finished fleshing out the plan, Hank offered to teach me some French. "One useful phrase a day," he said.

"Such as?" I said.

"*Ne bouge pas d'un poil.*"

"What's that supposed to mean?"

"Don't move an inch."

It was useful, I conceded. He had me repeat the phrase five times, using different tones of voices.

"Still American, but whoever you talk to will get the message."

"Thanks."

"So here's the bonus for your diligent effort," he said. "This is important to remember."

I nodded my head.

"A *preservatif* is not a *confiture.*"

I knew that *confitures* were the preserves, the jellies and jams that you spread on bread or croissants. So what the hell was a *preservatif?*

Hank could see the puzzled look on my face.

"A condom, my man. A rubber."

"Oh, that's why the room service operator was shocked when I asked for *préservatifs* to be sent up with my breakfast."

I had moved the OP to the small sidewalk café on the *Quai de Valmy*; where I sat in plain view, sipping a coffee. Hank was down at the other end of the quai, at an Indian restaurant, doing the same. If Blondie came out, no matter which way she turned, we'd pick up her trail and follow. But she needed to come my way for the plan to work

The waiter brought my coffee. He was doubling as the barman. It was the ubiquitous Parisian hangout—six stools along the bar and three bistro tables along the opposite wall, one of them covered in a blue and white checkered cloth. Maybe Nicolas Sarkozy would be popping in for a *pression.* Outside, red formica tables. I was sitting at one of these. The skies were dark and cloudy and it was cool in the open air. Still, it was Sunday and more people were out. Joggers, bicyclists, residents of the neighborhood. The *quartier*, the map in the Metro station called it.

A *maman* with a soft cocoa face, all dressed in white silk from head to toe, walked by, teenage daughter in tow. The woman had a long ankle length skirt and silk shirt with orange brocade on the left arm. Below her head wrap, gold ball earrings dangled. There was a gold band on her left hand; the 18k variety, and a silver coin ring on her right. Her daughter was clad in designer denim jeans and jacket with a revealing black silk top, a daringness offset by studious horn-rimmed glasses.

A few minutes earlier, I had slipped into the armory and went to the bedroom closet and pried open the weapons cache under the floorboards. I took two of the Berettas, one for Hank, one for me, plus a box of cartridges, and then started to seal the cache back up.

Hell, no. I changed my mind. I wasn't leaving the *plastique* for these clowns. I grabbed the brick of brown putty and shoved it under my jacket. Then I left the floor boards loose and dragged the carryon suitcase to the middle of the bedroom floor.

Now, I was back at the OP, waiting for Blondie to show on the set.

A man passed by, casual in tan slacks laden with cargo pockets, white shirt and a sweater tied around his neck. He paid no attention to me, just yapped into his *portable*.

I ordered another coffee and watched a female jogger in a gray t-shirt and shorts run along the street, her ample breasts heaving with each pound of the pavement. Sports bras must be out of fashion this season. Not too far behind her, a grizzled bicyclist in workingman's blue clothes pedaled by.

After about an hour or so, Blondie came down the street, casual, unconcerned. She was wearing a powder blue tank top and tight, white slacks and jogging shoes, all of which added spice to her saunter. When she reached my café table, I stood up.

"Hi, beautiful," I said in English.

She gave a startled look which changed to a glare of pure hatred.

"Long time, no see." I kept a smile on my face.

She turned and stormed off, hurrying to her building. When she reached the front door, she turned and looked back at me. This time the hate on her face was replaced by worry.

I walked across the street and stood where I could see the window to the Mistral Jihad armory, and more importantly, where Blondie could see me. I leaned against the iron fence and looked up, being as obvious as I could be. The curtain on the window pulled back and when I saw the corner of her face peeping out, I gave a jaunty wave of my hand. The curtain quickly dropped back.

Hank was watching from his table at the Indian restaurant. He was no longer interested in his *roman policier*, he had also seen Blondie come down the street and my approach to her.

About ten minutes later, she was looking out the window again. I gave another wave of my hand and the curtain dropped back.

A man with gray wavy hair and beard and wire rimmed glasses, and wearing a black sports jacket and tan pants, passed by. He was carrying a market sack with some items in it. He saw me looking at Blondie's window and looked up to see what I was looking at; saw nothing, and then looked at me.

"I'm American," I said, with a goofy grin.

He shrugged, satisfied with my explanation and walked off.

I went back across the street to the café and ordered a *pression* and waited. Blondie couldn't see the table from her window and I figured my disappearance from view would unnerve her just as much as her seeing me watch her.

It did.

An hour later, she came storming out of the building, hauling the carryon suitcase behind her. She scowled at me when I stood up and then she hurried off in the other direction; straight toward Hank. We had spooked her alright, though she didn't know there was a "we." Only knew about me as she hurried past Hank and crossed the street. When she glanced back she didn't even notice my ghost falling in a few feet behind her.

I started up the street towards her, a broad smile on my face, and that spooked her even more. Dodging a pair of youths rollerblading down the street, she dragged the carryon case up onto the sidewalk and hurried across the bridgeway to the *Quai de Jemmapes* on the other side of the canal. Blondie looked back at me again, still scowling, and I smiled and quickened my pace behind her while Hank passed by on the left, putting her in a neat surveillance squeeze. He had his book open, reading like some distracted intellectual with nothing else to do on a Sunday morning in Paris.

She rushed into a small community sports park and I followed, making it real obvious, waving my hand yelling, "Yoo-hoo" to her, as if I wanted her to stop and give me her number. We were walking on a quiet path overlooking basketball courts and an asphalt soccer pitch. She kept glancing back at me, not noticing Hank up ahead. All around us were tall apartment complexes—worker housing from the 1960's—elegant with curved terraces that looked out on most of Paris. The basketball court below was deserted, but some kids were practicing soccer kicks on the asphalt.

No one else was on the path and when we reached the *Place Robert Desnos*, there was a large flea market in progress. Residents raising money for a community health project. The *place* was actually a series of circular areas that rose uphill to the *rue Albert Camus* and the whole pavement was covered with household flotsam and jetsam.

Blondie had to struggle and wrestle the suitcase around the vendors and up the steps of each circle to the next higher level, bumping into two little girls, knocking their display of books over onto the ground. She cursed and glared at them, then back at me.

I was no longer smiling, my face hard, and my right hand hovering menacingly by the hem of my jacket, where she thought I was carrying a Beretta. She was moving at half-gallop now around the rim of the *Place Colonel Fabien*, me right behind her, and she stormed down the steps of the Metro station, stumbling, almost falling, as she looked back at me and missed a step.

Recovering her balance, she reached the bottom and fed a ticket into the turnstile and dashed through just before I reached her. I slapped my head and swore because I had no ticket; would have to wait on the Sunday line to buy one. Blondie threw me a triumphant leer and hurried off. She never saw, not even sensed, Hank right behind her.

I went back upstairs and sat outside at the Café Fabien and ordered a large Stella Artois *pression*. Even though it was still cloudy it was a fine day to sit and relax.

14.

I spent the rest of the afternoon at my café OP outside the Mistral Jihad armory, waiting to see if Blondie returned or if anyone else showed up. No one did. The place was abandoned. She, they, had flown the coop.

After an early dinner of steak tartare frites and most of a bottle of a good Châteauneuf-du-Pape, a young Domaine du Pégau Cuvée da Capo, I was back in my room watching one of the World Cup playoff games on the TV.

It was England against Ecuador and the match was being played in Stuttgart. I drowsily followed the action as the teams moved up and down the pitch. Then suddenly England's Number 7, the great Beckham, was caressing the ball with his feet, running through the defenders, and kicking in a goal with sixty minutes gone. The stadium erupted with the banging of drums and a mighty chanting of God Save the Queen. I was getting interested now. For England, like me, it was either a win or go home. Or die.

My cell phone went off at seventy-eight minutes into the match. It was Hank.

"Still alive, I see."

"Yeah, alive and kickin' back."

"Where are you?"

"Marseille, bro. Sitting at a café on the *Vieux Port*, enjoying a Poire William and watching the sunset."

"Blondie there too?"

"Right on my lap. Nah, she's in an apartment up in the *Panier*." The *Panier* is one of the oldest sections of Marseille, situated on the northern side of the *Vieux Port* harbor. A rabbit warren of hilly, narrow streets. It had been almost totally destroyed by the Germans during World War II in a pique of revenge against both the French Résistance and the Jews that were hiding there. During the vacation Dana and I had spent in Provence ten years ago, we'd wandered those quaint streets. I wondered how much it had changed.

"Where are you staying?" I said.

"I've checked into the La Residence du Vieux Port. A suite on the top floor. When are you coming down?"

"Tomorrow morning."

"Flying?"

"No, I'm going to take the TGV; I'm bringing presents."

The TGV was France's express train, capable of going one hundred and seventy miles an hour. And the presents were the two Berettas and the *plastique* which I knew I could never smuggle onto a plane.

"That's how I came down. Same train as Blondie; same car as a matter of fact."

"Anybody meet her at the station?"

"Two men and a woman. They grabbed a cab and went to the apartment. Haven't seen her since."

"She must not care for the tourist attractions."

"A couple of those attractions just sauntered by, so let me get off the phone."

"Okay. See you TMW."

"Room 907," Hank said. "What are going to do with all those fancy threads you bought?"

Good point. What was I going to do? I couldn't drag my wardrobe around on a surveillance to God knows where.

"I'll think of something," I said.

"I hope so," Hank said. "It's about time you stopped dressing like a civil service mouthpiece."

"Well, since you insist." I left the conversation at that, but instead of setting the phone back in its cradle I called Sylvie at her *portable* number.

When she picked up, I asked her to make TGV reservations for me and to arrange to have my clothes and Hank's gym bag picked up at the Lutetia.

I only packed a few items in my overnight, placing the clothes on top of the guns and the brick of explosives. Then I went out for a long stroll and when I reached the middle of the Pont de Bercy, I tossed the sand-gritted Beretta way out into the Seine.

The train station in Marseille was small by Parisian standards, its few tracks occupied mainly by traffic from four commuter lines. I took a cab from the station to the La Residence. We skirted the *Panier* on the way, the taxi driver desperately seeking to avoid the famously horrendous

Marseille congestion. The honking of horns and screeching of brakes and the strains of hoarse Gallic cursing didn't disturb me though. I had nothing but fond memories of the days Dana and I had spent here. And even more fonder memories of the nights. The driver pulled up at the corner of the hotel, and I paid him and got out.

The La Residence was an older hotel but it had the best view going of the *Vieux Port* and the *Panier*. When I checked in, the clerk told me that they were expecting me and I slid over the Milligan Foundation bank card to take care of the suite and incidentals.

The first thing I did when I got up to the room was pull open the drapes and look out onto the harbor. Since ancient Greece, this cove of water had been a thriving commercial seaport. Before it became too big for its britches. Now, it was just a large marina surrounded by hotels and a myriad number of restaurants and cafés. Still, it was terrific. My kind of place. Lots of good seafood, wine and prima pulchritude.

I'd check with Hank later; right now I wanted a long hot shower to wash the heat and dirt off of me; then a cold beer and a quick snooze. I put the little suitcase inside the bathroom and turned on the water. Then I wondered if the heat would affect the *plastique*; so I wheeled it back out and put the guns and explosives under the mattress.

About four o'clock, the room phone rang. I was groggy from the sleep and I almost knocked over the beer bottle reaching for the receiver.

"Speak to me."

"It's *moi*, blood brother. I'm back upstairs, in the suite."

"I'll be up in a minute," I said, reaching under the mattress for my stash.

When I got there, he had a bottle of champagne on ice and two glasses ready for action.

"Pour me a couple of those," I said.

"Trip that bad?"

"No, I'm just ready for action," I said, setting the guns and the brick of explosive down on the table. "I remembered you too." I slid one of the autos across to him.

Hank smiled. "You're so thoughtful," he said.

"That's me, Mr. Thoughtful," I said, as I took a glass of champagne. "This hits the spot." I walked over to the window and looked out, sipping the bubbly, comparing the view from Hank's suite to mine, three floors below. "Is that the Chateau d'If way out there in the water?"

"The one and only," Hank said.

93

"Dana and I had wanted to go see it but the ferry boat operators were on strike that week."

"This is France," he said.

I shrugged. "C'mon; let's go for a walk, let the champagne chill some more. Show me Blondie's hideout."

Hank led me to the other side of the *Vieux Port*, to the narrow hillside streets behind the Hotel de Ville, that ancient city hall the Germans didn't get around to destroying before they beat a hasty retreat. We passed the *Place de Lenche* and a crowded café, and then we were deep in the rabbit warren called the *Panier*. The streets were even more narrow here and shady, many of the buildings old and decrepit. We passed a *Santoun* shop, an establishment that sold the large dolls of Provençal characters. In the window, there were a group of them: card players at a table.

Hank stopped a few doors down and gestured with his right thumb at a gray stone three-story building across the street.

"She's in there," he said, stepping up on the curb.

"You followed her here?"

"Watched her go inside. That was yesterday afternoon. She hasn't shown herself since."

"Could they have set up countersurveillance? Maybe they spotted you?"

"On this narrow street? I stayed down at the corner. They'd have to open the shutters and stick their heads way out in order to spot me." Hank pointed to the closed wooden shutters on the second and third floors.

"Which apartment?" I said.

"That's for you to find out, counselor."

"Anybody else go in or out?"

"Just a couple of dudes, one chick."

Back at the hotel I spread out the DST enhanced photos of the remaining Mistral Jihad suspects on the bed. Hank sifted through them and set aside two men and a woman. AGNES, CALVI and RONDO; their *noms de guerre* read. AGNES? What's in a name?

CALVI and RONDO were young, like the others, the newly dearly departed. Except they were still around to do some damage. I hoped they were as stupid as the others but I couldn't count on it.

I picked up AGNES's photo. She was sitting at a café, a demitasse cup in front of her, shades over her eyes, beret over the hair.

"How do you recognize her, all covered up like this?"

Hank laughed. He tapped the photo, his finger hitting her ear. "See that sparkler? One carat diamond stud. Don't see many of those going in and out of the *Panier*."

I nodded. "Okay, she's the play. Does she go around alone or with CALVI and RONDO?"

"Sometimes with one of them; sometimes alone."

We had finished the champagne and now I was inspired.

"I'll make the approach. We grab her and get her to give up the apartment."

"Then what?"

"Then we go in."

"Like a SWAT team, you mean?"

I nodded. This time I was a little dubious though.

So was Hank. "If Vanessa Milligan is in there, they might kill her."

"Do you have a better idea?"

"As a matter of fact, counselor, I do."

Hank ran down the plan while I listened. I had to agree his idea made more sense than my gangbusters approach."

"So let's do it," I said.

"Now?"

"It's starting to get dark. Might as well."

He rubbed his chin. "Here's your French lesson for today, then."

"What?"

"C'est moi qui tire les ficelles."

"What's that mean?"

"I'm running the show."

15.

I left the La Residence and walked along the *Quai des Belges*, past the ferry boats that carried the tourists out to the Château d'If and the Île de Porquerolles. There was a demonstration going on, a protest against an incinerator plant and the intersection with *La Canebière*, Marseille's main drag, was jam-packed with protestors and plainclothes cops. I skirted the crowd and went along the *Quai du Port*, moving past the cafés, now filled with locals and tourists having an early evening drink. I turned at the *Hotel de Ville* and walked up the hill toward the *Place David*. A maroon Mercedes sped by me and reached the *Place* ahead of me and stopped. I slowed my walk and when I passed the Mercedes, I threw a sidelong glance at the driver, catching a large bulk and sunglasses. Could be RONDO, I thought.

As per Hank's plan, we had our cellphones turned on, with Hank connected to my number. I slid my hand into my pocket when I passed the church.

Two taps. The warning signal. I heard a tap back, Hank was ghosting me, hovering somewhere in the background as my security and he was signaling that he had picked up my watcher. I kept wandering the narrow streets, looking like a lost tourist, gradually bringing myself closer to Blondie's hideout. When I reached the *Santoun* shop I stopped, pretending to look in the store window. My four wooden card players were still there, at the table drinking *pastis* and looking at their cards.

One, in a black turtle neck sweater and white sailor's cap, seemed to be rearing back in his seat, laughing at my predicament.

I looked down the street towards Blondie's hideaway. A black Peugeot sedan pulled up at the far corner. A man and a woman got out and the man moved slowly toward me, keeping to the middle of the narrow cobblestone street.

They were putting me in a bind. Whichever side I moved to, he could cut me off. And if I barreled past him, AGNES was waiting for me and I was sure she was armed. They probably had orders to take me alive so that I could be interrogated, but if they had to kill me, they would.

I looked behind me. The maroon Mercedes was blocking the street. The driver was out, lumbering my way; young, with dark eyes much too small for his large shaven head. Below the bowling ball skull he was massive; shoulders, neck, chest and arms all molded into a solid muscle machine. RONDO moved like an up and coming pro wrestler; I wondered who his steroid supplier was. If his size wasn't enough to buffalo me, RONDO pulled back the side of his leather jacket, letting me see the butt of an automatic sticking up from under his belt.

He spoke to me in fluid French. I tried to think of something Hank had taught me to fire back at him, but I came up blank and answered him in English.

"Excuse me, could I take your picture next to the *Santoun* shop? It would make a wonderful souvenir of my trip to Marseille."

RONDO had his hand on his gun now, letting me know this conversation was basically going to be one-sided.

I smiled at him. "Yeah, good, props will make the picture even better," I said. "Maybe your friends can get in too? A group shot." I gestured at AGNES and CALVI.

The gun came out of RONDO's waistband and I let him shove me up against the wall.

"Put AGNES in the middle; it'll make a better photo," I said. I was going to make some more suggestions but a fist slammed into my kidney, causing my head to snap back and my legs buckle. I was on my way down when another punch, this time to the back of the neck, drove me forward, into the wall.

I could see the laughing card player in the window just before a soupy blackness enveloped me.

Blondie's hideout was on the second floor. I dimly remembered them dragging me up one flight of stairs from the street. When I regained some of my senses, I was slumped on a couch, facing the windows to the street. I knew it was the street because I caught a glimpse of the corner of the sign for the *Santoun* shop through the shutter just before RONDO yanked me to my feet and slapped my face.

He got my attention. I looked around the room. It was a sell-out crowd. Besides RONDO, CALVI and AGNES, Blondie was there. And a mystery guest of honor. A tall slender man, middle-aged with close-cropped hair, graying at the temples. He came over to me and cupped my chin and peered into my eyes. I recognized his face from the DST collection. THIERRY.

"Mr. Doherty, you are a royal pain in the arse." He spoke in English; a trace of British accent, the kind I figured Continentals picked while visiting the UK.

"I try to be," I said.

HONDO's fist slammed into my chest, sending me sprawling back on the couch. I let my hand fall to my side. Nothing there. Of course not, Doherty. Didn't you think they'd frisk you?

HONDO raised his fist as to hit me again but THIERRY held his hand up. "Not yet," he said. Turning back to me, "You see, Monsieur Doherty, your sense of humor doesn't go over big with this audience."

I tried to sit up but the pain in my side kept me doubled over.

"Does this mean they won't stick around for my second act?"

THIERRY let out a short laugh and brushed the side of his head with his hand.

"I'm afraid this will be your final performance, Monsieur Doherty. And my associates will be sticking around to ensure that it is a good one."

He was trying to stare me down now but I kept my eyes focused on his body, memorizing his build, the clothes he was wearing. He was clad differently than the others and it intrigued me. CALVI, AGNES, even HONDO were dressed upscale casual. But THIERRY was dressed more workmanlike. Not an industrial laborer but it seemed more like a farmer or maybe a construction worker.

Someone who spent his days outdoors. Yet, he was the leader of this pathetic band of Euro yuppies, at least what was left of them.

"Why are you so desperate to get Vanessa Milligan back?" he said.

"Why do you think?" I said.

HONDO stepped over and yanked me up and slammed a fist into my midsection. I had tensed my muscled to lessen the solar plexus blow but the big guy really packed a wallop and I felt a rib crack before I dropped to my knees.

"I ask the questions, Monsieur Doherty," THIERRY said.

Still holding my midsection, I eased myself back onto the couch. "She has a mother who loves her very much and she wants her daughter back. Unharmed."

"So she hired you to find the girl?"

"Yes."

"It seems Judge Milligan likes to approach problems from a long, convoluted and difficult position," THIERRY said.

"I don't get it? Are you telling me there's another way?"

"You mean you don't know?"

I shook my head.

"Too bad for you, Monsieur Doherty," he said. "You should have asked your client."

"Let me call her now," I said. I was trying to think of a plan.

A big blank.

"I'm afraid it's a little late for that," he said. "But you will have to answer a few questions before this all over."

"I really don't know all that much."

I tried to listen out for Hank. Nothing.

"Well, I'm very interested in what you do know."

"And if I don't tell you, HONDO here will hit me again."

THIERRY smiled. "Hondo? Is that what you call him? How quaint. Like some American cowboy movie."

"French, actually," I said.

THIERRY shrugged. "Well, no matter. He is capable of breaking every bone in your body. And he will. Then he'll start on the rest of you."

I held up my hands. "There's no need for violence."

"Violence? You've killed four of my associates."

It was actually three; the fourth was assisting the DST with their investigation. But I wasn't going to correct him.

"Who tried to kill me," I said. "After she fingered me. Her, Blondie."

"Blondie? Another quaint American name. Do you do this with everyone?"

"It's a New York thing."

"So you decided to follow her and get the rest of us."

"If need be," I said. "But I really just want Vanessa Milligan back."

"Are you working alone?"

"Of course." I spit the words out. "Do you think I want to share a fat fee with anyone?"

"I wish I could believe you, Monsieur Doherty," THIERRY said. "But I really must make sure."

He nodded to HONDO. "Leave his face for last. I want him able to talk."

HONDO broke into a wide grin. He obviously loved his line of work.

I looked over at AGNES. "You seem like a nice girl," I said. "Are you going to let them do this to me?"

Her eyes narrowed.

"She's not going to help you, Monsieur Doherty," THIERRY said. "She's going to participate in the festivities."

I looked into AGNES's eyes again. I believed him.

HONDO yanked me off the couch and hit me again. This time in my left side, just below the heart. I would have collapsed but he was still holding me up, fist drawn back for another punch.

Blondie stepped toward me, ready to get her licks in but suddenly I lost sight of her in a bright flash of white light.

Good. I was going under. To that safe place, that deep dark cavern where I could feel no pain.

HONDO let go of me. Then my eardrums split. I thought THIERRY had told HONDO not to hit me in the head. Then the white light faded and I could see the others holding their heads too, blood trickling down from their ears. Clothes torn. Stunned.

The sound of an automatic spitting as Hank stepped inside the blown off door, and a part of HONDO's skull shattered before Hank turned away. CALVI was reaching for my Beretta on the table but took two rounds in the chest before he could grab it. He floated backwards with glazed unseeing eyes until he slammed into the wall and sank.

I was on the floor now, sprawled out flat. More gunfire. Shrieks. Then AGNES's lithe body sank, her gun falling next to her. I crawled over and grabbed it, looking around wildly.

"Two more left," I said.

"They're gone," Hank said. "We'd better split too." He helped me up to my feet. "Get my gun," I said. "Fingerprints."

I could hear sirens wailing in the distance as he lifted me up onto his shoulders. "*Tu m'en bouches en cœur*," he said.

16.

"You think France has a shot at winning the World Cup?" I said.

"Odds are 12-to-1," Hank said.

We had the Marseille newspaper spread out in front of us on the coffee table. The front page was covered with soccer stories; Ribery, one of the Marseille club's star players was on the national team and a double dose of pride was involved with the city.

Down below on the right hand side of the page were photos of the Jihad Mistral's hideout in the *Panier*. One of the photos showed bodies being carried out of the building on stretchers; the other showed the blown up apartment, with HONDO's bulky corpse propped up against the couch. According to Hank, the police said the killings involved the drug trade. It would take awhile for the details to work up the bureaucratic pipeline and for the DST to put two and two together.

"How much of that stuff did you use?" I was talking about the *plastique* I had given Hank.

"Not much," he said. "I shaped it to the molding so the door would blow inward."

"Enough to rough me up." I touched the abraded skin on my forehead and nose where some splinters of wood had struck me.

"Had to shock and awe," he said.

"That you did."

Hank dunked one of the *pains au chocolat* in his coffee and took a bite, chewing slowly and swallowing. When he was done, he said, "What do you think THIERRY meant when he said Judge Milligan wanted to do this the hard way?"

"I have no idea," I said. "But it's something to think about all right."

While we drank our coffee and watched the news on CNN, we thought about that.

And while we thought, my cell phone rang.

"Doherty?" It was Carlton Andrews, the bean counter.

"Speaking."

"Alive and well. I hear you've been doing good work."

"I've been busy." He must have heard from Sylvie. Or from Cynthia Milligan who had heard from Sylvie. Well, for the money Milligan was paying she had the right to keep close tabs on me.

"Any purpose to your call?" I said.

"Of course. I'm a busy man myself."

"Well, get to it then." I was still jumpy from last night and my voice had a hard edge to it. But if it upset Andrews, tough.

"The ATM withdrawal you were concerned about; remember that?"

I didn't answer.

"Well, it turns out that the bank card belongs to a close corporation involved in French agribusiness."

"Agribusiness? Where?"

"In northern France. The company is owned by the family of a right-wing politician. Name of Jacques LaPlume. Anti-immigrant, really anti-everything not French. Some say he's pro-Nazi."

That threw me for a loop. French neo-Nazis and Islamic jihadists didn't run in the same circles.

"What else?" I knew there was more.

"This might interest you," Andrews said. "While the company is based in Normandy, there's been a flurry of activity from its bank cards in a small town near Bordeaux. Name of Pauillac. Ever hear of it?"

Damn right I did. Anyone who knew anything about wine did. Lafite-Rothschild, Mouton-Rothschild, Latour, Chateau Palmer, Lynch-Bages, all top growths, all in Pauillac; and all in my cellar.

I took a deep breath. "Pauillac. Yes, I've heard of it."

"I rather thought so," Andrews said. He gave me the address of a building and I wrote it down. He said it belonged to one of the LaPlume family businesses.

I thanked him and hung up the phone.

"You heard?" I said to Hank.

"Pauillac," he said.

"You know it?"

"Only from your cellar," he said.

"My cellar?"

"Yeah, the Clerc-Milon 2000."

"You drank my Clerc-Milon 2000? It's not ready yet?"

"Don't worry, I decanted it and left it open for a couple of hours."

"Damn it. When was this?"

"Remember when you had to go to Savannah and you left me to watch out for Dana?"

That was when Jimmy the Toad Murphy had sent his assassin Seamus after Dana and me. I shrugged. It was a cheap price to pay for Hank's bodyguard service.

"I didn't touch the Mouton," he said.

"You know your Pauillac, I see."

"You buy it, I try it," he laughed.

"I hope you had a good meal with it," I said.

"Porterhouse. Medium rare. Baked potato and an onion and tomato slices." Hank's face was lit up with the pleasure of the reminiscence of it all.

"You ate my steak too? That was $24 a pound at the Grand Central Market."

He nodded.

"Well, you're going to have to replace the wine," I said.

"You mean we're going to Pauillac?"

I told him what Andrews had said about the bank cards and LaPlume and the building in Pauillac.

"LaPlume, huh?"

"You know him?"

"A real piece of racist shit. He shoots off his mouth to all the other pieces of racist shit."

"We have anything to worry about?"

"Not with what I've seen so far," he said, "but you never know."

"How much of that *plastique* is left?"

"Most of it?"

"With that and our Berettas, we're ready."

He smiled at the thought. It was the same smile he had when he was thinking about the steak and wine.

I called Sylvie at the Milligan Foundation in Paris and asked her to make reservations on the TGV to Bordeaux. For two us. I gave her Hank's name and fended off her curiosity about him. This was strictly business.

Sylvie called back about twenty minutes later. Our tickets were waiting at the Marseille station. Train 4758, she said, leaving at 12:54 p.m. and arriving at Bordeaux at 6:28 p.m. A Mercedes minivan would be waiting when we got there. She had also made a room reservation for us, a suite at the Hotel Burdigala. Bordeaux's best, she said.

Good girl, that Sylvie.

I ran down the plan to Hank, how we would set up surveillance all over again in Pauillac; this time double-checking for counter surveillance.

"If Vanessa Milligan's there, we get her and go home."

"What about the other five?" Hank said. "Don't you want to collect the bounty on them?"

I walked over to the window and looked out at the harbor. It was a beautiful day. Sailboats were motoring out past the fort, heading for wider water to unfurl the canvas. I turned back to Hank and said, "If we have to kill any of them to get the girl back, fine. Otherwise, we'll let them go."

"Don't like leaving loose ends," Hank said.

On the way out of the hotel, I dropped the envelope with three more photos in the mail slot. Maybe Hank was right. Why leave any loose ends? Particularly at twenty-five grand a pop.

17.

When we arrived at the Bordeaux station, the rental car Sylvie had arranged for us was waiting outside the station. A Mercedes mini SUV, cute as bug with one of those fancy transmissions that let you shift out of automatic into standard without using a clutch.

I let Hank drive, my ribs were still sore from last night's Q & A, and he played with the shift, getting the feel of how the vehicle accelerated in standard and automatic.

"Not impressed with the standard," he grumbled. The gears were whining and I had to admit that I wasn't too impressed either.

"Sounds like a semi going upgrade," I said.

Hank laughed. "We'll just keep it in automatic. Makes things easier, anyway."

The drive to the Hotel Burdigala seemed like a Sunday cruise in the country after the traffic of Paris and Marseille. The hotel was on the *rue Georges Bonneau*, near the *Place Gambetta*, in the heart of Bordeaux. Burdigala, a pamphlet in the hotel lobby said, was the ancient Roman name for Bordeaux.

"This Sylvie has class," Hank said. "I've got to meet her when we get back to Paris."

"After the assignment is over," I said. "It's a promise since it seems to mean so much to you."

He was right. Sylvie was classy. I had thought about it too. More than once, in my suite at the Lutetia. But then I thought about Dana waiting for me back at my house and I toughed it out.

Our suite in the Burdigala was on the fifth floor, the clerk said, confirming we were staying for five nights. He didn't bat an eyelash when he saw we were just carrying my overnight bag.

The accommodations were spacious with modern leather furniture and two queen-sized beds. There were wide windows with heavy drapes which I pulled back to expose a view of the street and the downtown area beyond.

We ordered champagne and foie gras sent up to the room. After we unpacked, we spread out the Michelin map of the Gironde on one of the beds and ate and drank and mulled over what we were going to do next.

It was still light outside and would be for another couple of hours. We had the car in the garage and the addresses of the LaPlume building and the ATM machine in Pauillac.

"Road trip?" I said.

"Road trip, it is," Hank said.

We drove out of Bordeaux, taking the *Avenue de la Liberation* to the *Route du Médoc* and turning north onto the *Route du Pauillac* which became the D2, or unofficially the *Route des Vins*. Bordeaux's urban sprawl had reached out to these *communes*, spreading packed houses and apartment buildings like cement tentacles into the vineyards.

The hamlets flew by: Macau, with its Chateau Cambon La Pelouse; Labarde with its Giscours; Cantenac and Margaux with their dozen or so grand crus, all headed by the magnificent Chateau Margaux; Moulis and its Chateau Poujeaux, and Arcins with the chateau of the same name. Then Lamarque, Cussac. We swerved in and out of the little villages, the scenery framed by the setting sun. It was as if I was touring my wine cellar.

Suddenly Beycheville loomed ahead with its *commune* of St. Julian. Here were the great wines of Ducru-Beaucaillou; the Bartons; Leoville-Las-Cases, and just across the communal border sat the Pichon Longuevilles. I thought about the bottle of the Pichon-Comtesse that had been smashed in the shootout at the Bon Marché. We would be coming to Pauillac soon, with its tiny hamlet of Daubos and the superb Chateaus Latour and Lynch-Bages. And beyond those vineyards, the port of Pauillac and Blondie,THIERRY and, hopefully, Vanessa Milligan.

When we pulled into the center of Pauillac, the sun was still shining on the Gironde; the river's wide waters sparkling blue. Hank parked the Mercedes in a public lot near the marina and we walked across the road. There was a string of restaurants over there, all starting to fill with evening diners.

"Make like a tourist." Hank said. He took out the map of Pauillac and we looked at it, facing the Gironde as if comparing the river and the town. Orienting ourselves, we marked off the locations of the LaPlume company building and the ATM machine. Both were only a few blocks away.

Most of Pauillac was compactly built. In the center of town there were rows of attached stone houses lining both sides of the narrow treeless streets that meandered back and forth along the gentle hillside. The streets were crowded with ambling tourists mulling the scenery until dinner time, perhaps hoping for a bargain purchase from some merchant who was having a slow day.

It only took a couple of minutes to reach the target site. We walked along the *rue des Moineaux* which curved sharply and we split up, each taking one side of the street, then criss-crossing and doubling back, then doubling back again, meeting finally at the corner of the *rue Rabie*.

The building was a small three-story stone affair on a short street just off the *rue Jean Jaurès*. On both sides were two-story buildings, erected from the same stone, but sealed up and in a partial state of repair—or disrepair. I couldn't quite make up my mind. We passed by and went to the end of the block.

No sign of surveillance.

We blended in with a throng of tourists, strolling with them along the *rue Georges Clemenceau* until we came back to the *rue Jean Jaurès*. There we split up again and ran another SDR.

Nothing. No hits. No one watching us.

I pointed to the church. The Église St. Martin. It was a light gray stone structure with a two-tiered octagonal steeple on top. A clock in the front said 8:15.

We stood at the other corner after doing a quick walk by. Hank was on one side of the street, I was on the other. I nodded to him with my head and started walking back. When I reached the side door of the church, I ducked in, blessed myself with holy water and moved quickly over to a dark corner in the back. A minute later the door opened and closed; and then Hank was beside me in the shadows.

"What do you think?" I said. "Anyone home?"

"Only one way to find out," he said.

I was huddled up against the confessional, a large wooden box that announced *M. Le Prédicateur* on the front. I kept my eyes on the entrance door while we talked.

"I don't want to get caught up in a surveillance box like Marseille. Fool me once, etcetera," I said.

"You thinking about going in the back way?"

"If there is one."

"Except that's what he expects us to do."

"Booby-trapped?"

"What makes you think you got all of their *plastique*?"

I didn't answer him. I couldn't.

There was a large model boat dangling by a wire from the church ceiling. I stared at it. Stared at the three-masted ship of the line for a long time, wondering why it was hanging in this little village church. Wondering if Hank was right; that we were expected; that the LaPlume building was rigged to blow any intruders to kingdom come.

I finally said, "We could just wait for Blondie or one of the others to come out. Jump them and learn how to get safely inside."

"Could take a long time," Hank said. "You're not planning on pulling all-nighters, are you?"

"Hell, no," I said.

"Smart idea. The street's too small. Won't be long before the locals figure out we're not tourists admiring the architecture."

I sat straight up. "Hear that?" I said.

"What?" Hank said.

"My stomach growling."

"There were a ton of restaurants back on the quai."

"It's always best to plan things on a full stomach."

We walked back down to the *Quai Albert Pichon* and searched for a restaurant that had an open table on its terrace. The river at twilight was beautiful; a smooth slate gray below the dusky sky, and lights twinkled from far across the water. The restaurants were all crowded but we finally squeezed into a small eatery run by two middle-aged ladies who also served as the waitstaff.

We ate crevette salads followed by coq au vin, washed down with a bottle of local rosé. The sky had turned darker, the lights across the water brighter.

"We'll come back tomorrow," I said.

"What if nobody shows?"

"Then we come back the next day."

"How long do we keep it up?"

I looked around. "There are five restaurants in a row here."

"So five days then?"

"When in Bordeaux, do as the Bordelais," I said.

"*Tu parles, Charles*," Hank said.

"Huh?"

"You said it."

18.

The next morning we were back in Pauillac, bright eyed and bushy tailed, running counter-surveillance patterns on all the streets surrounding the LaPlume building. Then, while Hank watched the front, I checked the back street again for any hidden exits. Nothing. If anyone was going to leave, it would have to be past Hank.

I came back around to the front of the building and walked down to the corner where there was a *boulangerie*, its presence announced way in advance by the aroma of freshly baked bread. I stood there, looking through the window at the breads and pastries, my stomach concentrating on the goodies while my brain scanned over the street scene. As hard as it was for us to conduct surveillance on this short narrow street where everyone must know everyone else, it was just as easy for the Mistral Jihad to run a counter-surveillance operation. Probably ongoing right now.

And more manpower wouldn't have done us any good. Just make more targets for the bad guys. No matter how well we planned; how much time we had, it just wouldn't work. And even if we could hide in plain sight, it still was dicey. As soon as Blondie or THIERRY made a move, we'd have to break cover in order to follow them. As I was glumly mulling over our problem, Hank's shadow fell on the window of the bakery.

He sidled up next to me. Hank was wearing a blue workman's uniform that he had picked up in Bordeaux. A tool belt hung from his hip. "These pastries sure look good," he said. The store was also doubling as a *patisserie*; probably had to in a small town like this.

I suddenly jerked my head at the sound of a car coming down the street.

"Don't worry," Hank said. "You haven't left enough of their cadres alive for them to put up a moving counter-surveillance."

He was on point, if the DST was correct that the Mistral Jihad group numbered only a dozen. But this was their ballpark and their game so I couldn't allow myself to relax.

"Let's break up our routine," I said, "and watch the ATM machine."

"From one of the restaurants," Hank said.

There was a small restaurant across the street from the ATM. "Le Yachting Club," said the letters on the half-unfurled canvas awning out front. There was an open table in the corner, in the shade under the awning and I squeezed behind it and sat facing the bank. Hank pulled out a chair diagonally across from me.

We ordered light lunches: tuna salads and a bottle of rosé. Afterwards, I went next door and bought the Trib. When I returned, Hank had a book out and was reading. Simenon. *Le Voleur de Maigret.* I suppressed the urge to call him a showoff and opened up the newspaper.

"I ordered more coffee," he said without looking up.

We sat there for a long time, reading, drinking coffee and watching the ATM machine.

"Anything new?" Hank said. He was asking about the news, not the ATM.

"More dead in Iraq."

Hank shrugged and turned a page of his book.

"Ever been there?" I threw the question out like a fishing line.

He raised his eyebrows, letting me know I should know better than to ask.

"I was just curious."

"Why?"

"When I was up in the mountains in Korea I was cold all the time. Just wondered what a year in the desert's like."

"Sandy." Hank smiled but said nothing more. He didn't take the bait. Knew better. I hadn't really expected him to.

I went back to reading the newspaper. More of the same. Politics heating up back home. But on page three there was a blurb about the shootings in Marseille. Almost a day-old rehash of what the local paper had reported. Except that now the police were working on the theory that it had involved warfare between Corsican and Maghrebian gangs. We still had some breathing room. But for how long?

After I finished, I shoved the paper across the table to Hank in case he wanted to do the crossword puzzle. In his head, of course.

The waitress brought more coffee. It was late afternoon and there had been no serious hits. Only two people used the ATM machine. I followed the first one, a middle-aged man with a balding head and spectacles, back to a real estate office. Probably putting cash down for a rental.

110

The second, a young woman, touristy in attitude, led Hank back to a jewelry store where she bought a pair of gold filigree earrings. Heavy, he said; probably she wangled a nice discount for paying in cash.

At five, we ordered *pastis*.

At six we decided to pack it in. After an early dinner and a bottle of Duhart-Milon we drove back to the Burdigala.

The next morning we reversed our surveillance pattern, starting out having coffee and watching the ATM machine. Nothing. No one showed. At least no one who remotely looked like any of the Mistral Jihad cadres in the DST photos Pasquier had given me. I kept the photos with me in a folder on my lap and kept looking at them; comparing them to the ATM users.

"Aren't the images burnt into your mind yet?" Hank said.

"They might use prosthetics," I said. "Just trying to recognize any similarities."

"Prosthetics?" He laughed. "We're not dealing with the Russians or the CIA here. These folks aren't up to that." He rubbed his chin. "There's something more here though."

"Deeper than just a terrorist cell?"

"No, not deeper. Just tangentially different."

"How?" I was clueless. Hank was the veteran gladiator in this arena.

"I don't know," he said. "But I keep asking myself what's the connection to LaPlume. Seems like oil and water trying to mix with his anti-immigrant, Holocaust denying, race baiting political platform linked to some jihadis."

"This is France," I said. "They make Middle-Eastern politics look like the Boy Scouts." I was half-joking but I was wondering myself about the LaPlume connection.

We dropped the subject and walked up to the safehouse and ran surveillance patterns for the rest of the afternoon. No one emerged. No one went in.

At five we called it a day.

The next morning was glorious with a bright sun and clear blue sky, but we had no time to enjoy it, we were right back at our surveillance.

"This freaking sun is right in my eyes." I was speaking into the cell phone, sweat dripping from my forehead. I tried wiping it away with the back of my free hand.

Hank was at the other end of the short street, in the shade on the opposite side. Our positions didn't really matter. If the Mistral Jihad was running a static counter-surveillance from their safehouse, they would have spotted both of us by now. We had no choice except to continue our watch; we had to wait them out. Sooner or later someone would emerge. But that could be later. Much, much later. How much we had no idea. I chose to ignore the negatives of this operation. On the plus side was the conclusion that if we had been spotted, that each time we disappeared from view, they could never be sure whether we had left the area or were readying a try at penetrating the building. They would have to treat it as a 24-7 surveillance. And that meant the pressure was always on them.

Not on us.

"Let's take a break," I whispered into the phone.

"Roger that," Hank said.

We drove over to the quai and parked and walked along the shoreline. The tiny port was crammed with pleasure boats, all moored, their absentee skippers off somewhere making money like good little burghers. The estuary was fairly wide at this point, with the river split by an island directly across the gleaming water. The Paulliac map called it the *Île de Patiras*. There was a hiking path that followed the shoreline and we took it, walking among reeds and tall grass, past a series of wooden fishing shacks that sat on short piers protruding out onto the water. Large nets and poles hung ready from some of the piers. But no one seemed to be fishing. Far out in the estuary, I could see a large ship dredging the channel. Otherwise, the river was still.

We stopped in the *Maison du Vin de Pauillac*, which had an excellent display of local winemaking as well as bottles of wine for sale.

Hank selected a Clerc Milon 2003. "Here," he said. "Your replacement."

I put it back in the bin. "I've got a better idea."

I went over to the circular counter where a young man stood by a rack of pamphlets.

"Can we make tour reservations of chateaus here?" I said in English.

"Of course. Where?"

"Lynch-Bages would be nice. For today, if possible."

The clerk said he'd call and see. When he set the phone down he had a smile on his face.

"Noon sharp. Is that okay?"

I gave him the money. Just under eight Euros and he printed out two tickets. Then he took a small map off the pamphlet rack and drew the route for us in red ink. Lynch-Bages was close and we could have walked there except for the damn sun.

The tour was interesting and informative, the young Lynch-Bages guide speaking in English for my benefit, even though she and Hank prattled along in French, smiling and joking. Afterwards, we tasted the wine and I made Hank buy two bottles of the 2003 to replace the Clerc Milon he had guzzled with one of my porterhouses.

"*Regium mensis arisque deorum*," I said, finally able to get my two cents into the conversation.

"What's that mean?" Hank said.

"For the table of men and the altar of gods," I said. "Latin."

"Yes," said the guide. "And the motto belongs to the Chateau d'Issan, a Margaux. But it is appropriate for Pauillac."

Outside, the sun was straight above us, its bright glare turning the sky pale blue. Beneath it the Lynch-Bages vineyards seemed to stretch all the way into Pauillac, the octagonal steeple of St. Martin anchoring the far end of the vista.

"Where to now?" Hank said.

I looked at the map the man at the *Maison du Vin* had given us. "There's a couple of nearby chateaus on the D2 in St. Lambert. We could grab a couple of bottles for tonight."

"You mean we're not going to drink the Lynch-Bages I bought you?" He caught the scowl on my face and knew the answer.

When we reached the end of the long Lynch-Bages drive, I stopped at the large stone crucifix, and then turned right.

"The Chateau Gaudin is right up the road and Fonbadet just beyond it."

"You're the boss," Hank said.

I made a right turn and accelerated. "We'll take a quick look-see, pick up the bottles of wine and drive around a little before lunch."

Hank didn't answer. He wasn't listening to me. He was looking at something in the back seat. Only the something wasn't in the back seat; it was a platinum Peugeot sedan. It came right up on my rear end, and then zipped around us, cut in front and suddenly stopped. I jammed my foot on the brakes and noticed that Hank had his Beretta out and ready.

I threw the gears in reverse and started to back away when Hank's left hand grabbed my wrist.

"Look," he said, pointing at the Peugeot. Two men were getting out, the driver and one from the back seat. The one in the back had a woman with him, her head hooded and all trussed up, like a birthday present. The men were armed, I was sure, but they didn't have their guns out. Instead, they were half-prodding, half-dragging their captive towards our car.

One of the men, the driver, waved and yelled something in French.

"What'd he say?" I asked Hank.

"You want her, you can have her."

"What should we do?" They were giving us Vanessa Milligan.

"On this job, I'm taking orders from you. But if it were me, I'd get the girl and get the hell out of here. We can debrief her later if you still want to get the others."

The driver yelled again. The other man prodded the hooded woman forward, shoving her shoulder with the palm of his hand. She stumbled and fell onto the pavement.

"I don't like this, they're getting too close," I said, opening the door.

"I got your back," Hank said, opening the passenger side door for cover.

"Stop right there," I said to them. "Let her walk forward by herself."

The driver put his palms up in the air in acquiescence and the other man yanked Vanessa to her feet, whispering something in her ear.

"Keep walking forward, Vanessa," I said. "Slowly. I know you can't see but I'm right in front of you. It's going to be all right. You'll be safe soon."

She hobbled slowly; her hands were tied behind her back, her handbag looped around her neck, and she had to struggle with every movement to maintain her balance.

"Come on," I said. "They're not going to hurt you." As she neared, I moved toward the center of the road so she wouldn't come between me and the two thugs. I wanted a clear shot if I had to take one.

I didn't have to. Vanessa was about five feet from me when I heard the double crack of rifle fire and saw the side of the Peugeot driver's head come off. His partner was already prone on the road, lying in a pool of blood.

114

I dove for the girl, tackling her, sending her tumbling to the ground, and pulled her up against the side of the car and covered her with my body.

Hank? Where was Hank? How many shots had there been? Two, three? It was only a couple of seconds ago but I couldn't remember.

"Hank. Are you okay?" I yelled under the car.

"Yeah. Do you see anything?"

"No, let's get the hell out of here."

"Stay down," he said.

I kept my head just above the hood of the car and watched as Hank quickly belly crawled over to Vanessa. He ignored her and grabbed her handbag, ripping it away from her and started rummaging through it.

He threw out her compact makeup case and her eyebrow pencil.

"Don't move," he said. He sat the eyebrow pencil down behind him and opened the compact case, and then shut it.

"It's okay," he said.

I peeped up over the hood of the Mercedes again. In the distance, through the vineyards, I could see a truck speeding away. "They're gone," I said. I looked down at Vanessa. She had fainted, was out cold.

Hank rifled the dead driver's pockets, found the smart key and popped the trunk. We shoved the bodies inside.

"What about Vanessa?" Hank said.

"We better revive her now." I pulled off the hood covering her face, letting her get some fresh air and Hank laughed as he saw the shock on my face.

I wasn't holding Vanessa Milligan. I was holding Blondie.

"Sonofabitch," I swore. "Dump her in the trunk with others."

Hank laughed again. "She's going to have a surprise when she wakes up."

"Easier to debrief her," I said.

"What do we do with them and the car?"

I pulled out the map. "Take their car. Daubos is just up ahead. Go down the *Grand Rue* until the road forks and wait. I'll catch up to you and we'll work out a plan."

I stayed behind Hank until I reached the Chateau Gaudin. I stopped and ran into the tasting room and wine shop and took out some money. I tossed it on the counter and grabbed two bottles and left, saying "merci."

The proprietor looked at the money and said "merci" in return.

I caught up with Hank at the fork in the road. It was actually a small triangular park in front of a broken down, deserted chateau. Hank was standing outside the Mercedes. I pulled up next to him and got out and scoped the area. There was a park bench under some trees and I walked over and sat in the shade. Cigarette butts and empty wine bottles littered the ground.

"How's Blondie?" I said.

"Still out cold," Hank said. "Looks like we're not heading back to the Burdigala."

"Any ideas?"

"Yeah. Get as far away from here as possible."

I took out the Michelin map and looked at it. "Let's get on the D206 and head west, taking whatever roads come up. The Atlantic coast isn't far and it looks like there's a forest. We can bury the bodies and ditch the Mercedes."

Hank took the map. "I know the area," he said. "Did a joint exercise with the French *troops du choquer* a few years back. There is a forest there and the soil's sandy. Easy digging."

"Okay. Then that's where we head. When we reach this village Carcans," I pointed at the map, "we'll regroup on the other side."

"Roger. D206 to St. Laurent; D104 to the 207 to Carcans. You keep the map, counselor. I don't need it."

I looked at the peaceful hamlet scene, at the litter on the ground, and at the trunk of the Mercedes with two dead bodies and a trussed up blonde inside. Country life's not so idyllic after all.

The pounding in my head was getting on my nerves. It was coming from my temples and I couldn't will it away. And now Blondie was awake and kicking. Literally. She kept slamming her feet against the inside of the trunk and making muffled sounds which I knew were curses.

"We could make for Biarritz," Hank said. He had the Michelin map spread out and was ignoring Blondie's commotion.

"And then what?"

"We come back in country. Maybe through Switzerland."

"And go where?"

Hank looked at the trunk of the Peugeot. "We haven't debriefed Blondie yet."

"And afterwards?"

"We can't haul a prisoner all around Europe."

116

"What are you saying?"

"It's your call, counselor."

"I'm getting paid well for this, but not well enough for cold-blooded murder."

"Murder's a legal term," Hank said. "She's a killer, remember that. And remember who set you up twice."

"Still not enough."

He shrugged. "Like I said, it's your call. Let's leave first things first, then," he said, popping open the trunk of the Peugeot with the smart key.

19.

"*Con*! *Fils de pute*!" Blondie snarled the words at me. She was leaning up against the side of the Peugeot. Her hands and feet were still tied but Hank had removed the tape from her mouth. Now, she was making the most of it.

"You're getting your French lesson for the day." Hank was grinning.

"What'd she say?"

"You're a bastard; a son of a whore."

I laughed.

Blondie tried to hock a loogie in my direction but Hank shoved her off balance and she fell.

"*Putain de trou du cul*," she hissed. Hank pressed her face down in the dirt with his foot.

"What she'd call you?"

"A fucking asshole."

"Sorbonne graduate, I see."

When Hank removed his foot from the back of Blondie's head, she spit out dirt and scowled. But she didn't say anything more.

"Did you pat her down?" I said. "Who knows how good those two guys were at doing their job."

Hank hauled her back up to her feet and gave her the once over. She twisted and grimaced when he ran his hands along her inner thighs.

"She's clean," he said.

"*Touche-cul*," she spat him. Ass wipe. I figured that one out by myself.

"Tape up her mouth again," I said.

Blondie tried twisting her face away from Hank but he managed to get the tape back over her lips and pressed it down tightly.

I motioned to him to leave her and come over to the Mercedes. Hank pushed Blondie back to the ground and got in the front seat next to me.

"Let's talk this out," I said.

"We need a compressed interrogation," he said.

"How do you want to work it?" I said. My expertise was in cross-examination, not field debriefing. And this was about as far from a court of law as you could get.

Hank's face was grim. His eyes had turned hard, the soft dark brown of his pupils now fused into glistening ebony orbs of fury.

"What's eating you?" I said.

He took out the eyebrow pencil and makeup compact he had rifled from Blondie's handbag.

"See this?" he said, holding up the eyebrow pencil.

"Whaddya gonna do? Make up your face?"

"This little baby is a pencil fuse."

"Pencil fuse?"

"You got it now. Would have made up both our faces. Into hamburger."

I took it from him and held it in my hand and looked at it closely. I didn't see anything. "But where are the explosives?" I said.

"Right here." Hank popped open the compact case. Inside, instead of a makeup pad and powder was a pressed down patty of a brown clay-like substance.

"What is it? RDX?"

"Like the brick you lifted from the armory." Hank took back the eyebrow pencil fuse. "This will detonate the explosive after a set time, giving those two bozos in the trunk time to clear the area."

"Except LaPlume or whoever had other plans for them."

"Looks like he's eliminating all his connections with the Mistral Jihad. Taking Blondie and us too for a bonus."

"How the hell does this infernal contraption work?" I said.

"See the red band around the middle? That indicates the time delay before the acid corrodes the wire inside."

"What then?"

"A striker's released that hits the percussion cap and detonates." It was scotch taped to the inside of the compact case."

"Yeah, but what gets it going?" I said.

"Damn if I know for sure," he said.

"Really works though, you say?"

"Rudimentary, but an effective time honored method of assassination. Count von Stauffenberg used a captured British pencil detonator inserted into a block of *plastique* when he tried to kill Hitler. Commandos used them in raids on Norway and St. Lazaire. The French Résistance used them to blow up railway tracks and bridges. Hell, we trained the Mujahadeen in their use during the Soviet-Afghan War. Used the Paks as middlemen so our hands wouldn't get dirty."

"Just bloody," I said.

"We don't make the rules," Hank said. "We just have to play by them."

"Only there seems to be a lot more players clogging the field these days."

"You got that right," Hank said. "Actually these are what the terrorists in Pakistan are using these days to try and destabilize that country."

"What goes around, comes around."

"Only sometimes, bro; only sometimes."

"How the hell did the Mistral Jihad get training in this technique?" I said.

"What makes you think they did? Were there ever any bombings by them?"

"No, Pasquier just said there were some bank robberies and a botched attack on a police station."

"Probably only the top guy knows."

"How did he develop the expertise? From the islamofascists?"

"Fascists, anyway," Hank said.

"How so?"

"During the Battle of Algiers, the French used bombings as a counterterrorist weapon. Had the Foreign Legion and the security services carry them out. Used the same assassination technique against the Vietminh in Indochina."

"So? Where is this going?"

"LaPlume."

"The politician?"

"Yeah. He served in the French Army in Algeria and Indochina. Probably picked up the expertise along the way."

"That doesn't make any sense," I said. "A right-wing racist politician in bed with a Middle-Eastern terrorist cell? Where's the connection?"

"See anything Middle-Eastern about this group other than the name?"

Hank had a point. We had killed eight out of the twelve Mistral Jihadis; the DST had a ninth, and I had Blondie as a POW. And they were all European. I looked out the window at the pines rustling in the breeze. The forest was thick and you couldn't see more than twenty yards ahead. Just like the quandary we were in. Push back the heavy boughs and you only found more. And if you let go, they snapped back and hit you in the face.

If the kidnapping of Vanessa Milligan wasn't a terrorist strike, then what was it? There didn't seem to be much planning in the Mistral Jihad. It wasn't a deep-set organization. Amateurs. Dedicated but undisciplined. I had to face the fact that even if I could hunt them all down and kill them; I might not get Vanessa back alive. Oh, I'd get the two-hundred-and-fifty thou but I could never look myself in the mirror again without being sick.

Okay, Doherty. So with nine down and a bird in the hand, you better go slow and sure from now on.

I looked over at the Peugeot and Blondie writhing in the dirt, struggling to get to her feet, her face red with exertion and rage.

"Maybe she can give us some answers." I said.

"I'll ask the control questions," Hank said. "You play the tough guy."

We got out of the car and walked over to Blondie who had managed to get herself into a kneeling position.

"We don't want to hurt or kill you," I said, yanking her up. I pushed her against the side of the Peugeot and removed the tape from her mouth.

"*Envoyez-vous faire foutre,*" she spat.

"She said go fuck yourself."

I retaped her mouth and pinched her nose with my thumb and forefinger. Her eyes went wide and she tried to twist her head away. I just pinched tighter.

"Listen up. I want the girl back. Alive and in good health."

Blondie kept trying to twist her head but I held onto her nose. Her eyes were dilating with fear and lack of oxygen and she began to heave her chest and make chugging noises in her throat.

"You think I'm fooling?" Hank held her shoulders while I squeezed her nostrils tighter.

She shook her head.

"Are you going to cooperate?" I said, letting go of her nose.

She looked away.

I reached again for her nose and she nodded her head.

"Good," I said. "If I take off the tape, are you going to give us any more bullshit?"

She shook her head no.

Hank popped open the trunk of the Peugeot and I dragged Blondie around and shoved her head inside. She struggled, trying to shrink back, horror on her face. Hank rattled off something in French and she shook her head again, making little moaning sounds under the tape.

I looked at him.

"I told her that if she fucked around with us anymore, she'd be joining her friends."

I yanked her back up and removed the tape from her mouth. This time she didn't say anything. Her eyes were tearing, hate and fury now replaced by fear; mucous was dripping from her nose. She kept her head lowered, gasping for breath; licking her lips where the tape had pulled away some of the skin and tiny spots of blood appeared.

"We don't have to kill you," I said. "My associate is going to ask you some questions. I know you understand English."

"My wrists hurt," she said. "Untie me."

I started to seal the tape back on her mouth.

"No, please," she said. "I'll tell you whatever you want."

I went over to our Mercedes and came back with the portfolio of DST images. I pulled out the photos of the two dead men in the trunk and stuck them in front of Blondie's face.

"Who are they?" Hank said.

"Jean and Domingo."

"Jean Who and Domingo Who?"

"I don't know their last names. We only operate on a first-name basis."

"And those are their real names, Jean and Domingo?"

She shook her head. "No, those were the names we were given. Our operational names."

Hank came close to her. "And what is your real name?" he said. His voice was low, cool, almost conversational in tone.

"Dolores." She said the name so softly I could barely hear her.

"Speak up," I said. My voice was deep and rough, contrapuntal in tone and pitch to Hank's interrogatory dulcetto.

"Dolores," she said again. This time here voice was a little firmer.

"That's your operational or real name?"

She said nothing.

I slapped her head with the photo and she cringed. "Don't make me tape your mouth back up," I said.

"Operational," she said, after taking a deep breath.

"Your real name then."

"Astride."

"Astride what?" I slapped her head again with the photo.

"I'm not going to waste any more time with her," Hank said. "She's all yours. Have some fun before you finish her off, if you want." He started to walk away. "I'll be back in an hour."

I smiled and started to pull down the straps of her turquoise tank top.

"Oh, no, please don't," Astride said. She looked wildly at Hank, at his receding back. "Don't leave me alone with him."

Hank turned and shrugged. "Why not? If you don't answer my questions, you're of no use to me."

"Please," she said, "I'll cooperate. Astride Pelletier. My name is Astride Pelletier."

Hank came back to her and caressed her cheek with his hand. She kissed his fingers.

"Please," she said again. "Just don't leave me with him."

"As long as you talk to us."

"Yes, yes."

"That's fine, Astride. Now, tell us about the Mistral Jihad."

She looked down.

"They're almost all dead," Hank said. "No reason not to talk now."

"We are, were all university students," she said.

"What are your aims?"

"To combat imperialism and racism, to make France a leader again in the fight against American hegemony in the world."

I laughed. I guess Astride and the other Mistral Jihad clowns hadn't been watching what was going down in Iraq the past few years. Hegemony, my ass.

"Who's your leader?" Hank said.

She was quiet for a moment, and then finally spoke. "He's a great man. A man of ideas and honor. Martel."

"Martel?" I said.

She nodded at me, almost defiantly.

I had only two other DST photos beside those of the dead men in the trunk and Astride. I held the images up in front of her.

"Which one is Martel?"

She nodded at the one the right. It was the photo of a man in his mid-thirties. Prematurely balding with a round, pudgy pasty face and horn-rimmed glasses.

"This is your hero?" I said.

"Yes." She spat the word out. "He is a brave man, a fighter. Not like you American cowards with your nuclear missiles and your stupid cowboy president."

She was so clueless that it made me sad. We were just going to have to wise her up.

20.

"Recognize these?" Hank said. He was holding up Blondie's eyebrow pencil-detonator fuse and the compact makeup case filled with *plastique*.

"Those are my things," she said.

"I want you to pay close attention," Hank said. He walked about a hundred feet away from us and opened the compact case and set it on a rock. Then he jammed the eyebrow pencil down into it, gave it a twist and ran back to the Mercedes and ducked around to where Blondie and I were crouched.

"How long is the timer?" I said.

"Have no idea," Hank said. "Don't even know if it'll work."

"You could have been blown up."

Just after I uttered those words there was a large bang and rocks and dirt splattered the cars. If we had been standing next to the explosives when they went off then . . .

I looked at Astride's face. The horror etched on it told me she was unaware of what she had been carrying, that she was intended to die along with Hank and me.

"*Oh, merde,*" she said. "*Oh, merde et contre-merde.*"

"Yeah, that's right," Hank said. "Oh, shit and double-shit. Your hero, your knight in shining armor, this Martel, was going to blow you up into a thousand bloody bits of flesh and bone." His voice was soft but firm.

"*C'p'tit merdeux d'Martel.* He was going to kill me."

Hank smiled at her. "The little shit. He's really made you mad. Was he your lover too, your hero?"

"*Henri? Je l'emmerde.* Screw him."

"Henri?" I said. "Who's Henri?"

"Henri LaPlume." Astride spat the name out.

"Any relation to the fascist LaPlume?" Hank said, coldness in his voice now.

"His younger brother."

"Are the two of them in on this?"

Astride laughed. A bitter laugh. "*Jacques LaPlume? C'est l'roi des cons. Il est con comme la lune.*"

"What she'd say."

"She says LaPlume is the king of assholes."

"Are they connected in this? Just answer the question," I said to her.

"LaPlume hates Martel, excuse me, I mean Henri. He thinks his little brother is a traitor to the old Europe; the true Europe."

"And you know this how?" I said.

"Henri told me."

"And you believed him?" I nodded in the direction of the explosion; the blown plastique that had been intended for us, for her too.

She shrugged.

"You knew nothing about that?"

"Henri told me there was a transmitter buried in the compact case and that the eyebrow pencil was really an antenna. That after they turned me over to you, I was to jam the pencil into the compact and he would follow the signal and kill you both as soon as he had a chance."

"By himself?"

"No, with Richard."

"This Richard?" I showed her the last unidentified DST photo. It was the terrorist the DST had named THIERRY.

She nodded her head.

"What's his role in this operation?"

"He's Martel's, I mean Henri's personal bodyguard. He's very good with guns."

"As your two friends in the trunk suddenly found out," Hank said.

"I guess they died for the cause," I said.

Astride snorted.

"Do I sense a note of disbelief?" I said.

"I don't know what to believe," she said. "My wrists really hurt. Can't you untie my hands?"

Hank turned her around and sliced the ropes with a gravity knife. Where the hell did he pick that up? Paris?

"Don't try and run or I'll clip you," he said.

"I won't." She rubbed her hands and wrists. "I'm hungry and thirsty," she said with a pout.

"Maybe in a while we'll get you something to eat," I said, "but now you answer questions. How did Henri get onto me?"

"From the flyers. Another student mentioned it to me and I went and ripped it down and gave it to Henri."

"Then he used you to finger me?"

"What?" Astride had a puzzled look on her face.

"Used you to point me out to him and the others. At the Hotel Lutetia."

"Yes, at the hotel." She was still rubbing her wrists.

"You knew they were going to kill me, didn't you?"

She lowered her head and nodded.

"Because I was looking for Vanessa Milligan."

She nodded again.

"Why was Vanessa Milligan abducted?"

"I don't know."

I cupped her face with my hand. "Think," I said. "Martel—Henri LaPlume must have said something about it."

Astride looked away, like she was searching her memory, than faced me and shrugged a little shrug, more with her mouth than her head.

"The mother," she finally said. "Henri said something about the girl's mother."

"What?" I said.

"I'm trying to think. I just don't remember. He was talking to one of the others; Calvi, not me. I wasn't really paying attention."

Hank grabbed her and dragged her back to the open trunk of the Peugeot. Blood from the dead men had pooled on the carpet and its sweet sickly odor seeped into my nostrils, making me want to retch.

"Maybe a few hours visiting with your friends will help you remember," Hank said. He hefted her up and made to drop her inside the trunk.

"No, please; please don't," Astride said.

Hank set her down. She started to shake all over.

"We're wasting time," I said. "Let's put her in the trunk with the others and dump the car in the lake and get the hell out of here."

"No, please," she said. "I remember something else now. Something Henri said."

I stared at her, my hand on the trunk lid. "I'm waiting," I said, letting a rough edge creep back into my voice.

"Henri said that if the girl's mother made the right decision, the girl would be unharmed."

"Right decision? Who'd he say this to? Calvi?"

"No, he was speaking on the phone. In English."

"To whom?"

"I don't know. He mentioned a name though. Aziz Sharif or Sharif Aziz, maybe."

"Did he ever ask for ransom?"

"No, this is political, I tell you. We're not criminals."

I didn't want to waste any time debating the obvious with her. "Where is Vanessa Milligan now? In the house in Pauillac?"

She didn't answer.

I tried another tack. "After you spotted me outside the apartment on the Canal St. Martin, why did you run to Marseille?"

"To meet with Henri and the others."

"How did you know to go there?"

"I called him on my *portable* after I saw you had taken some of the guns and the *plastique*."

"And he told you to go to Marseille?"

"I was to lose you first."

"Why was Henri in Marseille?"

"That's one of the family properties."

"The apartment in the *Panier*?"

"The whole building. The LaPlume family is not poor."

"I thought Henri didn't get along with his brother."

"They don't; but the businesses are family run and Henri has a share, whether that *connard*, Jacques, likes it or not."

"And the little stone house in Pauillac? Henri owns that too?"

"He manages it. One of the companies is restoring the old buildings. To keep France beautiful, the way it once was before the Anglo-American infection."

"And he spotted us watching the place?"

"Yes. Henri is quite good at clandestine things."

Hank looked at me. "Probably made us from the gitgo," he said.

"So he tried to set me up again, using you, letting us believe he was giving Vanessa up."

"Yes."

"But killing your two friends wasn't part of the plan, was it? At least not the plan outlined to you."

"No," she said. She started to shake again. I held her shoulders to steady her.

She took a deep breath. "At first I thought they were killed by friends of yours. When I was in the trunk, I wanted to signal Henri; have him come and avenge them; but I couldn't find my handbag with the compact and the eyebrow pencil."

"Lucky for you," I said.

"So now who do you think killed them?" Hank said.

"Richard. I told you he was an excellent shot."

"Let's get back to the girl, Vanessa Milligan. Is she in the house in Pauillac?"

"She was."

"Was?"

"They're long gone by now."

I nodded, cursing silently to myself. She was right, of course. Henri LaPlume and Richard wouldn't have waited around for the explosion; they would have taken the girl and split.

"Where did they go?"

"I don't know."

"What about their plans?"

"He didn't tell me." She started to cry; soft, sad sobs. As dim as she was, Astride was finally starting to see the picture. She was a loose end and what better way for her lover, her hero, the man who had held her tightly in bed at night and whispered soothing words softly in her ear, to get rid of her than to use her as a sacrificial lamb to destroy his pursuers?

"Look at me," I said. "How do you contact him?"

She sniffled. "By *portable*. His number is preprogrammed."

Hank laughed. "There's no phone in your handbag."

Her face reddened, the sadness replaced by anger. *"Quels bands de cons, nous.* What a bunch of idiots we were. We believed in Henri and what he was doing."

She smiled a bitter smile. "If I could help you, I would."

It was almost dark when Hank returned. Astride had been right. LaPlume, his bodyguard and Vanessa Milligan were long gone from the Pauillac safehouse.

"This was all that was there." He dropped a copy of *L'Équipe* on the hood of the Mercedes. The lead story was again about the World Cup soccer tournament.

"Mean anything?" I said to Astride.

"Henri is a fanatic for the sport. Goes to a match any chance he can get."

I looked at Hank and Hank looked at me. The semifinals matches were in two days in Germany; the final this coming weekend in Berlin. And the French national team would be playing in one of the semifinals.

"I'm hungry." She was whimpering again, really starting to annoy me. But she had a point. We all needed to eat something.

"There's a town back there, Maubuisson." I tapped my finger on the map, showing Hank. "Go get some food and I'll stay here with our newly found friend. I have some calls to make."

After he left, I called Carlton Andrews, the Milligan Foundation bean counter.

The phone connected after two rings.

"It's me," I said.

"Still busy, I see, according to the papers," Andrews said.

"I'm on the trail." I gave him the code names of the dead men in the car as well as Henri LaPlume and Richard. "Nine down, one in hand, and two to go."

"Very good," he said. "And Vanessa?"

"I don't want to make any promises."

"I understand," he said.

"Berlin's the next stop," I said. "We need housing, a car and tickets to the World Cup tournament. Three of them for the finals. Can you fix me up?"

"I'll have to pull a few strings, make some quick calls, but yes."

After he hung up, I called Sylvie and told her what I wanted, gave her Astride's name; she already had Hank's.

"Three's company, but four is a party," she said.

"I'd love to take you up on that but I'm a good guy these days."

"What about your friend, Henry Lowrie Jackson?"

"Hank? Pure poison."

"Maybe I'm the antidote." Sylvie laughed and hung up.

21.

In the morning, we drove the Peugeot over to the edge of the lake. Hank rolled all the windows down and we got out.

I looked at Astride. "Life is full of choices. Yours is easy. You can go with us or try to run. If we don't kill you, the DST will catch you. And then you'll be begging to die."

From the look in her eyes, she had already made up her mind.

Hank opened the driver's door and placed a stone on the accelerator, and then shifted the car out of neutral and jumped back. We watched as it descended into the water, making just a few gurgling sounds before it disappeared under the surface of the lake.

"This'll buy us some time," he said, "but not more than a week."

"A week's plenty," I said.

We dropped our Mercedes mini-SUV back at the St. Jean railroad station in Bordeaux and went inside. The tickets to Berlin were waiting for us at the counter. Sylvie had done her job well; she had arranged for a comfortable sleeper compartment, a T-3 cabin with three berths. Only problem was that we had to change trains in Paris.

We pulled into the Gare Montparnasse at 6:55 p.m. and taxied over to the Gare du Nord, with enough time to grab a bite to eat in the brasserie before boarding Number 243. We left at 8:46 p.m. Hank had the steward uncork one of the bottles of Lynch-Bages and by nine-thirty, we were relaxed and enjoying the trip.

At ten-fifteen, Andrews called me back. He had made arrangements for us; gave me the address and told me the caretaker would be waiting for us at the house. Nothing left for us to do.

I poured some more wine into Astride's glass. "What's Henri's connection to Middle-Eastern terrorists groups?" I said.

"None that I know of," she said.

"Then why the name Mistral Jihad?"

"It was to show solidarity with the sufferings and aspirations of the people."

"Couldn't he just build a clinic?" Hank said.

"Why? So you Americans can bomb it?"

We dropped the subject. I sipped my wine and came back at her from another angle.

"You said Henri was good at clandestine work. Who trained him?"

She looked puzzled, a little confused, pursing her lips. "I don't know. He never really talked too much about himself."

"Not even pillow talk?" Hank said.

Astride made a face.

The sleeper beds were comfortable and by eleven we had shut down, Hank staying near the door in case Astride had a change of heart and tried to make a run for it. At seven a.m. the steward awoke us for breakfast and at seven-fifty, we pulled into the Berlin-Spandau station. I used the ATM, withdrawing a thousand Euros.

The station was jammed with European football fanatics and it took us twenty minutes to grab a cab. Outside, as the taxi wended its way through the streets, we passed throngs of raucous revelers fueling themselves up to cheer on their countries' teams. I wondered how many would be happy when the tournament was over.

The Foundation house was a neat stone and brick structure. It was situated on a quiet residential street, just off of the Koenigsallee in Grunewald, not far from the large forested park. The caretaker was a tall, silver-haired man dressed in a livery costume that made him look like a Long Island lawn jockey.

Kurt, he said his name was, showed us around the place; the kitchen where he said the housekeeper, a Frau Helfing, cooks. She had already prepared something for us to eat and would cook again tomorrow; this was her half-day off. Next, he showed us the upstairs bedrooms and then the garage where a green BMW M-series sedan was waiting. After Kurt left, Hank took the car out for a spin while Astride showered. I waited outside the bathroom door; keeping her on a short leash was the order of the day.

When Hank returned, he had bottles of beer to drink with the meal.

We sat around the kitchen table, eating the food Frau Helfing had readied for us. Nothing fancy; just a heap of solid German burgher cooking: a large pot of egg noodles, cabbage, a roast chicken, a thick sausage, potatoes and a loaf of dark sweet bread. Astride sat there picking at the chicken while we men gorged ourselves. The Kloster beer that Hank had graciously supplied cut the garlic edge to the sausage and I ate more than I should have. I hoped I wouldn't pay for it later.

When we were done, Astride was still picking at the chicken, pushing the meat around on her plate like a little kid who didn't like her meal. She had put her clothes in the washer and was clad only in a pink silk nightie she found in one of the bedrooms. She left the nightie open at the top and kept stealing peeks at Hank while we ate and talked but he ignored her.

After we finished eating, I rummaged around in the kitchen cupboards and came up with a stoneware bottle of jägermeister.

"Save it for later," Hank said. "Let's go for a drive. I've got something to show you."

Hank drove while Astride and I sat in the back. Her clothes were still damp, not fully dry from the washing and she kept shifting uncomfortably in the seat, a pout fixed on her face.

"I don't see why I have to come with you," she said. "I could have stayed back there at the house and watched television."

"Sure," Hank and I said in unison.

He drove the sedan down the Richard-Strauss Strasse and into the Grunewald. We eased our way along a curving drive; Hank seemed to know where he was going. Bicycle lanes and paths on both sides of us were being used by cyclists and joggers. Not everyone here in Berlin was a World Cup fanatic. At least not 24-7.

"That's the Teufelsee," Hank said as we passed a lake. He pointed at a large hill that loomed up ahead. "And that's the Teufelsberg. The Devil's Mountain. We're going to take a walk up to the summit."

We parked the car and got out. At the top of the hill was a large domed building that looked like a hybrid between an igloo and a Kremlin church.

"What's that?" I said.

"The subtle invention of genius," Hank said with a wry smile. "When Berlin was reconstructed after the war—the real one—they had to do something with all the rubble; so they built a small railroad line from the center of the city and dumped it here."

"You mean that hill is man-made?"

"All one hundred and seventy-five meters of it."

"That's over five hundred feet high," I said.

"And there's a great view of Berlin up top."

"You mean we're going to climb up there?" Astride said. "I just took a shower and washed my clothes."

"Stop complaining," Hank said, giving her rump a sharp slap. "The exercise will work off some of this baby fat."

"Are you always such a brute?" she said to him.

"Only on my best days."

The view from the top was worth the walk. Even though the air was hazy, you could see for miles. Hank pointed out the Olympiastadion, where the World Cup finals were to be played. From a distance it looked like Giants Stadium to me.

"And this building?" I asked him about the dome-shaped building near us.

"This was a National Security Agency field station. One of the premier listening posts our country had during the Cold War. All closed down now. This used to be the British Sector of Berlin and they had their own building on the Teufelsberg, as well."

"How do you know so much about this?"

He looked out to the east, quiet. Finally, he said, "The NSA turned over operations to the Army; to INSCOM. The Intelligence and Security Command. We had all kinds of ELINT and SIGENT equipment up here. Lot of the buildings are gone now. Just like us."

"So what's left?"

"Besides happy memories? Just the Arctic Tower, the Computing and Analysts Building and the British installation."

We left these relics of struggles and times past and drove back to the house.

Hank and I had a shot of jägermeister while Astride drank a bottle of beer. Then Hank and I took turns showering, one of us watching our new friend at all times.

I had the window open and cool air filled the room and moonbeams gradually played across the bed. I was in a light sleep, comfortable but wary, the same sleep my cats go into at night; always on the alert for prey—or danger.

A rustling noise in the hallway caused my eyes to blink open. I heard voices murmuring and then the slap of a hand.

"Ow." Astride's voice came from outside my room.

"Go back to bed," Hank said.

A door slammed.

The moon had moved its gleam across the room and away from me. It was higher in the sky now and its glow partially obscured by wispy gray clouds.

I heard the door creak open and a shadow split the vague moonlight in half. It was gliding silently towards me. I was face down, one hand underneath the pillow, resting on the Beretta. I kept breathing slowly and softly, feigning sleep while I squinted with one eye at the shadow. When it reached the bed, my free hand snapped out and grabbed a wrist, yanking the arm toward me. At the same time I brought the Beretta up and jammed it against a set of ribs.

"Don't shoot, lover," Astride moaned, her lips and tongue searching my face; her sweet breath warm and wanting. She was wearing the pink silk nightie she had on earlier. Nothing else. I yanked her back by her hair and forced her onto the floor.

"Yes," she whimpered. "Take me here; take me now."

"No," I said. I pulled her up and dragged her over to the door. "Be good or I'll have to tie you up again."

"Promises, promises," she said.

I closed the door and went back to my bed and picked my cell phone. I ran down the directory and punched the name.

After three rings, I heard Dana's sleepy voice. "Hey, Doherty. What's up?"

"I just wanted to hear your voice," I said.

22.

I awoke to the smell of coffee and frying ham. My watch said six o'clock. Why in the hell does Hank always have to operate like we're still in the service? Breakfast at this ungodly hour. Then I realized that the housekeeper, Frau Helfing, had returned to prepare our meals for the day.

Frau Helfing was a plump middle-aged woman with rosy cheeks and ash blonde hair that had once been golden. She enjoyed cooking for us, complaining mildly that the Milligans had rarely used the Grunewald house and there really wasn't much for her to do. When I explained that we would be staying for several days at least, she absolutely beamed and began talking out loud about food shopping.

We ate scrambled eggs and thick slices of ham along with buttered pumpernickel bread and cups of coffee, protesting when she said she wanted to brew us a fresh pot.

After cleaning my plate, I reached into my pants pocket and took out my wallet. Counting off three hundred Euros, I slid them over to Hank.

"What's this for?" he said.

"To get yourself and Astride some new clothes."

"Not enough."

I took out the rest of my money and slid the wad over. "There's another six hundred, that's all I have."

"We'll have to make do for now," Hank said. "Remember, my per diem is adding up."

"The job is almost finished, I hope." I looked over at Frau Helfing who was puttering around the large double-doored stainless steel refrigerator.

"Where can they buy some clothes?" I asked her.

She wiped her hands on her apron. "Bleibtreustrasse in Charlottenberg is closest. But my daughter shops in Mitte. Lots of local stores. Good, but not so expensive."

I turned to Hank. "You heard the lady. Nine hundred Euros is your budget. So it's your decision."

"Aren't you coming with us?" Astride said.

"I have other things to do."

"You mean I have this brute all to myself?" She smiled sweetly at Hank.

"Use him as you wish," I said.

"I've got enough on my plate without this," Hank said.

"For now, make her a happy camper."

Hank said, "Okay, beautiful, it's show time."

"I like silk," she said with a wicked grin.

"You'll like what I buy you," he said.

"When you talk like that I get chills," she said.

He pushed her towards the garage door and I watched as the two of them drove off in the Beemer.

After Frau Helfing left to do the food shopping I called Carlton Andrews. It was nine-thirty in the morning here in Berlin, two-thirty back in New York, but Andrews picked up on the third ring.

"Still the dedicated professional? I figured you'd be up this late," I said.

"My responsibilities to the Foundation are time-consuming," he said.

"That's why you get paid the big bucks."

"That is precisely why," he said. "Where are you now?"

"I'm in Berlin; at the house. I'm hoping to get the last parcels and bring back the package you want." I was speaking in code; all that talk about the Teufelsberg listening post had made me a little edgy. I didn't know who might be intercepting my cell-phone transmissions.

A little late to be worrying about that, Doherty.

Better late than never, I told myself.

"Judge Milligan has the utmost confidence in your ability to fulfill the contract," Andrews said. "but she would like to see photographs of the last two items before . . ."

I cut him off. "And I'd like to talk to Judge Milligan. Today. Now."

"Concerning?"

"Some questions have arisen that need to be answered before I can obtain the final package. I assume she's still interested in making the acquisition?"

"Her Honor has made all the additional contributions to bring your account up to date, save the last two installments. She is fulfilling her end of the bargain and fully expects you to carry out yours."

"And I intend to. But I need to speak to her now."

There was a pause and then Andrews spoke again. "She does not engage in telephone conversations on matters of this nature. And in any event, she's asleep at this time of night."

"Wake her up and tell her we need to talk. Then get back to me. Tell her it's urgent; go earn those big bucks."

I told Andrews I'd be waiting here in Grunewald and to have her call the house number if she can't get me on the cell-phone. I didn't want any excuses about not being able to reach me.

That done, I went over to the stove and pressed my cup under the coffeemaker and let it fill. I sat and drank it black, ruminating. I was getting really good at that.

If Henri LaPlume and his bodyguard were here in Berlin with Vanessa Milligan, then Henri would want to see the World Cup final.

Especially if France was playing.

This was working out in my mind as several scenarios. Henri could go alone to the stadium, while Richard guarded Vanessa at some Mistral Jihad safehouse. Or they could both come if the girl was secure—or already dead. Or maybe they would bring the girl with them. I wanted to throw this last option out; it sounded too risky for them, but I couldn't. I still wasn't sure where Vanessa Milligan stood in all this. For all I knew, she was one of them.

I was still mulling all of this over when my cell phone buzzed. It was Andrews.

"Judge Milligan would like to see you," he said.

"I'm not flying back to New York."

"She knows that; she doesn't expect you to. She will videoconference with you from the Paris office. Sylvie will make the airline reservation for you."

I hung up and called Sylvie. She booked a flight for me on Air France 2035 leaving Tegel at 3:55 p.m. She apologized because the return flight would be tomorrow but said my seat was in business class. Could she make up for the delay in any way?

Don't tempt me, I told her. After ending the call, I tried to reach Dana at our house. No answer and when the machine picked up I left a message that I'd call back later.

I was sitting there, staring at the phone in my hand, when Hank and Astride returned. They stormed into the kitchen carrying a bunch of boxes.

"Man, you can't believe the hordes of soccer nuts out on the streets," Hank said. "I had to cut the spree short and get the chick back here before some half-soused stud tried to abscond with her."

"At least European men know what to do," she said, flouncing upstairs with her packages.

"She wants you," I said.

"You too," he said.

"She's all yours tonight," I said. "I'm flying to Paris this afternoon, coming back on the morning shuttle."

"A little rendezvous with Sylvie?" Hank was grinning.

"No, strictly business."

"A new lead?"

"I have to talk to Judge Milligan."

"She's in Paris?"

"Videoconference. From the Paris office. She wants to see my face and I want to see hers. Can you hold the fort while I'm gone?"

"No problem with the ducats she promised you, is there? Like I said, my per diem is growing."

"She's straight there," I said. "Something's bothering me about this whole thing. Why hasn't there been a ransom demand?"

"Or a dead hostage with a note or videocassette," Hank said.

"Exactly."

"So I'll just hang out here with the little wannabe while you're gone."

"You could take Astride over to the Olympiastadion and scout the place. Maybe get inside for a peak."

"What if your boy LaPlume shows?"

"Trail him."

"She might act up when she sees him."

"Cold-cock her if you have to."

Hank grinned. "That's about all she'll get from me." He went over to the fridge and took out two beers and opened them. "What do you think Judge Milligan can tell you?"

I took one of the beers from him and tilted it up for a long swallow. "I don't know," I said. "Any scratch left from the Euros I gave you?"

"A little," Hank said. He had a pained look on his face.

"Fork it over. I'm taking a cab to the airport."

At Tegel I used another bank machine and replenished my hungry wallet, and then caught my flight. At seven p.m. I was at the front door of the Milligan Foundation office on the *Boulevard St. Germain.*

Sylvie answered the door. "Monsieur Doherty, good to see you; please come in." She led me down the hall to a conference room where there was a computer and speaker phone hooked to a large wide screen plasma television.

The screen was blank but after Sylvie punched a number into the phone, the plasma did its thing, lighting up. The face of Carlton Andrews appeared.

"Doherty, are you there?" he said.

Sylvie went over to the computer and swiveled a camera on top, aiming it at me.

"Ah, I see you now," Andrews said. "Judge Milligan will be here in a moment."

We both sat there, staring at each other over the electronic ether, saying nothing. After a while, Andrews turned and looked to his right, then stood up and moved away from the chair. Suddenly Cynthia Milligan replaced him.

"Good evening, Your Honor," I said.

"It's early afternoon here in New York, Doherty," she said. Her tone was business like. She sat down and folded her hands on the table.

"Sylvie, are you there?" Milligan said.

"*Oui, madame.*"

"You may excuse us; I need to speak privately with Mr. Doherty."

"*Oui, madame.*" Sylvie nodded to me and left the conference room, closing the door softly behind her.

"You too, Carlton," Milligan said.

Andrews said nothing, just moved off camera in the same direction that Milligan entered from. The judge's eyes followed him for a moment, and then turned back to me.

I kept looking into the camera and saying nothing.

Finally Milligan said, "Well, what is it, Doherty? I'm a busy woman."

"I take it this is a secure conference line," I said.

"You may take it as such."

"Then why in the hell are you screwing around with me?" I didn't bother to add your honor.

"I don't care very much for your tone of voice, Doherty."

I ignored her comment. "The name Aziz Sharif or Sharif Aziz mean anything to you?" My voice was cold and sharp.

Cynthia Milligan jumped in her chair as if I had plunged an icicle into her. She twisted her hands and a grimace replaced the anger lines in her face. She looked down at the table, then up at the camera, at me, and nodded faintly.

"What the hell is going?" I kept a steady look into the camera, not moving, not even blinking. Even over the thousands of miles separating us, Milligan seemed disconcerted by my stare. She looked away and fidgeted, then started to speak, cleared her throat and started again.

"He's a terrorist," she said. "We seized him last year in Europe with some help from our friends after a tip the CIA received about a ricin plot."

"Ricin?"

"An attack was planned against the U.S. somewhere."

"Seems kind of vague," I said.

"That's why he was held for a lengthy interrogation and eventually flown to Guantanamo Bay."

"Where do you fit in?" I said.

"He was recently convicted by a military court and sentenced to death." Her voice was quavering now, the brusque business tone long gone. "He appealed the sentence; his attorneys maintain he was illegally abducted and brought to the U.S. and that the only evidence against him was his confession, which he claims was tortured out of him."

"Let me guess," I said. "This appeal has gone to the Second Circuit and has somehow wound up before you."

She nodded again. "I'm part of a three-judge *banc* deciding the appeal. The senior judge, actually."

"How does your daughter fit in all of this?"

The grimace left her face, replaced now by furrows of worry on her forehead. Her mouth was curving down as she spoke.

"After Vanessa was abducted, I received a call from her cell phone. It was a man speaking and he said that if I ever wanted to see her alive again, I better make sure Aziz was set free. Then he described what he'd do to her before he killed her."

She started to cry. "It made me sick, Doherty. It made me so scared for my little girl."

"Did you tell the FBI?"

"I didn't tell anyone."

"Not even your fellow judges?"

"I would have had to recuse myself from the case and then Vanessa . . ." her voice broke off.

"So you were going to vote to overturn the conviction?"

She shook her head. "For all I know, Vanessa was already dead."

"That's why you hired me to track these people down, instead of using the FBI and the CIA."

"Yes," she said. "It was the only thing I could think of."

"You knew that if you offered me enough money, I wouldn't ask too many questions"

She nodded glumly.

"And if I could kill them all and get Vanessa back, then you'd let Aziz's conviction stand."

Milligan said nothing. She didn't have to; I was figuring it out myself now.

"But if Vanessa was already dead, you'd have your revenge."

She started to cry again.

"And of course, her death would help your Supreme Court nomination."

She sat straight up, rage filling her face. "If you want to believe that, after all the time we worked together to do justice, go ahead and believe it."

The firmness in her voice surprised me; made me feel a little bit better.

"I just don't like being lied to; especially a lie of omission, when my life's on the line."

Milligan said, "I'll give you any help you need. I'll even double the money I'm paying you. Just get my little girl back safe and sound."

"I'll check my account balance in the morning." I leaned toward the camera, hoping my face would loom larger on her end. "I want the money upfront. Whether I bring her back alive or not. Otherwise, I'm flying back home tonight."

Milligan didn't hesitate. "Agreed," she said. "I'll have Andrews take care of the transaction immediately. Just get Vanessa back."

23.

Hank's voice was rough over the phone. After I finished with Cynthia Milligan, I called him and filled him in on what Milligan had said about Sharif Aziz. He wasn't buying it. At least not all of it, but when I told him that there'd be a big bonus if we got the girl back safe and sound, he said he was still in. I just wasn't sure whether I was.

As soon as I disconnected with Hank, my phone buzzed. A voice message and when I hit the play button, I heard Dana's sweet voice. "Doherty, I'm at JFK; I'm coming to Paris."

I tapped the return call option and she picked up.

"Well, this is a pleasant surprise," I said. "You finally decided Paris was worth a visit."

"I'm coming to rescue you, Doherty," she said.

I laughed. "Rescue me from what?"

"I'm afraid to imagine but I'm sure you're in some kind of trouble."

Dana was arriving on an early morning flight, so I asked Sylvie to cancel my return flight to Berlin and while she was doing that I called Hank back.

"I'm staying an extra day, good buddy."

"Something struck your fancy?"

"Dana's long legs."

"She's in Paris?"

"On her way. She'll be here in the morning," I said. "I don't want to stay at the Lutetia again. Any recommendations for something small, cozy and comfortable, and très romantic?"

Hank had just the place and I wrote the name and address down.

When Sylvie came back into the conference room she had a pleasant surprise of her own. My clothes. She had ordered the Lutetia to deliver them to her office and hadn't yet shipped them back Stateside. She had also kept Hank's gym bag.

I asked her to get out my pearl gray trousers and a blue shirt.

"Are we going out tonight, Monsieur Doherty?" Sylvie was smiling.

I chucked her under the chin. "I'm afraid not."

The smile changed to a pout.

I gave her the name and address of the hotel Hank recommended and asked her to call and reserve a room. A double.

Her face lit up again.

"It's not for us." I emphasized the "us."

She pouted again but did as I asked. When she returned I told her I needed the Foundation car and driver.

"I'm doing this in the cause of love, I guess, even if I'm not involved," she said.

"I owe you one," I said.

"Well you can send me your friend, this Henry Lowrie Jackson."

"We call him Hank."

"Hank," she replied. "*C'est bon.*"

"And he always dresses better than I do."

"*Toujours bien fringué. Oui, c'est très bon.*"

In an effort to avoid traffic, the driver skirted the center of the city with its ancient streets that twisted every way but the one you wanted to go; instead crossing the Seine on the *Pont de Sully*. When we reached the *Place de la Bastille*, he turned up the *Boulevard Beaumarchais*. We were heading to the Hotel Regyn in Monmartre, Hank's suggestion de la nuit.

At the *Place de la République*, the traffic was clogged and we barely moved forward, bunched in a morass of painted steel and sooty exhaust for what seemed like an eternity. I was realizing only now how much I missed Dana. And not just those long legs of hers.

Finally, the driver eased the Mercedes up the *Boulevard de Magenta*. The traffic was still heavy here, a cacophony of honks and bleats and Gallic curses, but we were moving at least. Reaching the *Boulevard de Rochechouart*, he turned left and then when we reached *Clignancourt*, turned right and headed uphill. I was losing track of direction, only trying to keep the names of the streets in my mind: *Custine,Caulaincourt, Joseph de Maistre,* then suddenly the *rue des Abbesses* and the *Place des Abbesses* which formed a small triangular square. In its middle was a tiny park with a small children's carrousel. Even though the sky was overcast, obscuring the low sun of early evening, hordes of people—couples, small groups—were moving to and fro. The hotel was right by the Art Deco entrance to the Metro and I thanked my driver, grabbed my clothes and Hank's gym bag and, easing through the throng, went inside.

Sylvie had arranged for a room on the fourth floor that looked down on the square and at the Church of St. Jean de Montmartre, just across from the hotel. The room had one of those old-fashioned double beds which was really two twin beds combined under a single headboard. I didn't care; I was planning on only using one side anyway.

I walked over to the window and drew back the curtain. The view expanded outward and downhill, displaying a panorama of Paris. The Invalides and the Eiffel Tower were in my direct line of view and I stood there looking for a long moment, drinking them in.

Finally, I tore myself away. Dana would be here in the morning and there was so much to do before then. The stores were still open so I decided to walk around and do some shopping. I skipped the retro boutiques, instead finding Tatiana Lebedev's shop on the *rue Houdon*. I went inside and bought an outfit for Dana; a black and white silk skirt and jacket and a black silk top. One of the advantages of making love to the same woman is that you quickly learn her clothing sizes. The saleswoman complimented me on my choice and asked if I would like it gift wrapped. I told her she needn't bother.

Next, I walked over to the Cave des Abbesses and bought two bottles of Laurent-Perrier Grand Siècle. I brought the clothes and the champagne back to the hotel. There was no mini-fridge in the room so I hurried out and bought some sausages and cheese and a large bag of ice. Back upstairs, I dumped the ice in the bathroom sink and scrunched the two champagne bottles deep down among the cubes.

I could hear the bells of St. Jean tolling and went to the window and looked out. Rain was moving swiftly across the Left Bank; it looked like a tornado. Under ugly, dark threatening skies, lights were flashing from the top to the bottom of the Eiffel Tower. I stripped and took a long hot shower, letting the water play on my face, trying to wash the fatigue away. When I came back out, the church bells were tolling again, mixed now with heavy thunder. The sky above was almost pitch black with storm, its inkiness only broken by shards of lightening.

Suddenly there was a harsh splatter of rain and I rushed to the open window and pushed it shut. Down below, gusts of wind whipped the street and the café terrace next to the hotel was deserted; the patrons who only minutes before had been reveling in each other's company now abandoned the evening's pleasure.

I unwrapped the clothes I had bought Dana and hung them in the closet next to the outfit Sylvie had unpacked for me. Flipping on the flat screen, I played with the remote until I found a channel showing soccer highlights. Any sport is better than no sport. I ate some of the sausage and cheese and drank a beer and tried to stay interested in the match.

The man's voice was annoying but I didn't mind the woman's. Still, I turned over in bed and pulled the pillow over my head. I was almost back asleep when the hotel phone rang. I tried to ignore it but gave up after the third ring. I reached over and picked it up; eyes still half shut.

"Yeah?"

"Doherty?"

"Dana? Where are you? At the airport?" I shut the TV voices off.

"I'm downstairs."

"Downstairs? What time is it?"

"Eight-thirty. Don't tell me you were still asleep."

Oh, hell. I sat straight up and looked out the window. The rain had stopped and the sun was up over the *Sacre Cœur*.

"Well, come on up then."

"The man at the front desk won't let me pass unless you tell him it's okay." I heard her say something, then the clerk came on the line.

"Monsieur Doherty, is this the lady you are expecting?"

"She's the one."

Two minutes later Dana was rapping at the door. I opened it, toothbrush still in my mouth. "Do you greet all your women like this?" she said.

I ran back into the bathroom and rinsed my mouth under the shower nozzle, and then came out and kissed her.

"So what other women were you expecting?"

"Huh?"

"The desk clerk was screening your guests."

"It's a Parisian thing," I said. She didn't get it so I added, "No one, he's just being careful."

She opened the closet and peered inside.

"What woman wears my size," she said, lifting the outfit I had bought her.

"The most beautiful woman in the world," I said, kissing her neck. "You can model them for me."

146

She put them back. "Later," she said, sinking into my arms and wrestling me toward the bed. Her lips were on my face and mouth, and then her tongue probed between my lips and dueled with mine, sending shock waves through my body. We held each other close and kissed deeply again before she sat up and took off her clothes.

"I need a hot shower first," she said. "The flight makes me feel grimy."

"Need me to soap your back?"

"No, but you can open up one of those bottles of champagne."

"At eight-thirty in the morning?"

"I'm still operating on New York time."

I poured the champagne and sipped some, feeling it go right to my head. I left the curtains open and reclined back on the bed. When Dana came out of the bathroom, her naked body was splashed in sunlight and shadow; an angel and a wraith both moving ever closer to me as I lay there waiting.

She crawled under the sheet next to me and picked up her champagne glass.

"To us, Doherty," she said.

"To us."

We drank in silence, the heat from her thigh burning into me.

"I'm so glad you're here," I said.

"Me too," she said. Then she laughed. "I never thought I'd be saying that about Paris."

"You'll just have to take full advantage of the situation," I said. My hand was resting on her smooth flat belly and I reached for the curve of her hip and pulled her against me and kissed her, first softly, and then searching with a sudden hunger.

"Wasn't this where we left off when I walked in the door?"

I kissed one breast, feeling the nipple harden between my lips. I moved my mouth over and nuzzled her arm. Her hand was between my legs, stroking me, and my breathing became deeper, matching hers. My hands moved to her thighs and the warm moistness between them. She murmured softly as I caressed her.

"I want you so much," I said.

She pressed her finger on my lips. "Enough talking."

I kept my eyes open as she shifted in the bed and straddled my body.

24.

"A ricin plot?" Dana said.

"That's what Milligan said."

"And the appeal is before her?"

We were still in bed, drinking champagne and eating food from the Osteria Oscolana. Our greediness for each other spent to exhaustion, we had fallen into a deep sleep. A close, warm, cozy sleep and it took an accordionist down below on the *Place des Abbesses* to awaken us with his music.

"Tell me what she wants you to do."

I stuffed a forkful of tortellini and chicken into my mouth, chewed and swallowed, and then polished off the champagne in my glass.

"Get her daughter back alive. Or in the alternative, kill them all."

"Go on," Dana said, "you're joking." She slapped my thigh.

I refilled my champagne glass.

"That's me," I said, "a regular kidder."

"Sometimes, I can't tell," Dana said. She drank the rest of her bubbly. "Fill me up again, please."

"Are you talking about your champagne glass?"

"Whatever suits your fancy," she said.

I poured some into her glass and we toasted each other silently.

"Why doesn't she just recuse herself?"

"This guy LaPlume will kill Vanessa. Or so Milligan believes."

"Isn't the President considering her for the Supreme Court?"

I nodded. "A law and order female judge from the opposition party would win him a lot of support in a Senate they control."

"So it would pay for her to come down hard on Aziz."

I thought about that while we showered.

Outside, we started to walk through the maze of streets, and then opted to ride the Metro Pigalle kiddie train, letting it take us up the sloping streets and narrow lanes. The sun was bright, it was noon, and when we neared the top of the butte, behind the *Sacre Cœur*, on the *rue*

St. Vincent, we hopped off the train and walked past the tiny vineyard, and then went downhill to the *rue des Saules*, past the Cabaret Lapin Agile, to the *Square du Mont Cenis*.

We stood among a throng of tourists and looked out over the rooftops of Paris far below.

"It is lovely," Dana said. "So lovely."

I pulled her close to me and we stood in silence for a long moment. I finally said, "Let's walk some more," and took her by the hand. We went inside the church of St. Pierre-de-Montmartre, letting its dark interior cool us. Then we stopped at a café on the *Place du Tertre* and I had a *café crème* while Dana drank a tea with milk. Refreshed, we followed the *rue Norvins* to the *rue Lepic* and took the *Lepic* downhill, past the Moulin de la Galette. We walked along the curving street until we reached the *rue des Abbesses* below.

Here, we strolled among the crowds, just two more tourists; a couple in love. On the *rue de la Vieuville*, we looked at the art in the Atelier du Silence; and the paintings on wood in the Dorure sur Bois on the corner of the *rue des Martyrs*. They all seemed to be antique surfaces, restored or redone in gilt paint to their original design. Mirrors, statues, huge barometers, even a console in the back. We walked down the *rue des Martyrs* and back to the *Place des Abbesses*. We stood there for a while watching the children's carrousel until we tired of the shouts and screams.

"Where to next?" Dana said.

It was hot and stifling in the afternoon sun and we finally sought refuge in the shade of the Houdon Jazz Bar. I had a small beer, a *demi-pression*, while Dana drank another tea.

My mind was still on Sharif Aziz; on what Dana had said about the appeal decision and how it could propel Cynthia Milligan to the Supreme Court.

Dana hadn't suggested it. At least not overtly, but the thought was in my mind and I couldn't get rid of it. Had Cynthia Milligan not informed anyone about LaPlume's demand because she wanted to render a tough decision in a terrorism case? A decision that might cinch her nomination to the Supreme Court? And kill her daughter.

"A farthing for your thoughts," Dana said.

"A farthing?"

"I'm trying to be continental."

"That's British."

"Close enough."

"Try telling *les Français* that."

She laughed and kissed me.

We watched the sunset turn the Parisian rooftops golden and the shadows creep over the trefoiled bell tower of the sandy-bricked Église St. Jean. I felt tired and lay down on the bed.

I turned on the flat screen. The World Cup was on. It was a semifinal match between France and Portugal, being played at Munich. If France won, they would be in the final in Berlin on Saturday. And I would have a date with Henri LaPlume.

Dana sat next to me on the bed as I watched. The full day, all of it, the lovemaking, the champagne, the long walk, had caught up to me. My eyelids weighed a ton but I forced myself to stay awake.

The match seemed slow, both sides moving the ball up and down the pitch. France was on the attack finally; the ball passed to Number 10, Henry, the striker and team captain. Suddenly he was down; the referee blows his whistle. I didn't see it but Henry was tripped and now France has a penalty kick. Thirty-two minutes gone.

Number 10, the great Zinedine Zidane will kick the penalty. He lines up to take the shot, runs forward, his foot smashing into the ball. It arcs toward the goal and is in. France leads 1-0.

Now, Portugal is on the attack. They move quickly, and only a desperate grab by Barthez, the French goalie stops them from tieing the score. But the Portuguese keep the pressure up and a minute later, Barthez has to make another huge save.

I manage to stay awake through the half-time yammering of the sports commentators. The resuming play is more of the same. Portugal on the attack; France trying to protect its lead. Portugal is really putting the pressure now; Pauleta kicks hard, striking the side netting of the French goal. Close but no cigar. They won't quit, though. Barthez makes another save, a push that sends the ball just over the top. Another lost chance for the Portuguese.

Seventy-eight minutes gone in the match. I need to close my eyes for a minute.

When I awoke it was pitch dark. I could see Dana's shadow by the window, and I got up and went and stood next to her. In the distance, the Eiffel Tower was all aglitter with flashing lights as if it were a Fourth of July sparkler. I dragged two chairs over to the window and poured the rest of the champagne and we sat in silence and watched and drank. The Tower's restaurants were only dark swatches in a sea of silver. It must be late, I realized, and looked at my watch. Five after midnight. The high aircraft beacon on top of the Tower, was turning, splaying a silver cone across Paris. Every time, it shined on us, we kissed.

"Remember how the Twin Towers used to look from Brooklyn Heights at night?"

"Yes," I said, wanting to say more but finding myself choking with anger and sadness.

We stayed there like that, in the quiet, for a long time. Then the Eiffel Tower no longer lit up and Dana spoke.

"Are you?" she said.

"Am I what?"

"Going to kill them all?"

I didn't answer her, deciding to deflect the question, changing the subject to what was still roiling inside my mind.

"You think Milligan really wants that Supreme Court seat?"

"What judge doesn't?"

"Badly enough to hire me to find her daughter and keep the FBI and the CIA out of it?"

"You worked for her, Doherty. You remember how the office was run. You tell me."

I looked back out the window at the darkness that was Paris. I didn't answer her. I didn't have to.

25.

The next morning Dana went with me to the airport. The early morning breeze was fresh and cool and we walked down the *rue Houdon* arm in arm, and with easy strides. The Metro station was at the bottom of the hill, on the *Boulevard de Clichy*, and there was a *bar tabac* at the corner. We had some time so we stopped and I drank a *café crème* while Dana had her tea with milk. A man at a nearby table was reading the morning paper. France 1-Italie 0, the headline blared. I knew I had a hot date coming up in Berlin but all I wanted to think about right then was Dana.

"Hank is concerned about us," I said, tearing off a chunk of croissant and dunking it into my coffee.

"Why? Does he think we're having problems? What did you tell him?"

"Not problems. He thinks we're going to tie the knot."

Dana looked down, and then up at me. "Are we?" she finally said.

"I don't know," I said. "Let me get back from Berlin first and we'll talk about it. If you want."

She said, "I want."

"To tie the knot or just talk about it?"

"I don't know either."

I nodded and finished my coffee.

We took the Metro Number 2 line to Barbès-Rochechouart and went downstairs and caught the Number 4 train one stop to the Gare du Nord. Dana was looking at the signs at the Metro stops, memorizing them, even though she had the little pocket tourist map they gave out at the Hotel Regyn. She was going to stay there, wait in Paris until I concluded my business in Berlin.

The Gare du Nord was crammed with early morning commuters rushing pell-mell, cell phones plastered to their ears. What in the hell people had to say to each other at 5:30 a.m., I didn't know.

We sat shoulder to shoulder in silence on the RER to Charles de Gaulle. There really wasn't much to say, other than how we would miss each other. She leaned her head on me and rested, staring out the window. We were on the express train and the stations flew by, platforms filled with Arab and black African men and women waiting for the local trains to take them into Paris for their daily grind.

It was only six when we reached the airport and I had plenty of time to catch the 7:15 Air France shuttle to Berlin; so we stayed on the RER platform, hugging each other.

"How long will you be away?" she said.

"Only a few days—not longer than the weekend."

"I won't check out of the Regyn, then."

I rubbed my face against her cheek and kissed her on the mouth, keeping my lips on hers, letting her kiss me back.

"I want you with me always," I said.

"And I want to be with you."

I kissed her again and rode the escalator up to the main level of the terminal. When I looked back, she was still standing on the platform watching me. She saw me turn to look at her and brushed her eyes with her hand and gave me a weak smile.

Ninety minutes later, I was disembarking at Tegel Airport and forty minutes after hailing a Berlin taxi I was in the Grunewald house, just off of the Koenigsallee.

Kurt the caretaker let me in and Frau Helfing prepared breakfast for me. Ham and eggs and sausage and potatoes and pumpernickel. After I finished, I skipped the coffee and went into the living room and flipped on the television set. Frau Helfing wanted to serve me coffee there but I told her no thanks, just please bring me a bottle of beer.

I was sitting there on the sofa, drinking an ice cold Kloster, just goofing the facts around in my head, when Kurt came in.

"Excuse me, Herr Doherty, but this arrived for you while you were gone." He handed me a small cream-colored envelope embossed with the Milligan Foundation logo and a Berlin address in Mitte.

I ripped it open with my thumbnail after Kurt went away. Inside were three tickets for the World Cup final on Saturday. VIP passes. I was turning them over in my hands, impressed, when Hank and Astride breezed in.

Hank went into the kitchen and came back with a cold bottle of Kloster. "So, is Dana as charming as ever?" he said. He was leaning up against the doorsill, unscrewing the bottle top. Astride sat beside me on the couch and started playing with the remote control.

"More so. She said not to worry."

"Worry? About what?"

"Her and me tying the knot. We'll manage okay if we decide to do it."

He laughed. "I just don't want to lose a workout partner. Besides, married life will be boring."

"Married to Dana? Boring? I don't think so."

"You think she's going to let you run around chasing missing teenage girls; getting shot up or blown to bits?" He took a long swig of his beer. "Dream on, pardner."

I shrugged. Hank had a point. A damn good one. So I changed the subject.

"Where were you guys? Sightseeing?"

"We were out checking the Olympiastadion. Took the U-bahn, getting a feel for the city." He drank some more beer. "Impressive. They really duded the old girl up for Saturday's match. Can hardly believe it's seventy years ago the Fuehrer was there, watching us kick Germany's ass."

"Here's to good old Jessie Owens," I said, and raised my bottle.

We drank in silence for a moment, and then Hank said, "The match has been sold out for weeks and the German police are real tough on scalpers. Not one to be seen."

I smiled and said, "Not to worry." I fanned out the tickets the Milligan Foundation had sent over. "I'm holding three aces. VIP seats."

"Well, that takes care of that." Hank said. "Now all we have to do is hope LaPlume shows up."

"Oh, he will, won't he, Astride?" I turned to the girl. She was still playing with the remote but I knew she had been following the conversation.

"Yes, he'll be there, *lui*. France is in the final."

"What about the Milligan girl? Will he bring her with him?"

She shrugged. "Maybe."

That would be a big plus. Almost too good to be true.

"Anything to eat around here," Hank said. "I'm starving,"

"Frau Helfing is making tonight's dinner; so why don't we head back into the city for lunch?" I said.

"You up for Indonesian?" Hank said. "I saw a great little place when we were shopping in Mitte the other day."

"Okay," I said, "but I need to shave and shower first."

The restaurant was on a short street off the Friedrichstrasse and it had no name in the front, just a large window filled with an attractive display of cooked dishes. We sat at a huge circular table and Hank ordered the rijstafel Padang style. The waitress brought us a deep bowl of saffron rice and three plates; and then she offered us the food selections in the window, one by one. Hank chose, warning us that the dishes would be flavored with hot chili sauces.

The waitress brought us beer, then went away and returned with the food. Astride pointed to one of the dishes in the middle of the table. "What's this?" she said.

"Gado-gado," Hank said. "Vegetables in a peanut sauce."

She speared a forkful and tried it. "Ow," she said, "it's hot." She took a swig of beer and smiled. "But it's good," and took another forkful.

Back in the house, I went down to the basement and used the sauna. I was dozing in the heat when the door opened and Astride stepped. She was naked except for the towel wrapped around her luscious curves. She lazily let it fall to the floor and smiled. "Hank said you might want some company."

I stood up. "Well, I don't."

26.

We planned to take the U-bahn to the Olympiastadion. Hank wanted to keep the BMW in the garage back in Grunewald, only using it for the final operation. We hoped that would be Saturday, which I reminded myself was tomorrow.

The U-bahn, U was for unter, was not really an underground subway line. Like New York City, the trains ran above ground some of the way. Only difference, Berlin had no Bronx, at least in the old western zones. We could change at Adenauer Platz and again at Wilmersdorferstrasse which was connected to the huge Charlottenberg Station. But the trains were so packed with fans that we opted to drive the Beemer after all.

My first look at the Olympiastadion up close made me realize how wrong I was when I first saw it the other day. It was nothing like the Giants football stadium, that awkward lump of circular cement plopped in the middle of a Jersey swamp.

There was nothing going on today, not even practice sessions, and I showed the uniformed security staff our tickets for tomorrow's final match. Hank asked them in German if we could go in and look around. Impressed by Hank's accent and maybe Astride's hip-hugging jeans, they allowed us in. A huge banner inside the entrance announced the Hertha BSC, Berlin's home football club.

The interior was huge. Even though the restoration of this ancient venue had reduced the seating from 100,000 to 76,000, it was still spectacular. At the west end there was an open gap and we could see the Glockenturm or clock and bell tower across the large meadow called the Maifeld.

This was nothing like the stadium where the monsters of the Third Reich paraded their buffoonery in front of the world. And where Jessie Owens, African-American extraordinaire won four gold medals in the 1936 Olympics, pushing the arrogant faces of the master race into the huge shit pile they were making out of their beloved Deutschland.

Astride stayed close to Hank as we walked around the interior corridor that circumnavigated the arena.

"She's nervous," Hank said. "She says Richard is a crack shot. Could take all of us down easily."

"Not if we see him first."

"Says he's an expert with a pistol as well as a rifle. Was on France's pentathlon team."

"Pentathlon?"

"Yeah, you know. Sniping for rich kids."

"In that case, you two walk in front of me. Earn your per diem."

"She says Richard is LaPlume's number one killer; the one he really relies on. If LaPlume is going be here tomorrow, he'd send Richard out to scout the place first."

"Just like us."

I took out the DST photo image of Richard. I hadn't seen him since all the fireworks back at the Mistral Jihad safehouse in the *Panier*.

I pulled Astride by the arm. "What happened to Richard after your buddies snatched me in Marseille?"

She said, "Henri sent him to Bordeaux, to Pauillac. Henri likes to move around a lot, not stay in one place too long; he always sends Richard ahead first."

"So if we see Richard in Berlin, that means LaPlume is here and planning to stay?"

Astride nodded. "At least for a while, anyway. He will want to see the championship match, I assure you of that."

"Let's split up," I said to Hank. "I'm going to head that way." I was pointing to a sign that said Ostkurve. "You and Astride go the opposite way and we'll meet up. Keep your cell phone turned onto my number; if one of us spots Richard, we'll give a tap. Otherwise, when we meet, we'll repeat the procedure at the next level up."

I watched as Hank and Astride walked off and then I headed down the Ostkurve. I took my time, checking behind me every few seconds. I was dressed casually like a soccer fan, wearing blue jeans, a gray sweat shirt and gold and blue running shoes. It was too warm for the sweatshirt but I needed it for cover, to fall loose over the Beretta holstered in the small of my back. I was glad I was wearing the Nike's. The long circular hallway was deserted and shoes would have echoed around the curve, announcing that someone, me, still unseen, was approaching. Every hundred feet or so a passageway led out to the stadium seating and I had to slow as I reached each one; edging along the wall and peeping around the corner, right hand behind my back, under the sweatshirt, fingers on the Beretta.

I was flattened against the wall like this when a worker dressed in a white kitchen uniform passed me, pushing a stainless steel cart loaded with linen. He gave me a strange look and I smiled back at him and tossed out a "Guten Tag, mate," hoping he just thought I was another English soccer nut. He watched me as I eased around the corner and walked down the passage and into the stadium. I stood there for a few moments, stretching my arms and breathing deeply, looking at the all-weather running track with its red and blue lanes, and the green soccer pitch and the Glockenturm in the distance. When I turned around, the worker was gone.

I went back down the passageway to the Ostkurve and resumed my patrol. I kept to the same pattern, taking it slow, and after about ten minutes I was facing a large restaurant. There were workers inside but no patrons. A sign on the door said, "Geschlossen." I didn't need a German phrase book to tell me that meant "closed."

There was a menu taped to the inside of one of the windows and I looked at it, picking out what I knew, starting with "Bier" and ending with "wurst." I was complimenting myself on my linguistic ability when a flash of color—yellow and green—caught the corner of my left eye. I rolled my eyeballs eyes left and glimpsed him heading my way. It was Richard, the terrorist leader's bodyguard, wearing a flashy soccer shirt, and he was alone, just like Astride said he would be. I bent over quickly, moving my head closer to the menu on the wall, as if I was studying it. I waited for him to pass, but he didn't. He was behind me now; there was no way I could grab my Beretta without him seeing me, without him putting a round, maybe two, into my back before my hand ever touched my weapon.

Sweat broke out on my scalp while simultaneously a chill seeped into my thighs. If he recognized me, it was over, I couldn't move, couldn't straighten up, couldn't even tap Hank on the cell phone. What good would that do anyway? He'd come on a run, pistol out but I'd never see him, never know it. I wondered if Richard would administer a *coup de grâce* while I was lying there on the pavement in a widening pool of blood. While I was thinking these happy thoughts, the restaurant door opened.

"Guten Morgen," a man's voice said.

"Guten Morgen," I said. "I'm sorry, I don't speak German."

The man was dressed in a blue business suit and red tie and he smiled at me. "I'm sorry, the restaurant is closed. I would tell you to come back tomorrow but we are completely booked. We have been for months."

I straightened up. "Well, maybe another time," I said.

"Of course," the man said. He was still smiling; a friendly host's smile.

I looked around casually. Richard was gone. But he didn't pass me, didn't go back down the Ostkurve. He must have gone out the connecting passageway to the stadium.

"Auf Wiedersehn," I said to the man who wanted to be my host and walked into the passageway. I tapped the cell phone and Hank's fingers tapped back. Message received.

I looked around, my eyes running over the stands, but couldn't see Richard. Then I glanced above me and saw him climbing the steps to the next level. He stopped at the top and looked at the overhanging ceiling, where floodlights were recessed into the surface. Then he scanned the upper tier where there was a row of glassed-in luxury VIP seating suites. I ducked back into the passageway, before his eyes turned downward again.

"He's going up," I said into the phone. "He's alone."

"Meet you up there; we'll try and sandwich him," Hank's voice came back.

I peeked around the corner and looked up. Richard had disappeared into the tunnel above me. I scooted up the stairs, pausing just before the top; flattening down with my Beretta out, unsure whether he was leading me into a trap. The tunnel was empty. I edged along it until I reached the second level hallway.

"I'm going left," I said into the phone.

"Roger that," Hank said.

I turned and looked back out at the stadium. The Glockenturm was standing tall beyond the Maifeld and I knew that direction was due west. So if I turned left on the Ostkurve, going down the circular hallway, I would be heading north, then eventually west.

I wondered why in the hell Richard was looking at the stadium ceiling and the luxury VIP suites. Maybe nothing, Doherty. Just waiting for you to catch up to him. Maybe he's waiting at the next passageway to clip you.

I have no choice, I answered myself; I've got to follow him.

You could take your four hundred thousand in the bank and go home.

And leave the girl?

Cynthia Milligan held back on you. You don't owe her.

What about the girl? Just let her die?

I didn't wait for an answer. I already knew what it would be.

I moved along the hallway, keeping to my routine. After about a hundred meters, I came to a large open space with stairways going up and down. Still no Richard. I moved quickly across the space to the stairway and caught a flash of yellow and green down below.

I tapped the phone again. "He's going back down. He's on the atrium stairs."

Hank tapped back.

When I reached the bottom of the stairs, Richard had disappeared. To my left were restrooms. I had no choice, I had to check them out. Men's room first. Why risk a fuss and screams and police if I didn't have to.

I stepped inside, Beretta out and down by my thigh. I could hear movement, then flushing from one of the stalls. I stuffed the gun back into the front of my waist band, not bothering with the holster, and ducked back outside. I hid behind the stairs and tapped the phone again. "I'm on him; by the atrium."

Maybe a minute later, Richard strolled out of the men's room. I checked my watch. 11:18. It should take Hank and Astride two minutes tops to reach us. Richard wandered along the hallway, not glancing back, no seeming purpose to his tour. I picked up the surveillance, stopping every twenty feet, letting him disappear from view around the curve.

I looked at my watch again. 11:20. "You should be coming up on him now," I said into the phone.

No answer.

Shit. I don't remember whether I said it to myself or out loud.

The Beretta was back in my hand and I charged around the curve of the hallway toward Richard, toward where Hank and Astride would be approaching.

Richard was standing there, right in the middle of the corridor, his pistol out in a two-handed grip, pointed directly at Hank. Astride was crumpled in a heap on the floor.

Shit, I said again. I'm going to have to kill him now; kill him before we ever have a chance to debrief him.

"Hey," I shouted.

Richard turned, just a nod of the head. But enough time for Hank to duck and roll to the side, his weapon out, before Richard's gun swung back to where Hank used to be.

Confusion was on his face as he looked around. Suddenly he sprinted down a side corridor that said VIP Parking. I ran after him, Hank hopefully somewhere behind me. Richard was fast, running the race of the doomed, and slammed into a steel door and bounced off it, aware too late that the door opened in instead of out.

I rammed my shoulder into his back, sending his face against the door. He was dazed but not out, and he turned to me and raised his pistol as I slammed into him again. I looped my right hand with the pistol in it towards his head, but he ducked and chopped his free hand at my throat. I twisted away but still took some of the blow and went down, getting kneed in the jaw on the way. The door sprung open and sunlight flooded my face, blinding me for an instant as it mixed with white jolts of pain running through my head.

"Stay down," Hank said as he bolted past me.

I wasn't listening, wasn't having any of that, and I pushed myself to my feet and stumbled outside after him. We were in the VIP parking area. Richard was sprinting for a Volkswagen van about a hundred feet away; Hank racing after him, wanting to take him alive if he could. I watched sickly as Richard reached the van door and turned and raised his gun. I heard the three sharp pops as Hank peppered his torso, and I closed my eyes and cursed. Richard slid down the side of the van, no use to us anymore. Then I heard the sound of the van's engine gunning as it went into gear; louder as it came around towards me, towards the exit gate. And as it passed by my face, I saw her driving.

"No, Vanessa, wait. You're safe now," I yelled, the squeal of the tires drowning out my voice.

27.

By the time we got back to the house in Grunewald, my head had cleared. Astride was beside me in the back seat, still unconscious. Richard hadn't shot her; she had fainted dead away when he pulled out his pistol and aimed at her and Hank. I had run over to the car and drove it to the VIP entrance while Hank went back inside the stadium. When I pulled up to the door, he was hurrying back out, Astride with him, slumped across his shoulders in a fireman's carry.

He threw her on the back seat and I got out and sat in the back with her while he drove. We could hear the annoying hoo-wa, hoo-wa klaxons of the Berlin Polizei in the distance as we sped out of the lot.

Hank headed away from the city, towards Spandau and just past the Zitadelle, he turned and followed the Havel until we reached the Grunewald. Skirting the forested park, he came out by the Hohenzollernstrasse and zigzagged through the streets, doubling back and redoubling again before we reached the safety of the garage.

"Is she awake?" he said.

"No, still out." My words were thick.

"We'd better wait here until she comes around. No need for Kurt and Frau Helfing to see her in this condition."

That was all right with me. I was still a little shaky from the chop to the throat and the knee to the jaw. I ran my tongue around my mouth and felt a loose tooth.

"Adjust the rearview mirror so I can look at myself," I said.

When Hank twisted the glass rectangle, I saw a fleshy gargoyle, lower lip ballooned up and a purple welt on the side of my neck. I smiled at myself in the glass but I didn't look any better.

Next to me, Astride was softly stirring.

Hank said, "I've got some questions for her."

"Me too," I said. "But later, after Kurt and Frau Helfing have left for the day."

We managed to get the girl upstairs and into her bed without Kurt or Frau Helfing noticing anything was wrong. While Astride slept, I washed the cut on my lip and then Hank and I went down to the kitchen and grabbed a couple of beers.

Taking the bottles into the living room, we sat on the couch and drank them. Hank flipped on the television, keeping the volume just high enough that our conversation couldn't be overheard.

"Whaddya think?" I said. I rubbed the cold bottle against my swollen jaw.

"I don't know," Hank said. "That was the girl, wasn't it?"

"Vanessa Milligan. I definitely saw her face."

"Driving Richard the sniper's getaway vehicle."

"Doesn't make sense," I said.

We nursed our beers for a while, saying nothing. When we finished, Hank got up and went to the kitchen and brought back two more.

"Stockholm Syndrome?" I said, unscrewing the cap on the bottle. Maybe LaPlume and his buddies had brainwashed the Milligan girl. Back in 1973 when some bank robbers in Sweden held the bank employees hostage, their victims wound up becoming emotionally attached to their captors.

"She was only abducted two weeks ago," Hank said.

"And the Swedish bank robbers only held their captives for six days," I said.

Hank took a swig of his beer and said, "Yeah, but they didn't let their captives drive around the streets unguarded. Who was watching the Milligan girl while Richard was scouting the Olympiastadion?"

I drank some of my beer before answering. I thought about Richard wandering the stadium, still wondering what he was looking at.

"Hell, look at Patty Hearst," I finally said. "She actually participated in Symbionese Liberation Army robberies after they kidnapped her."

"Sure but the SLA scumbags held her for months, terrorizing her. Sexual abuse and death threats. She was brainwashed."

"A jury didn't think so," I said.

Hank looked at me. "Get real, counselor," he said. "That was then. You know juries. No one today would have convicted her."

"So that proves my point," I said. "Vanessa could have been brainwashed like Patty."

"Not quite. The SLA never let Patty Hearst out of their sight, let alone gave her a Volkswagen van to drive."

I mulled that over, drinking my beer, saying nothing again. Why had Vanessa driven off? She must have known we weren't going to hurt her; especially after Hank plunked three rounds into Richard's chest. Or maybe she didn't. She might have thought we believed her to be part of the Mistral Jihad. So she split.

I played with the remote, switching channels, stopping on one that showed hordes of reveling World Cup fans drinking and dancing along Berlin's Fan Mile. This was a stretch of street the city authorities had set up especially for the revelers and which started at the Brandenburg Gate.

No fighting, no soccer hooligans, no German cops. Everyone was having a good time. I switched the channel to CNN. More babble about Iraq. Another violent day in the Fertile Crescent. More bombs blowing up civilians; more snipers downing American troops. It's going to get worse before it gets better, some White House mouthpiece was intoning, struggling to keep the know it all smirk off his face.

No shit.

"Elizabeth Smart," I said, turning to Hank.

"What about her?" he said.

"She had opportunities to get away from her abductor and she didn't take them."

"Okay, but that freak really did a number on her. Repeated rapes, threats to kill her, kill her whole family. He kept her tied up in a hole, in isolation." Hank swigged his beer. "Besides, she did try to escape once and remember, she was only fourteen, just a scared little kid." He gestured at me with his beer bottle. "And the freak never, ever left her side."

"What then?"

"Like I said, I have some questions for Blondie."

After Kurt and Frau Helfing left, we took Astride down to the basement. She was still pale and shaken from the day's activities. Hank turned on the sauna and ordered Astride to strip and get inside.

She started to cry but she did as she was told, never looking directly at us. Hank pushed her down on one of the cedar benches and stood in front of her.

We asked her again about Vanessa, demanding details. She told us the girl hadn't ever been at the apartment on the *Quai de Valmy* nor in the apartment in the *Panier*. Henri LaPlume had kept her separated from the rest of them. After the snatch by Richard and two of the others, she was taken to some hidden location.

"Why didn't you tell me this before?" I said.

"You didn't ask," she said, and started to cry again.

She was right. I hadn't asked. Hadn't taken the time to go back over what had happened. I was so busy looking forward, trying to chase down LaPlume and rescue Vanessa. But how do you know where you're going if you don't where you've been?

We sent Astride back to her room. I was sick about the way we had acted but I knew now she was telling the truth.

28.

The championship match was scheduled for eight o'clock but we reached the stadium early so we could scout the area again. We took a taxi; Hank's suggestion, in case a description of the BMW had been broadcast after yesterday's shoot out. I wasn't happy about packing my Beretta; worried that there might be extra security precautions because of Richard's killing in the VIP parking lot. But I had no choice. Hank left his piece back at the house, not wanting to be picked up carrying something that could be matched to the three nine mm slugs the Polizei would have picked out of Richard.

We had the driver drop us off at the northern VIP entrance. It was still light out, the sun sets late this time of year, and even though we were way early, fans were crowding into the stadium. We were dressed down, like real American football bums, but when I flashed the VIP tickets at the entrance gate, the guard smiled at me and stepped aside to let us through. He kept his eyes on Astride's butt the whole time.

Inside, we circled the interior corridor, and then moved out into the open arena, looking around. It was only six o'clock but the place was already half-filled. We stood at the tunnel entrance for a while, scanning the seats.

"See him?" I said to Astride.

She shook her head.

We walked up to the next level and circled along the hallway, and went back outside again. Still no LaPlume.

"He'll show up," Astride said. "I swear it."

Yeah but he'd be the proverbial needle in the haystack. "Hank, what's the German word for haystack?"

"*Heumiete.*"

"Well, we're looking for a needle in a *heumiete.*"

Astride laughed. A young, innocent, infectious laugh.

"Let's get something to eat," Hank said. We went back down the tunnel to the corridor and found a food stand. We ordered bratwursts and beer and stood there for a long while, eating and drinking and watching the crowd. It was as good a place as any to spot LaPlume.

France was playing Italy in the championship match and there were throngs of both nationalities wandering along the corridor or hovering around the food stands. Astride had to use the ladies' room and Hank went with her, standing outside. He still didn't trust her. Neither did I as a matter of fact, but I didn't expect her to bolt.

I stood there drinking my beer and watching faces, wondering what I would do, how I would take out LaPlume if I spotted him. I had my Beretta tucked into my waist band; the small belt holster had proved useless yesterday. But that was the sum total of our firepower; Hank was unarmed. It wasn't in the job description Judge Milligan had given me to take LaPlume alive but knocking him off here, in the middle of 76,000 maddened soccer fans was problematic.

While I was thinking this through, Hank and Astride returned.

"What next?" he said.

"The match is going to start in twenty minutes. Let's circulate again." I switched on my cell phone. "You take the lower level; I'll stay on this one. One sweep, and then we meet at the elevator to the VIP boxes."

Hank switched on his phone and the two of them went back out into the arena and down the stairs.

After fifteen minutes I had completed my route. No LaPlume. He hadn't showed yet. Or if he had, I sure hadn't spotted him; but I believed Astride; was sure he'd be here tonight.

"Anything?" I said into the cell phone.

"Nada," Hank's voice said.

"I'm heading for the VIP elevator."

I stood by the Dannemann Lounge, an upscale cigar bar in the VIP lobby, taking in the aromas of their Brazilian tobacco with its Indonesian wrapper. I wouldn't have minded spending a couple of hours over an H. Uppman Sir Winston and a snifter of Armagnac. Hank and Astride approached, breaking into this happy thought. I showed our tickets to the guard at the elevator and we rode up in silence. Our seats were in one of the more exclusive VIP boxes, which could seat ten. The white-gloved usher said with a smile, however, that it was reserved for only us.

The box was all that one would expect Milligan Foundation moolah and clout to procure. The walls were wood-paneled with accents of stone and the floor was dark parquet. There was a wide-screen plasma television on the wall for those crude enough to forego the stunning view of the football pitch below.

"Not even the K Street lobbyists could spring for something like this," Hank said, walking over to the window.

Our usher asked if we would like champagne and we graciously accepted. He brought us a bottle of Mumm's NV and poured. Before he left, he explained that if we wanted something else to drink or a bite to eat, there was a business lounge in the back.

"Well, we're in business today," Hank said.

The usher looked puzzled but Hank smiled and asked him if he could bring us some sports binoculars. I handed the man a twenty-Euro note. He thanked me with a smile and left; promptly returning with the binoculars.

Outside in the stadium, the air was filled with electricity and even though we were isolated in the thick-paneled room, you could hear and feel the excitement of the crowd.

The teams were on the field; the French in white, the Italians in blue. They had finished warming up and were getting their last-second instructions from their managers. The French manager looked like a university professor.

Astride pointed out the players to us.

"Look, Number 10, that's Zinedine Zidane," she said, gesturing at the middle-aged man with the shaved head. I remembered seeing him in the semi-final match against Portugal that Dana and I had watched back in the hotel room in Montmartre. Zidane had scored the only goal on a penalty kick.

"And Number 12, that's the captain, Thierry Henry, the team's only striker." Henry was a black man and I wondered if he was Caribbean or African-French.

"Why do you say the only striker? Is there usually more than one?"

"Yes, that's what Henri says. He always complains, saying that the French team should have two strikers; one of them at least should be a true Frenchman." She sneered. "That's his brother talking, trying to fill Henri's head with racist filth."

"Maybe he succeeded," Hank said.

Astride shook her head. "Never. That's why he formed the Mistral Jihad."

"Which was to do what?" Hank said. "I forgot." He snapped his fingers. "Oh, I remember now: to kidnap and kill people."

"Justice has a cost, Henri always says."

I stared at her, sickened by the platitude. "Nine of your group are dead," I said. "That's a pretty steep price to pay for Mission Not-Accomplished. And you would have made ten; remember that."

She fell silent, saying nothing, just looking out the window at the soccer pitch below.

The match had started, the noise of the crowd outside was a muted rumble through the thick pane of glass in the VIP box. I thought about the Dannemann Lounge below and sipped my champagne, wishing that I had that Sir Winston and Armagnac instead.

Suddenly, a roar from the crowd echoed through the VIP box. Thierry Henry, the French striker, was down, hurt. I looked over at the French bench; the manager, Raymond Domenech, was worried, fingers to his lips, biting his nails. Henry was up again now. Astride clapped her hands and shouted, that broad smile on her face again.

"We need him," she said, "he is one of the young ones."

"Young ones?"

"Yes, the French team has too many veterans, Zidane and Thuram, Makelele and the goalkeeper, Fabian Barthez, are all over thirty. Henry calls this team the golden oldies; they are at the end of their careers."

"Who's the tall skinny kid?" I pointed to a young black player.

"That's Patrick Vieira," she said. "The midfielder. He's the youngest player on the team."

The play resumed; the teams moving the ball back and forth, probing, testing each other's defenses. Then the French were on the attack again. Suddenly a French player was down, the referee blowing his whistle and signaling a penalty kick.

I didn't see any foul but what the hell did I know?

Zidane, the great Zidane, I remembered that the Marseille newspaper had called him that, was back, measuring the goal for the kick.

Silence. It was dead quiet. Zidane rushes forward, arching his steps at an angle, trying to fake out the Italian goalkeeper, Buffon. Zidane's foot strikes the ball solidly, sending it smashing into the crossbar, and caroming straight down into the goal. Zidane raises his hand in triumph and the stadium breaks into a roar; causing the window in our VIP box to vibrate in unison.

"*Vive les Bleues*," Astride shouted, jumping up.

"But they are wearing white."

"They are still *les Bleues*," she smiled. She jumped up again. "*Vive l'Algerie.*"

"*Vive l'Algérie?*" I said.

"Yes, Zidane's family is from the Kabyle, the mountains."

"Well, your friend LaPlume must really admire him, then."

"He says he should stay in retirement. It's his brother, the fascist, who hates Zidane. And Henry and Vieira and Makelele. All of them." She grimaced. "You know he says they should all be deported, expelled; along with the Jews. *Macacas*, that's what his party calls them."

Hank had been ignoring her, studying the stands through the binoculars, trying to spot LaPlume. He turned to Astride and said, "Who would work his family's agricultural operations if that happened?"

"Oh, they'd let a few stay, restricted to living in work locations."

"I guess nobody told him his ideas about race were already settled. It was called World War Two."

"Forget him," I said. "Let's concentrate on baby brother."

"Right," Hank said. "You know, after his bodyguard Richard didn't show up yesterday at wherever they're hiding out, and Vanessa told him what happened, LaPlume must have realized the danger."

"So you think he won't be here."

"Oh, he's here," Hank said. "But he's low key. Very low key. No way we'll be able to spot him."

A glumness overtook me. Hank was right. I had known all along how difficult it would be, with that stupid pun about finding a needle in a *heumiete*. Now, Hank was agreeing with me.

I was stewing in my juices about how impossible this task was when Astride suddenly punched me on the shoulder, shouting *merde*. I looked down at the field; the Italians were attacking, swarming around the French goal and the beleaguered Barthez. A cross kick in front of the crease sailed through the air. Materazzi pulls down a French player's shoulders, leaping above him and heading the ball in. No foul is called.

"*Merde et contre-merde,*" Astride said. The score was tied, one to one.

The Italians kept attacking for the rest of the first half. Materazzi again tries to push off a French player, this time from a corner kick but he's caught. Twelve minutes later, Luco Toni slams the ball towards the French goal but it hits the cross-bar and bounces away.

In the second-half, the French come back and Henry launches an arching shot skyward, and it sails over the Italian goal. Astride is on the edge of her seat. I'm actually enjoying the action, the champagne helping, and Hank is still scanning the crowd.

Italy is now back on the attack and they bring the ball quickly downfield and score; but the referee calls an off-side, nullifying the goal. Still one-one.

"I have to go to the ladies room," Astride said.

I looked at Hank. He shook his head, meaning he didn't think he'd have to go with her; she'd come back. Astride left the VIP box and I turned back to the game. Sixty-two minutes gone. They would play for ninety minutes plus time added on, maybe two or three minutes, for injury substitutions. Not much time left to catch LaPlume.

The time clock said sixty-seven minutes. Astride hadn't returned yet. Maybe there was a line at the ladies room but I doubted it. This was VIP seating up here. They would more than enough facilities for this class of spectator.

"I'm going to go check on Blondie," I said.

Hank nodded, his binoculars still focused on the crowd.

I started to get up when the door to our VIP box opened.

It was Astride, her face pale. "I saw him," she said. She was shaking. "I saw him."

I led her over to a chair.

"Where?"

She said nothing, still shaking.

"Where?" I said it again, this time louder. Hank had set down the binoculars and was watching her.

She lifted her finger and pointed. It was waving toward the door.

"Out there," she said. "Out there. I was leaving the ladies room and I saw him."

"Was Vanessa with him?" The cold steel in my voice seemed to shock her.

"No, he was alone."

"Did you see where he was going?"

She nodded her head.

"Well, where then, dammit?"

"Into a room. Like this one."

"Well, I'll be," Hank said. "The mickeyfricker has a VIP box, like us. No wonder we couldn't spot him."

29.

I eased the door to the VIP box open. Just a crack, maybe an inch. It hadn't made a sound. I breathed slowly, deeply; waiting, getting my heart rate and muscles under control. I had moved my Beretta from the small of my back to the front of my waist band so anyone passing along the VIP corridor wouldn't notice the bulge or me reaching for it when the time came. I could only see a sliver of the room through my tiny viewing space but it seemed to have the same layout as ours. Sounds came from inside, low murmurs of voices and a soft screeching, like someone washing a window or running their fingernails sharply down a blackboard.

Hank was backing me up, taking a post down the corridor, on the other side where he'd have a sure diagonal for a physical takedown of LaPlume if the terrorist got by me.

Get by you, Doherty? Don't you mean if he kills you?

No need to get technical.

I eased the door open another inch and waited, listening. I could see a little more of the room, a corner of the table and chairs but no LaPlume. Murmured voices, still so low I couldn't make out what they were saying, couldn't even tell where they were coming from. I heard no movement but the roar of the crowd came sharply through the window, blocking any noise from inside. I waited for the noise to die down. When it did, I looked back at Hank and nodded. He nodded back.

I had the Beretta out now, in my right hand; my left still on the door knob. I pushed it open further, just enough to ease myself through. As I started to close it behind me, I stopped, standing there stunned.

LaPlume was kneeling on a chair in front of the window. A rectangular piece had been cut out of the glass; I could see it lying on the table. He was holding a rifle, poking through the opening. It was one of those fancy jobs, the ones you only see in movies—or in special forces, like the French Foreign Legion. The kind with the detachable stock and a two-piece barrel that screwed together. He had a scope on it; was looking though it, but there was no sound suppressor. Made sense; LaPlume was looking for the long shot and the suppressor would alter the trajectory. Besides, with the pandemonium of the fans in the stadium, he really didn't need one.

But this wasn't what had shocked me; had stopped me dead in my tracks.

Next to him, holding a glass cutter, was Vanessa Milligan.

She must have heard me or maybe only sensed my presence, because while I was standing there, still staring at them, she turned and saw me.

I put my finger to my lips, gesturing to her to stay quiet.

Her eyes widened and then she half-screamed, half-shouted, "Henri."

LaPlume took his eye away from the sight and started to turn. I couldn't shoot, the girl was too close. I bulldozed across the room, slamming my shoulder into him, spilling him and the chair over. I was on top of him, punching, but he clubbed at me with the rifle. I blocked the blows with my left arm, at the same time trying to get my pistol close enough to his body to squeeze off a killing shot.

Suddenly Vanessa leapt on my back like a hungry cougar taking down its prey. She was slashing at my face with the glass cutter but I twisted her wrist sharply, forcing her drop it. She yelped in pain then sank her teeth into my shoulder, deep and hard. Her hands raked across my face, ripping flesh; fingernails searching for my eyes. I kept twisting my head back and forth, at the same time pounding LaPlume with both hands. He wasn't soft, his body holding up under the blows and I knew I couldn't fight the two of them for much longer. Sooner or later one of Vanessa's nails would find an eyeball, giving LaPlume enough of a respite to reach my gun.

Where in the hell was Hank?

I slammed my fist into LaPlume's ribs and he grunted and tried to roll away, causing my follow up punch to glance off him. I swung again, the punch misdirected as Vanessa hooked an arm around my neck, and my fist bounced off the wall, the Beretta clattering as I lost it. I tried to shake her off me but I couldn't; tried to butt LaPlume in the face but missed. He was moving his hand along the floor, feeling for my pistol. I was tiring fast, worried that Vanessa's teeth would cut all the way through the top of my trapezius muscle, and my right arm would be useless.

She was growling through her clenched teeth, still trying to rake and gouge my eyes. I was down now, panting for breath. LaPlume had rolled away; crawled under the table. His rifle was underneath me and I could see my Beretta lying in the corner, out of his reach, but I didn't know what other weapons were in the room.

Vanessa was still on me, feral sounds erupting from her throat. Then I heard a sharp crack and her teeth let go and her body crumpled to the floor next to me.

I rolled over and saw Hank standing there, my pistol in his hand.

"Did you kill her?" I said.

"No, just laid a good lick upside her head." He looked around. "Where's LaPlume?

The door slammed. While Hank was rescuing me, the terrorist or whatever he was had slid out from under the other side of the table and had made a break for it.

"Stay here with the girl," I said. "Getting that sonofabitch is my job. Get Vanessa away if you can."

"I know every kaserne in Deutschland," Hank said.

"And you probably snuck some frauleins into them all."

Hank laughed and handed me the pistol. "You better move then, blood bro."

I was out the door and in the hallway. I could see LaPlume by the elevator, frantically pushing the down button. He spotted me and broke into a run and I chased after him. A sign on the wall said we were heading toward the Atrium.

There were stairs there, I remembered, and if he could reach the ground floor he could lose me in the crowd, or get outside and disappear into the night. I picked up speed and started to gain on him; voices behind me; shouts in German along the corridor. I reached the stairs and saw him on the landing below. I took the steps two at a time, almost losing my balance and caroming off the steel railing. The bounce hurt but I was closing the distance and closing it fast.

As I reached the bottom I could see LaPlume making for the door to the VIP parking area. Hands reached out, trying to grab me, stop me but I shook them off only to watch LaPlume disappear beyond the door.

I started running again, remembering the door opened inward and yanked it. Outside, I looked around. The area was lit up and I spotted LaPlume running about two hundred feet away, making for what looked like the same Volkswagen van I had seen Vanessa drive away in yesterday.

I chased after him, lifting the Beretta, stopping and trying to get a bead on him. He was zigzagging and nearing the van and I couldn't get a steady aim so I gave up and started the chase again. My lungs were burning from the deep gasps of air and I winced as my ankles twisted under the slam of my feet against the hard pavement, but I was so close to my prey that I wasn't calling off the hunt.

LaPlume had reached the van but instead of getting inside and driving off, he ran around to the other side and yanked open the door. I tried to aim at him through the windows but he ducked down. I slowed, moving cautiously forward, arms out with my pistol up. He was trapped; all I had to do was get close enough to force him to surrender or down him with an easy kill shot.

Suddenly LaPlume's head popped up along with his right arm. And in the right arm was an automatic. That's why he ducked; the bastard was looking for a gun he had hidden in the van. I dove for the pavement as his pistol spit twice, kicking up bits of concrete around me. I rolled to my left and looked around, my pistol arm extended. My Beretta pointed to where LaPlume was.

Only he wasn't. He was gone.

I scanned the lot again and spotted him running fast, making towards a large grassy area. The Maifeld. A huge lawn once used by the Nazis for their annual May Day celebrations. Like they really cared for the working-classes.

The twilight sky had long vanished, its pink glow now replaced by the inky blackness of night. The VIP parking area was bright but the Maifeld was an ominous void of deep dark space, with only the lights of the Glockenturm glowing like a distant nebula.

I wasn't sure where LaPlume was heading but I knew that if I let him get far enough into the grassy field, he could turn in the darkness and aim at me from a prone position, my silhouette a sure target. I picked up my pace and as I reached the edge of the lawn I could make him out, heading straight for the Glockenturm. I ran after him, knowing that if he turned and stopped I could get off at least two good shots before he could aim.

But he didn't stop.

He was at the door of the Glockenturm now. I could hear two shots and instinctively hit the ground. No whistling rounds went by me; no clumps of dirt flew up. He wasn't firing at me, I realized as I watched him duck inside the clocktower. I moved after him, my feet thudding on the soft grass, enjoying the run now, adrenalin pumping as I knew the hunt would lead to a kill.

When I reached the tower, I flattened myself against the wall and waited, catching my breath. The lock was shot off and the door pushed open. I crouched down near the ground, working myself up. Then I dove inside and rolled across the floor, muscles tensed, waiting for slugs from LaPlume's gun to rip into me.

Nothing. I looked up and saw a tiny light glowing and heard a soft hum and a cable whirring. LaPlume was taking the elevator to the top. I lay there on the floor, resting, knowing he had no other place to go. He would know it too and would be waiting for me. I scanned the lobby, and then looked outside. No one anywhere. Far across the Maifeld the lights of the stadium glowed and a might roar erupted. But that was there. Here, I was alone. Berlin was just like New York. Never a cop around when you need one.

I pressed the elevator button and waited for the car to come down. I timed it. Twenty-five seconds. I ducked inside and pressed the button. As the elevator closed I started counting again. When I reached twenty, I flattened myself on the floor and aimed the Beretta at the door.

At twenty-five, the car stopped and the door opened. I squeezed off three quick rounds. Nobody home. The walkway was deserted. I stepped outside and crouched against the inner wall. Across the narrow platform was an iron railing. Above me was the bell, enclosed in a square frame by the walkway.

LaPlume was nowhere in sight; maybe hiding around the left corner; maybe hiding around the right. I didn't know; didn't have any idea. But I had to make a decision. Not the first time I flipped a coin.

I was sweating hard from the exertion, my clothes damp and heavy around me. I could stay here by the elevators and wait for LaPlume, but what good would that do? Just give him time to recover his bearings, regroup and come after me again. No, I had him on the run; had to keep up the hunt.

I chose moving left, keeping my gun hand on the outside, hoping for a better shooting angle if I glimpsed him. I reached the first corner; jumped out in a crouch, hands in a firing position. No target. I moved softly but faster to the next corner. I knelt down, and then rolled out, gun aimed. Still no LaPlume.

Maybe he was moving away from me, moving faster so he'd come up behind me. I looked up at the bell. If I could get up there next to it, I could see all four sides of the walkway. I jammed the Beretta into my waistband and leaped, catching a wooden post and heaving myself up and over it. I lay there, next to the bell, in the darkness of its shadow, forcing my breathing to become shallow, through my nose, silent. Then I rose to my knees, gun back out. No movement below. No noises.

Where the fuck are you, LaPlume?

As I stood and peered out and down at the walkway, I got my answer. His shadow caught my eye, a split second before he rushed from the other side of the bell, like Quasimodo, all hunched over in an attacking stance.

I braced myself for the onslaught but when he slammed into me, the force pushed me over the side. I tried to grab onto the wood, anything, to keep from falling, a chill running through me when my hands only clutched air.

The next thing I remember I was flat on my back, the wind knocked out of me, my gun lying a few feet away.

Another roar erupted from the stadium.

I looked up towards the bell, only to see LaPlume leaping down and landing next to me. He aimed his gun at my head and smirked.

"One less *sale Américain* sticking his big nose where it doesn't belong."

I moved my hands; my fingers reaching, groping desperately for the Beretta, but they came up empty.

I closed my eyes and thought of Dana waiting for me back in the hotel room in Montmartre; thought of my cats who only had enough food and water for a week. Thought how much I wanted to kill that sonofabitch standing in front of me. My nose wasn't big.

"Henri," a woman's voice yelled. It was Astride. Blondie. How in the hell did she get up here? LaPlume turned to look and she rushed him before he could fire, clawing at his face. He tried to push her away, but she kept clawing, yelling at him.

I stuck my foot out to trip him and it worked. He lost his balance, stumbling against the railing. Astride shoved him and he started to topple over the side, his gun falling away as he clutched frantically for her. I became sick as I watched his hand clasp her wrist, knowing what would happen next: He falls back, yanking her over the side with him before I can grab her. And then I see it happen.

Another roar. Not from the stadium; from inside my head.

30.

When I came out of the fog there was a shroud hovering over me. I blinked and realized it was a nurse in a white uniform, giving me an injection in my arm.

"Stay still," she said in English. American English.

They had shaved my head and sutured the scalp where the bullet had creased me. I reached up and touched the bandage, feeling good because there was no handcuff attached to my wrist. But the effort tired me out and I dropped back off to sleep.

When I awakened the second time, my tongue was thick and fuzzy, my throat dry. I needed water, a gallon of it. I looked around the room and saw Hank sitting in a chair by the window.

"Where am I?" I said.

"Hey, blood brother, welcome back to the land of the living," Hank said.

"Water," I said, surprised at the slurring of my voice.

He picked up a metal carafe and poured some into a glass and handed it to me. "Compliments of the American Clinic," he said.

I struggled to sit up and with Hank's help, got myself into a position where I could sip the water.

"How'd I get here?" I said.

"Vanessa regained consciousness back in the VIP box and started to put up a fight, so I clipped her again with the gun butt. She wasn't going anywhere so I went looking for you and LaPlume."

I sipped some more water and let him continue.

"There was pandemonium outside and people were pointing towards the Atrium. I ran downstairs and saw that the door to the VIP Parking was open. I went outside but I didn't see anything; then I heard gunfire from the Glockenturm. Three shots."

"That must have been me."

"So I started running in that direction, then I heard another shot and saw Blondie and LaPlume falling from the top."

I shuddered, remembering the scene. "I hope it was quick for her."

"It was."

"So how did I get here?"

"The polizei were right behind me. When we found you, you were in bad shape. They called for an ambulance and I told the driver to bring you here. The polizei wanted to arrest you and take you to a local butcher shop but I gave them Pasquier's name and said he would vouch for you."

"Pasquier vouched for me?"

"*Oui, Monsieur Doherty.*" I turned my eyes toward the sound of the voice. It was the French magistrate. I was so weak that I hadn't noticed that he was in the room.

"What's this all about?" I said.

"False flag," Hank said.

"What?"

"The Mistral Jihad; LaPlume used it as a false flag to recruit his young sacrificial lambs, tricking them into believing they were fighting for world justice."

"Instead?"

"Instead, he was pushing his older brother's fascist agenda."

"How is that piece of puke connected with all this?"

"One theory we have, and we believe it is a good one," Pasquier said, "is that LaPlume planned to assassinate one of the non-European players on the French team, hoping to provoke bloody rioting throughout France. Chaos so devastating that it would bring the government down and new elections would be held."

"Like the student demonstrations brought down DeGaulle in 1968?"

"Yes, these types always look for crises."

"And LaPlume the Elder hoped the French would want to put a strong man in charge, someone who would clamp down on the foreign 'criminal element,'" I said.

"That would have been only his first step, I'm afraid. First mass arrests, then deportations."

"Just like under Vichy," Hank said.

"Does LaPlume really believe that the French people would go along with this?"

Pasquier shrugged. "People have short memories. And he hopes that enough of them will go along to keep the rest silent."

I lay back down in the pillow. My head was throbbing. Not in pain but in turmoil, trying to process all the craziness I had just heard.

"So his brother Henri was doing just the opposite of what Blondie believed," I said.

"Who?" Pasquier said.

"Astride. The dead girl. The DST called her BLONDIE, so I picked up on it. Henri LaPlume recruited her into the Mistral Jihad and she really believed she was fighting for social justice."

"In the end, maybe she was," Hank said.

"How so?" I said.

"After you started chasing LaPlume, she came into his VIP box and saw the rifle and the cut glass. Probably put two and two together. Knew he was up to no good."

I nodded, wincing from a jolt of pain in my skull. "That's why she came after him, I guess. She saved my life." I said this last bit for Pasquier's benefit.

"As far as the French authorities are concerned, the girl was not a terrorist," he said. "She was *une patriote*."

"Where did Vanessa Milligan fit in the terrorist's plans?" I said.

"Oh, that was LaPlume's trump card. After he shot the player, he was to kill Vanessa and leave her there with the rifle. Imagine the outcry when everyone learns the daughter of an American judge was involved in the assassination of one of our north-African or black players."

"LaPlume wanted to blame the U.S.? I don't understand."

"He hates America," Pasquier said. "To him, you're a mongrel nation run by Jews. They're his other favorite target."

I had heard it all before, too many freaking times. "What happened at the football match. I kept hearing the crowd roar."

"Two overtimes and we lost," Pasquier said.

"How'd that happen?" I said.

"In the second OT, Materazzi cursed at Zidane, something terrible, *raciste* we believe, and Zidane head butted him. After the OT, France lost on penalty kicks. We should have won."

I nodded at Pasquier, and then started laughing.

"What?" he said. "France goes down to defeat and you laugh?"

I laughed louder. "No," I finally said, catching my breath. I told them about my struggle with Henri LaPlume in the VIP box. "I tried to head butt my fascist and missed. At least Zidane got his."

I started laughing again and Hank and Pasquier joined in.

We enjoyed the joke for a long moment, and then I said, "What's going to happen to his older brother, the French fuehrer?"

"We're watching him closely," Pasquier said. "He made a lot of enemies in the DST with this episode. We can't prove anything but there is always *la justice des rues*."

Street justice. Sometimes I loved the concept. This was one of them.

"What about Vanessa?" I said to Hank.

"She's here," he said. "In the clinic; in a room down the hall. Her mother is with her now."

"Judge Milligan is here?"

"Yes," Pasquier said. "And the German authorities have been decent enough to release the Milligan girl into her mother's custody. They think of her more as a victim than a participant."

"Hank, do me a favor, go tell Judge Milligan I'd like to see her."

After he left, I told Pasquier that if Astride's family needs any help with the funeral, to let me know.

He said that was kind of me and got up to go.

"Look me up the next time you're in Paris, *Monsieur Doherty*," he said. "But leave the Beretta home."

I gave him a weak salute with my hand as he left.

I was lying there with my eyes closed when I heard a rap on the door. It was Cynthia Milligan and I motioned her in. Hank was right behind her, pushing Vanessa in a wheel chair. The girl's head was bandaged, probably from when Hank whacked her with the gun butt.

Milligan was beaming as she came to my bedside.

"Doherty, thank you so much for saving my baby," she said.

I wanted to say it was nothing, but eleven people were dead, maybe twelve by now, and I was lying in a hospital bed. So I said, "That's what you paid me for."

It was the truth, wasn't it?

Milligan turned to her daughter and said, "Vanessa, don't you have something to say to Mr. Doherty?"

Mr. Doherty? I had known Cynthia Milligan for fourteen years, and for nine of them she had been my boss. This was the first time I ever heard her call me Mr. Doherty. Decency to the line troops had always been in short supply in the D.A.'s office.

"That's okay," I said.

Hank wheeled Vanessa over to my bed.

The girl smiled. It was a shy smile and I suddenly realized how pretty she was, even with her bandaged head. And I wondered if her mother had once been like that.

"I'm sorry, Mr. Doherty," she said.

I looked at her face. It was filled with sorrow; genuine emotion. "What for?" I said.

"For causing all this trouble. And thank you for saving me." She began to cry.

I reached over and held her hand. Just yesterday, a few hours ago, she had been a brainwashed terrorist. Now she was only a scared little girl.

But what about tomorrow? "It's all right," I said. Was it?

I let go of her hand. "Hank, could you wheel Vanessa around for a while? I'd like to speak to Judge Milligan alone."

After they left, I asked Cynthia to hand me the water glass so I could drink. When I finished, I handed it back to her.

She was still smiling at me. "Doherty," she said, "I once called you a one-trick pony. I was so wrong."

"No you weren't," I said. "You always gave a good snow job, Cynthia." I hoped my tone was as bitter as the taste in my mouth.

"Whatever do you mean?" she said.

"The phone call, Cynthia. The one you received after Vanessa was abducted."

"What about it?"

"It wasn't LaPlume talking to you, threatening you; it was Vanessa, wasn't it?"

Her face paled and she sat down on one of the chairs.

"You don't know what that monster did to her. He kept her in isolation, raping her every day, sometimes more than once, torturing her; I can't even talk about that. Keeping her awake for days, hungry and thirsty. He told her if she tried to escape, he'd kill her, than he'd kill me."

I watched her sitting there, wringing her hands.

"But you didn't know that at the time she called, did you?"

"She was reading from a script; he had her tied up and was holding a gun to her head."

"Like I said, you didn't know that."

"I knew she was in danger," Milligan said.

"Her life wasn't the only thing in danger."

Milligan was looking away from me, not answering.

"Cynthia," I said sharply, bringing her attention back. "That wasn't the only thing you were worried about, Vanessa's well being."

She nodded slowly.

"The Supreme Court nomination. As soon as word got out that Vanessa, your daughter, was running around Europe with a terrorist group named Mistral Jihad, the President would shit can your future."

"I really didn't care about that."

"Don't bullshit me," I said. "I used to work for you, remember."

She said nothing.

"Do you want me to tell you the rest?"

She was still silent, a sick look on her face.

"So you hired me to get her back and to kill her abductors. Only I was really killing witnesses, wasn't I? Not that they didn't deserve it.

"Oh, you might have suspected she was being brainwashed, turned like Patty Hearst, but you couldn't really be sure, couldn't take the chance. If the story came out, your shot at the Supreme Court would've been longer than Kim Jong Il's.

"And if she got killed, well then, you could always get the sympathy vote in the Senate. You made sure to tidy up ahead of time, didn't want to leave any possible dirt lying around Paris; that's why you had Vanessa's belongings shipped back to New York right away." I took a long sip of water. I was just getting started. "For most of us time moves on; we change, adapt, mature, whatever label you want to put on it. Look at you, Cynthia. Once you wanted to do justice; you used to call it God's work, remember? Then one bright shining day you grew up and only wanted to be reelected. And now? Now you'd trade your daughter's life for a shot at the Supreme Court. I guess you'd call that a metamorphosis."

I drank some more water and went on. "But me, I always wanted to put the bad guys under the jailhouse; that was my noble cause. My sum and substance. So you added it up. One and one makes $250,000, just in case I had any moral qualms about playing executioner."

I set the glass back down. The water hadn't washed away the bitterness in my throat.

"Cynthia, I remember when I first started in the D.A.'s Office and I was assigned to the Criminal Courts Bureau in that rat hole on Schermerhorn Street."

She smiled faintly. "That was eons ago, it seems."

"You came by one day to give us a pep talk. All the rookies squashed together, battered metal desks crammed next to each other, four to a room. Do you remember what you said?"

She nodded. "It's not the quality of furniture you bring to the office that counts, it's the quality of justice."

"So I did quality justice here. No qualms. I am a one-trick pony."

She sat there taking it, saying nothing. What could she say? I was telling her the truth about herself and she really didn't give a shit. She'd get what she wanted now.

I just felt sorry for that girl in the wheelchair.

"I'll make it up to her, Doherty, I swear," she said.

"Yeah," I said, turning my head and looking out the window.

The summer sunlight splayed through the blinds, and I welcomed it, let it warm my face, pretending that it was cleansing me of all the filth I had been through.

When I finally turned back, Cynthia Milligan was gone.

31.

We stood arm in arm on the *Pont de Sully*; Dana's face a soft reddish glow in the late afternoon sun. Below us, the dark water of the Seine was deep, with a strong dangerous current. After it hit the prow of the Île St. Louis, the river rushed angrily down the narrow walled passageways that flanked both sides of the island.

I leaned on the bridge, taking pressure off my left ankle, still bandaged but sore. I was wearing the pearl gray silk suit and a navy and silver polka dot tie. Dana had on the black and white silk Tatiana Lebedev outfit I had bought her, accessorizing with a pair of one-carat diamond studs. She had her jacket off and the white silk top exposed her slender arms, already tanned a deep bronze from the early summer sun.

We watched the water, saying nothing, ignoring the passersby, lost in the world that was Paris. A constant breeze blew along the river and even here, in the midst of the city, with its exhaust and smog, fragrances of summer wafted over us.

I squeezed Dana's waist and kissed her neck, catching the scent of her perfume, the Issey Miyake she always wore.

Dana looked at me and kissed me. "I'm glad I'm here with you," she said.

"I'm glad you're with me anywhere." I kissed her back, leaving my lips on hers for a long moment. We walked to the other end of the Île St. Louis and sat on the small treed terrace of the brasserie that is there. I ordered a *bière blanche*, the Belgian wheat beer the Flemish called weisse bier, and Dana had a *kir royale*.

"So Milligan's on her way back to New York with her daughter," Dana said.

"The girl is going to need a lot of help," I said.

"Think Milligan's going to give it to her?"

"I hope so."

"You sound dubious."

"She's only thinking about the Supreme Court."

"Even she can't be that cold of a bitch."

I shrugged and sipped my beer. "What did you say to me once? 'Remember, you worked for her.'"

We walked over to the Pont Louis Philippe. The sun was starting to set, lighting up the windows of the Hôtel de Ville with a golden glow.

One of the cruise boats was approaching us, heading downstream. It was filled with tourists but I was sure I recognized two of them on the upper deck.

"Look," I said, pointing down.

"That's Hank," Dana said. "Who's the woman with him?"

"Sylvie, from the Milligan Foundation's Paris office. Both of them were clamoring to meet the other, so I played cupid."

As the boat passed, we could see Hank whispering something in Sylvie's ear. She was smiling. Then he looked up and gave a slight wave. I smiled back and pulled out a piece of paper.

"What's that?" Dana said.

"My French lesson for today."

I read the words to myself, then crumpled up the paper and tossed it over the bridge and watched the current pick it up and carry it away. I wouldn't need it tonight.

"Are you hungry?" I said.

"Not really," she said.

"We could take a cruise on the Seine like Hank and Sylvie."

"If you want to."

"Or we could catch a cab back to the hotel."

"When it gets dark we can watch the Eiffel Tower."

"Only on the hour when it glitters," I said.

"What will we do the rest of the time?"

"Elevate my sore ankle."

IN THE OLD DAYS

The Hotel George in the old days was called the Bellevue and it was the sort of place that politicos would take their mistresses, and lobbyists (they called them bagmen back then when honesty about one's station in life was easier to come by) would slide little white envelopes across the table with a smile. Even earlier in the Bellevue's career, or the really good old days, Soviet defector Walt Krivitsky was found shot dead in one of the upper rooms, a .38 caliber Savage revolver, serial number 43907 clutched in his hand, and an assortment of purported suicide notes scattered about. Was it suicide or murder? It all depended on your point of view.

Making the affair even murkier was the fact that Krivitsky, who directed Soviet military intelligence in Western Europe before he defected, had been driven to nearby Union Station the previous night by the wife of a former Nazi storm trooper. Adding another strange twist, Krivitsky, who was supposed to take a train to New York where he was scheduled to testify before a committee investigating subversion in the New York City Public School system, instead registered under an alias at the Bellevue.

These days, with new owners, a new name and a sleek new stainless steel and coral façade, and an upscale bar and restaurant connected to it, and with a more cheerful and pleasant staff, the slitherati and spies have been replaced by a more urbane clientele. In the old days, no one talked politics; it wasn't that sort of place. These days, the restaurant and bar is the place for Capitol Hill staffers to go for a drink after work and for politicians and influential visitors to Washington to dine in streamlined elegance.

The restaurant, called the Bistro Bis, if not the best in Washington, is certainly the tops on Capitol Hill. That makes it the place to go on weeknights. It is even better than a health club because when administrations change like they are doing now, the club memberships change as well. Not at the Bistro Bis whose regulars hang on like upper level British civil servants, dining well through the vicissitudes of their erstwhile political masters. Sure, some faces fade and new ones meld in.

Yet, the critical mass of talent and wit of its patrons remains on a steady level.

Hank Jackson had checked into the George that afternoon and after a long hot shower and nap, he went down to the Bis for a drink and some light food. He draped his cashmere top coat over one of the chairs at the bar and sat in the chair next to it. His olive-cuprous face was framed in soft light from stainless steel lamps on both sides of him, their glow muted by peach colored shades. He ordered a plate of crab fitters and a glass of viognier. While he waited for his food, he sipped the wine and watched the crowd of patrons through the large mirror behind the bar. He had been back in country for less than five hours after spending a year overseas. Still, as he listened to the raucous Friday night laughter from a group drinking champagne at one end of the bar, he felt as if he had never left.

Outside, snow was starting to lightly fall and limousines and taxicabs were pulling up and disgorging passengers. A white-haired limousine driver named Alex, whom Hank had known in the old days when Alex hadn't been a limo driver, came inside and approached the bar. The old man ran his hands along the sides of a huge vase filled with artificial red flowers resting not far from Hank's right shoulder. The flowers were attached to thick green stalks that reminded Hank of the rhubarb his mother used to grow on the side patch down the hill from their house. That had been in even older days.

After a few moments, the limo driver stopped frittering with the vase and came over to Hank. "You know what happened, don't you?" He was speaking in Farsi, his native language.

"No," Hank said, "I've been away."

The limo driver whispered something to Hank.

"You're kidding me. I don't believe it."

"He's got a helluva nerve coming here," Alex said. "He's sitting down there right now."

"The past is the past," Hank said.

"Yes, you're right."

Alex went away. Hank couldn't help himself and stood and peered down into the lower level dining room. Alex was right; Skipper Lane was sitting there, his back against the partition separating the dining room from the kitchen. There were two young men with him and a bottle of champagne rested in an ice bucket next to their table. All Hank could say to himself was: the stupid little bastard. The arrogant stupid little bastard.

The bartender had set down the plate of crab fritters and silverware and a napkin on the bar in front of Hank. Alex returned as the bartender left.

"Have you seen the papers?" he asked.

Hank shook his head and stabbed one of the fritters with his fork.

Alex took out a newspaper clip from his jacket pocket. "See. Pardoned by President. Other legal issues remain."

"How long has he been back in town?"

"They say he really never left."

"Has anyone else from the old days seen him?"

The limo driver shrugged and left. Hank rolled his fritter in the aioli sauce and chewed it. After a few moments Alex returned again. "Perhaps he has regrets."

"No. His kind never does," Hank said.

"Still, it must not be easy coming here."

Hank chewed slowly and swallowed. "Skipper still has lots of friends on the Hill."

Alex wanted to say something but just then a young man whom Hank was supposed to meet came into the bar. He too had worked with Hank but that was long after Alex. The man was now a courier for one of the contract corporations that employed Hank in the new days. He had two women with him, a blonde and a brunette, and he took them to the vacant end of the bar and ordered drinks. Leaving the women, he approached Hank, who removed his coat from the chair next to him, and the man sat down.

"How's everything, Ray?" Hank asked him. "Want to try a taste?" He raised his glass of viognier.

"What is that stuff, Hank?"

"Viognier."

"What the hell is that?"

"White wine."

"It looks golden. Piss golden."

"Try a glass."

"No thanks, I'll stick to a beer." Ray nodded to the bartender who poured a glass of Stella from the tap and brought it over and left again. He picked up the glass with his thumb and two fingers. That was all that was left of his right hand.

"Will the surgeons give you new fingers?" Hank asked him.

"They say they have some kind of experimental electro-mechanical device that looks like skin and fits like a glove. They want to try it on me. If it works, the manufacturer will offer it to the V.A."

"Go for it then."

Ray shook his head slowly. "It still won't get me back in the field. Besides, this is a babe magnet." He held his hand up and twirled it around in a signal to the women at the end of the bar. One of the women, the brunette, raised a martini glass and signaled back. "See what I mean."

"Well, that's something to be cheerful about," Hank said.

"Why are you so sour?"

Hank waved his hand. "Some old unfinished business just came up."

Ray started to say something but Alex the limousine driver returned.

"You remember my sister?" Alex said. "Her son was an engineer in Tabriz. He has disappeared."

Hank rolled another of the fritters around in the aioli sauce and bit into it. "Do you understand Farsi?" he asked Ray.

"No," the younger man laughed. "I barely understand Pushtu and I was up in the mountains for over a year." His face was still dark from being in the high altitude sun, even though his injury had brought him back months ago, and it made the twinkle in his eyes even brighter as he spoke.

Hank told him the story about Skipper and the betrayal and the pardon and Alex and Alex's nephew.

"They say two Iranian nuclear scientists were arrested, tortured and killed because of that business," Ray said, this time with no twinkle in his eyes.

"Yes, they say that," Hank said.

"And a Russian microbiologist was a hit and run victim."

"They have a lot of drunk drivers in Russia."

Ray made a face, swallowed some of his beer, and then made another face.

"How in the hell did that sniper damage your hand?" Hank asked him.

"Had the radio to my ear."

"Lucky for you."

"I want something stronger than beer. How about you?"

Hank signaled to the bartender. "Two Bellinis," he said when the man neared.

"If it's true, it would be terrible," Alex said in English after the bartender left.

190

"If it's true."

"And there could be more."

"Or less." Hank wasn't going to make it easy for the old man. He looked up at the flat screen television in the corner. A Hornets-Celtics game was on.

"My nephew," Alex said. "You remember him from the Bekaa?"

"Yes," Hank said, "I remember him."

"My sister says he is dead."

Above them a trio of stainless steel ceiling fans twirled silently, pushing a cool soft breeze onto Hank's neck. It chilled him as he told Ray about the nephew who had saved Hank's butt by hiding him in a truck and driving him out of Lebanon and into Syria.

"I should take care of this myself," Alex said.

"Don't be stupid," Hank said. "Here in the middle of town? Besides there was a trial."

"And a pardon."

"And a pardon." Hank wasn't trying to talk him out of it, only wanted the old man to think it through logically.

"What about the others? There was no trial for their deaths."

"He didn't kill them."

"Didn't he? If the runt hadn't shot off his big mouth, they'd still be alive."

"He's a politician, a political operative, that's what they do, shoot off their mouths. This town is full of them." He looked Alex in the face. "Besides, you don't know that for sure."

The old limousine driver laughed. A harsh, almost bitter sound. "We've been in this business together, what, thirty years now?" He touched his nose with a finger. "I know. You know."

Hank was getting tired of this. He looked at the large Christmas wreath behind the bar. "Well, anyway, it's not up to you. Why don't you just let it drop?"

Ray had been listening to the two of them. "He has a point, Hank."

"It's not up to you, either. Why don't you just enjoy the company of those two ladies you came in with? Or are they just cover?"

Ray looked down the bar at the women. One of them, the blonde this time, waved at him. "Let me go make sure they're okay," he said. He walked to the end of the bar and kissed the brunette on the cheek and hugged the blonde.

"Their screams," Alex said finally. "Do you think Skippy hears their screams as they are being tortured? As they are taken to the hangman?"

"No, I don't," Hank said. He was becoming uncomfortable now. He could see how the old man was working himself up to doing something; already calling the little bastard Skippy.

"It could have been me," Alex said. "Or my family." He was rubbing his chin now, as if thinking it through, making up his mind.

"This is not your responsibility," Hank said.

"In the old days, it would have been the responsibility of all of us."

"In the old days Skipper would have never dared to shoot his mouth off."

Alex went off as Ray returned. "What was that all about?" he asked Hank.

The bartender set their Bellinis down in front of them. After he left, Hank explained about Alex's nephew.

"This is a bad thing," the younger man said.

The old limousine driver came back. "I should make the call," he said to Hank.

"Someone should." Hank stared again at the large Christmas wreath behind the bar.

"If I don't, who will?"

Hank took a long sip of his drink. "If you call, don't call across the river." He took out a pen and wrote a number on a cocktail napkin and slid it in front of Alex. "Call this number," he said, "if you insist. Tell whoever answers that you've seen Skipper here. Let them take care of it. Repeat the number." When the old man did so, Hank took back the napkin and rubbed it over a wet spot on the bar and watched the ink turn into a smear.

Alex nodded and left; Ray went back to his female companions at the end of the bar and Hank sat there silently, nursing his Bellini, still uncomfortable.

Alex returned later. "I made the call," he said.

Hank nodded.

"And when he leaves—"

Hank held up his hand. "I don't want to hear the details."

"That's right, don't get involved." There was a bitter tone in Alex's voice.

"No, it's just better if I don't know."

The old man looked at Hank's face for a moment and nodded. "Yes, you're right. I shouldn't have told you." He signaled to the bartender to bring them another round of drinks. When the man set the drinks down and left, he said, "Skippy shouldn't have come here."

"You're having second thoughts? That's no good."

"You are right. It's in motion."

"I told you not to tell me about it."

"It's just that, well, do you think it will be quick?"

"When we were in ops together, did you ever ask that question?"

"I am asking it now," Alex said.

Hank still wasn't going to make it easy for him even though the old man had already made the call. "You should have thought about that before."

The old man fell silent. He was turning morose.

Hank slapped him lightly on the shoulder. "In the end, fast or slow, what does it matter? But if you insist, it probably will be fast."

He stood again and looked down at the table where Skipper Lane was sitting. A congressman had joined the group and there was a fresh bottle of champagne in the ice bucket. Alex's eyes followed Hank's gaze.

"Strange, in the old days, the Hill used to clear out on Friday nights and we could slip in for drinks and no one would pay any attention to us."

"In the old days we could do a lot of things and no one would pay any attention to us."

"Maybe I should wait outside," Alex said.

Hank put his hand on the old man's shoulder again. "Don't get involved. You made the call."

"That's it. I am involved."

"Well, don't get more involved, then." Hank was starting to become irritated about the whole business.

"You're right, Hank." The old man looked out the window. The light snow was still falling and had covered the sidewalk. A couple entered the bar, their coats dusted with a fine white powder.

"Is he still there, Hank?"

Hank looked down into the dining room. Skipper Lane was still seated with the congressman and the two young men. He recognized one of them as a staffer on the House Intelligence Committee and felt sick. Skipper was sleek and well-coiffed, a far cry from the real old days when he and Hank were in their first year at Columbia Law. Skipper wasn't so sleek and well-coiffed then. Hank had only that one year. Every morning he would cross the plaza to the old law building, passing the awkward Alexander Calder sculpture that was dedicated to Wild Bill Donovan.

And then one day he knew what he really wanted to do. But Skipper had stayed and graduated and joined a white shoe law firm with a big lobbying practice.

"Yes," Hank said when he came back to the bar. "A congressman is with him."

"Do you think that will change things?" the old man asked.

"No," Hank said. "It changes nothing."

Ray left the two women and came back over. "The girls are hungry. Want to go into the dining room for some steak tartare and good red wine?"

Hank shook his head. He was watching Skipper Lane get up and leave the table; the runt was wearing lifts. A young woman at the front desk retrieved Lane's coat and helped him on with it. On the sidewalk, he hailed a cab and disappeared inside.

"Let's go to the Old Ebbitt instead and lose ourselves in the crowd."

Ray laughed. "What the hell, I'll go get the ladies."

Alex, who had been standing in the hotel foyer, came back over to Hank. "How do you think they will do it?"

"Why do you want to know?" Hank was tired again. "If you want vengeance, it matters. If you want justice, then what's the difference?" Hank wanted to get out of there now.

"My sister wants vengeance for her son. And I am the oldest man in the family."

"You should have killed him then instead of making the call."

"Perhaps again you are right." Alex walked away.

"Is he still carrying on about Skipper Lane?" Ray had returned to finish his drink.

Hank stepped out into the street. The snow was heavier and the sidewalk was deserted. He punched a number into his cell phone, waited a moment, and then said, "Is he still alive?"

"Oh, yes," a voice said. "For now."

Hank said nothing. He had known all along that it wouldn't be fast. These jobs never were. He had known it back at the Bis and so he had lied about it to Alex, trying to calm the old man, to ease his conscience for making the call.

"We have some more work for you," the voice continued.

Hank broke the connection.

Back inside the Ebbitt, he joined Ray and the women at a table.

"Why in the hell would that little sonofabitch dine in the Bistro Bis where he was sure to be recognized?" Ray asked.

"He was arrogant."

"That's the trouble with this town," Ray said. "Too many arrogant bastards."

"Ray," Hank said. "Why don't you just shut up about it." The cold tone of his voice shocked him and he said nothing more to the kid. He knew why Skipper Lane had gone to the Bis, he couldn't help himself. He had been a major player in this town and the Presidential pardon had put him back in the game. Like the old days. He could have gone to the Monocle or Charlie Palmer's but this night he had gone to the Bistro Bis.

Hank looked over at the women sitting on each side of Ray. They were beautiful, two of ten thousand beautiful women in Washington, and they were having a good time. In the old days, he would have come to Ebbitt's with Alex and some of the others and they would talk about the Redskins, or sailing, or skiing, or their own business, which they weren't really supposed to talk about, even among themselves, but did anyway. It was better then and he wished he could talk about any of those things now instead of Skipper Lane.

NO LOOSE ENDS

1

"I'm ready to retire," the slender well-dressed man said.

"No one ever retires from here," the middle-aged olive-skinned woman said. "Lots want to, but it's not permitted. You should know that."

"All I know is that I want out. Now," the man replied softly. "Just tell me when I can go. Next week? Next month? Whatever cases I have left someone else in the Unit can handle."

The olive-skinned woman shook her head. "The Chancellor won't give her permission. As long as you have open cases, you remain in the Unit. And you will always have open cases."

"There are only four left; give them to a newbie."

The woman laughed harshly and shook her head again. A sickly light shone from the sterile fluorescent tubes hanging above them. In the sunlight her complexion would have been pleasant, healthy, even attractive, but under the pale feeble rays her face was a leathery lattice of angry age lines.

"It doesn't work that way in the Unit. It never has. You knew that when you signed on." As the woman spoke, she slouched back in her chair and regarded him with the annoyance of a petty bureaucratic boss required to listen to a subordinate. The man was in his late forties, with close-cropped ash-blond hair showing streaks of gray at the temples, the color matching his mustache, which was kept at a military trim. Rummaging around in the clutter on her desk, she picked up a file folder, the legal kind called a Redwel, and glanced at it casually.

"See this?" she said, holding it out to him. "Now you have five cases. And we'll be getting plenty more at the end of the month."

The slender well-dressed man did not take the file folder from her, only staring calmly into her eyes, saying nothing. Finally, the woman set the folder back down atop the clutter of her desk.

"I want out," the man repeated, his voice still smooth.

"You know the Chancellor doesn't like loose ends. And you have five open cases. Can't be done." The women's eyes avoided him, were fixed on the file folder as she spoke, as if she could see inside it and read its contents.

"There must be a way," the man continued gently. "All we have to do is think."

"You *think*," the woman snarled. "That's what you're paid for. I'm paid to supervise."

The slender man didn't move, just smiled at her, saying nothing.

"What?" the woman finally asked.

"If all the cases were closed by the end of the month, before any new cases come in, my case load would be zero, right?"

"Yeah," the woman said. "If. And that's a big if." Her voice was shaky as she spoke, worried that the man might have gotten the upper hand, might leave, and she'd have to face the Chancellor alone.

2

"I said what happened," the little boy told the well-dressed man. "I said everything. First the lady asked me questions, then the man, and then the old man who was wearing a black robe. I said it over and over again while the other grownups listened. But they let him go."

"We can take care of him now," the well-dressed man said. "Your principal believed you. And your mother."

"Yes, but no one else," the little boy's mother said, her voice rasping with hate. "The trial almost destroyed Eric, the way he was forced to tell what that pig did to him. Over and over. I'm not going to let him testify again, even before an arbitrator. I won't put him through it."

"How long had he been tutored?" the well-dressed man said softly. "Before it started."

"Only a few weeks," the little boy's mother said.

3

"Are you the parent that called me?" the tutor asked.

"She's still at work," the slender, well-dressed man said. "She wants me to bring you to her house. Her son is at home now."

"She could have just given me the address. Why waste my time making an extra trip?"

"Don't worry, she said she'll pay you portal-to-portal. Hey, you're earning money right now. Besides, she was worried you might not find it; the streets are all awkward out here and run into each other at crazy angles. Let's take your car."

"No problem," the tutor said, smiling at his luck.

After about five minutes of twisting and turning through the streets, the two men were in front of a run-down tenement building. The slender, well-dressed man gestured for the tutor to enter ahead of him. Inside there were no lights and the hallway stank of urine. The tutor backed up quickly. "What the fuck is going on? Nobody lives here."

"But they die here," the well-dressed man said, producing an ice pick.

The tutor turned and started to say something, stopping when he saw the thin shiny piece of metal flashing towards his chest.

4

"I don't know why you asked me here," the pudgy-faced attorney said, downing his glass of Scotch. "I told you over the phone that my client is not interested in a stipulated settlement." His voice was bored, dismissive, matching his facial expression. "We're going to trial."

"I understand," the well-dressed man said. "It was a mistake."

"Well, why don't you just withdraw the charges and put my client back in the classroom? Where he can be useful, instead of languishing in the Rubber Room."

"I'm retiring. I just wanted to have a drink with you before I pack it in."

"Well, all right then," the pudgy-faced attorney said, gesturing to the bartender with his empty glass.

"No, don't bother. I've got something better."

The pudgy-faced attorney's eyes narrowed warily.

"It might be the best you've ever tasted." The slender, well-dressed man smiled warmly. "Single malt Scotch. Abelour, aged sixteen years."

"You have some?"

"Sure, I have two bottles in my car. One's yours, a little going away present."

The pudgy-faced attorney licked his lips. His eyes were no longer narrow, instead they gleamed with anticipation. "Where's your car?" he asked, getting off his bar stool.

"Right around the corner, in the alley where it's shady."

He popped the lock with the remote key and reached in and brought out a blue canvas sack with the two bottles of Abelour.

"Enjoy," he said, handing one of the bottles to the pudgy-faced attorney. The other man greedily grasped it with a flabby, moist paw.

"You know I'm glad your client won't settle by stipulation. I'd like to give him this other bottle to show him there's no hard feelings."

"I could do that for you."

"It wouldn't be the same," the slender well-dressed man said, a real sincere tone in his voice.

The other shrugged. "Have it your way. But he's not in the Rubber Room today, called in sick."

"I'll just drop by his house then," the well-dressed man said.

The pudgy attorney turned to go. He hadn't started his second step when the long piece of sharpened steel sliced between two folds of fat at the base of his neck. He fell to the ground, the bottle of expensive single-malt still clutched in his hand.

5

"You say my attorney sent you?" the well-muscled gym teacher asked.

"That's right," the slender well-dressed man said, stepping quickly inside. "It's about your disciplinary case."

"But I'm not supposed to talk about it with anyone but my attorney." He was looking at the well-dressed man through slitted eyes.

"It's okay. Believe me, your attorney won't complain. The case is going away. That's why I'm here."

"About time," the muscled gym teacher said. "I've been sitting in the Rubber Room for almost two years, waiting for a hearing to clear me." He was speaking in a flat tone, the jaw muscles barely moving as he squinted at the other. "Well, come on in."

The well-dressed man followed him into the living room.

"I guess this calls for a celebration. Do you want a drink?"

"Sure."

The muscled teacher opened up a cabinet and took out a bottle and two glasses. "Rum, okay?"

The well-dressed man nodded. "I'm just a little curious," he said. "Now that this is all over, why did the little girl make up stories about you?"

The muscled teacher handed him a glass and then put his glass to his lips and downed the contents. "You kidding? Have you seen the body on that little bitch? A real cockteaser, she was looking for it and when she didn't get it right away from me, she made up a bunch of lies."

"So you never touched her?" the well-dressed man said.

"Not that the little slut didn't want me to." The teacher laughed with a sneer.

"That's what I figured. Say, could I get a little ice in this drink?"

"No problem. Come on in the kitchen."

The well-dressed man watched as the muscled teacher took a tray of ice cubes out of the refrigerator.

"Help yourself," the teacher said.

While the well-dressed man plopped a couple of the cubes into his glass, the teacher refilled his.

"Here's to you," said the well-dressed man, raising his glass. "Today's your day."

The muscled teacher clinked his glass against the well-dressed man's and drank. As he tilted his head to finish the contents at the bottom of the glass, the thin piece of shiny steel arced up under his jaw and drove straight through the flesh and cartilage until the tip hit the center of his brain.

6

"It was a false positive," the scrawny, pasty-faced woman said. "They screwed up the drug test and took me out of the classroom. I was just sick that day. Tired, you know how it is."

"I understand," the well-dressed man said. "But there's no sense standing out here in the hallway talking about it."

The scrawny woman smiled at him. A smile mixed with desperation and hope. "I was just watching the six o'clock news; I wouldn't mind some company."

The well-dressed man smiled back. "It would be my pleasure."

As they watched television, he asked her, "Do you have any smack in the house?"

The scrawny woman's face twisted up. "What the fuck are you talking about? Who are you? I'm calling my attorney." She started to punch numbers into her cell phone.

The point of the thin shiny piece of steel rammed into her forehead just as she tapped the last number. She dropped to the floor with unseeing eyes.

As the well-dressed man walked to the door, he could hear a tinny voice repeating, "Hello, hello."

7

"You don't look like you indulge," the oily man said. "This school's mine, you understand? I'm the chapter chair. Nothing moves here unless it's through me. Whatever you want to buy, I'm the one you have to see. But like I said, you don't look like you use."

"I like to relax," the well-dressed man said, "after a long day in the classroom."

"Hey, I can understand that," the oily man said.

"But I'd like some weight, I don't want to have to keep coming back."

The oily man scratched his chin. "How much?"

"A key."

"A kilo of heroin? I don't keep that much on school premises."

"I'll take what you have right now, the rest later."

"How much can you spend?"

"This," said the well-dressed man, taking the ice pick out of his pocket.

8

"Little kids," the Crone said, "mean big money. How old is your daughter?"

"Four," the slender, well-dressed man said.

"The market's strong for that age," the Crone said. "Can you bring her here to the school?"

"You do the films here?" The well-dressed man placed some shock in his voice.

"Can you think of a better place?" the Crone laughed. "We use an actual classroom. The freaks love the setting, it triples the selling price. How far can we go with your daughter? The real sickos will pay top dollar."

"Can I take a look at the set up first?"

Inside the classroom, the well-dressed man saw a video camera on a tripod and a pad stretched over the teacher's desk. Two spotlights on the sides of the desk were aimed down at the mat. "This is where it's done?"

The Crone laughed. "This is the money pit."

The well-dressed man walked around to the rear of the video camera and turned it on and looked through the viewing lens.

"Stand in front of the camera so I can focus," he said to the Crone.

"You want to make me a star?" she laughed, stepping where he directed.

"Sure. Just tilt your head to the side, close your eyes and look up as if you're dreaming."

The Crone did as he said and never saw the thin piece of steel arcing toward her left ear.

9

The well-dressed man stood at the end of the pier, overlooking the Hudson River. Placing the ice pick under his foot, he pulled up on the handle until it snapped. Then he tossed both pieces far out into the water, where he had thrown all the others. Using the ice picks had been a good idea. Why waste bullets. It took a little more time, going around to several hardware stores to buy the picks but the extra effort had paid off. He smiled at the thought; he had always put extra effort into his cases. He looked out at the fast moving currents, gray and ugly under low scudding clouds. He patted the inside breast pocket of his suit coat, where the last ice pick rested. His work day was almost over.

1 O

"You closed the five cases," the olive-skinned woman said, an annoyed tone in her voice. "And you closed them so fast. So I guess this is goodbye. I'll have to tell the Chancellor you will be leaving. She'll be pissed."

"Six cases," the well-dressed man said. "And she won't be pissed."

"Six cases? But you only had five open cases."

The well-dressed man pushed the clutter on her desk to one side and sat on the edge. He looked down at the olive-skinned woman and smiled his sweetest smile. "The Chancellor asked me to do her a favor. A very big favor," he said as he took the thin shiny piece of steel out of his pocket. "As you said, she doesn't like loose ends."

(This story first appeared in Hardboiled Magazine #39, January, 2009).

HOLDOUT

"We are unable to agree on a verdict, Your Honor." The forewoman's voice was short, clipped and in a frustrated tone. The air conditioning was not working well and the courtroom was hot and stuffy. She placed her hand on the railing in front of her, gripping its highly polished surface for support.

"Have you really tried?" The judge looked down at her.

"We have, Your Honor. The vote still remains eleven to one." She stared with anger-filled eyes at Juror Number Seven, a young thin man sitting erect.

The thin young man looked back at her with a blank expression. His face was well-tanned, the skin still smooth with youth, the only blemish a pale horizontal scar that ran along a slight indentation below his right cheekbone. He had been silent, unassuming, during the trial and no one in the courtroom had paid much attention to him until now.

The defense attorney stood and waved a sheaf of papers that he was holding in a finely manicured hand.

"Your Honor, I move for a mistrial. The jury has been deliberating for three days, it would be unconscionable to allow this travesty to continue."

His client, Booger Dave Jenkins, looked down, a tiny smile erupting on his face. He was surrounded by a trio of court officers, hands in a ready position. They had been expecting a guilty verdict and were hovering just behind Booger Dave in case he tried to make a break for it.

The young woman prosecutor jumped to her feet, anguish filling her soft ebony face. "Please, Your Honor, send the jury back for more deliberations."

The parents of the little girl were seated in the second row, they had been there every day of the trial. Juror Number Seven didn't look at them but glanced up at the wall behind the judge.

Justice is the Foundation of Society proclaimed large words carved into the paneling and lettered in gold paint.

"You have given the jury a lengthy Allen Charge, ordering them to try their best to reach a verdict. Telling any holdouts to try and agree with the majority. It has had no effect." The defense attorney patted Booger Dave's shoulder. "It is time to end this. Anything further would be a miscarriage of justice."

"I'm afraid, Ms Robinson that I must declare a mistrial."

"Your Honor, please."

"No, that's it. I cannot ask this jury to continue to deliberate." The judge glared at Juror Number Seven. "But if you feel there was anything untoward in the deliberations, that a holdout acted in bad faith, you can always conduct a grand jury investigation."

Booger Dave looked up at Juror Number Seven and smiled more broadly. The thin young man did not smile back.

"I wish I could thank all the members of the panel for their attention and time to this trial and their effort to reach a verdict, but I cannot, Madame Forelady. But I do thank you and the other ten members. I hereby declare a mistrial."

"Your Honor," the young black prosecutor said, "The People of this State want the defendant's bail revoked."

"I object, Your Honor," the defense attorney said. "My client has made every appearance and has been here for the duration of the trial. He has placed his Tribeca apartment as collateral to make bail, which is $1,000,000 I must remind this court. He is innocent and has no intention of going anywhere."

"Bail is continued."

Booger Dave looked at Juror Number Seven and mouthed silently, "Thank you, kind sir, thank you."

The thin young man still kept the blank look on his face.

The family of the little girl was silent, stunned by the judge's decision. Then the mother broke into loud wails, so piercing that one or two of the jurors flinched. The little girl's father said nothing, only stared at Juror Number Seven, then put his arm around his wife's shoulder and ushered her out of the courtroom.

Outside the Criminal Courts Building, television crews crowded the sidewalk, lining both sides of the main entrance as if they were some sort of ghoulish honor guard, ready to salute with microphones and cameras. When the jury emerged, someone shoved a mike in the face of an elderly man with tired eyes that folded into a lined, fleshy face.

"Why couldn't you come to a verdict?" the media genius asked the man, pushing the mike up to his mouth.

The old man swiped at the mike, looked over at Juror Number Seven and spit on the sidewalk. The crowd of media hounds followed his gaze, their eyes locking onto the blank stare of the thin young man. Suddenly, they swung en masse in his direction.

"Did you vote for acquittal?" someone shouted.

"How does it feel to let Booger Dave loose on the streets of the City?"

"Don't you have any pity for the family of that little girl?"

"The blood of Booger Dave's next victim will be on your hands."

The thin young man ignored them, turning and walking down the street towards the subway entrance. He was waiting to cross at the light when a beefy florid-faced man approached him, eyes blazing hostility.

He recognized the other as a witness for the prosecution, a homicide detective who had testified at length about discovering the little girl's body in the basement of Booger Dave's apartment building.

The detective came up close to the thin young man. "I don't know who's the bigger piece of shit . . . you or that maggot-ridden turd you just sent back into society." He looked away and then back at the young man. "There are only two things I wish. You know what they are?"

The young man's skin tightened along his facial bones but he said nothing. There was nothing he could say, nothing that would matter, that would make sense to the detective. He didn't even shake his head, just stood at the curb, keeping the blank stare on his face.

"Two things, I'm gonna tell you." The voice was a hate-filled snarl, yet so low and his face so calm that any passerby would think he was merely asking for the correct time. "Number one, that I live long enough to see that diseased punk's putrid face ground into a thousand pieces of flesh and fed to junkyard dogs; two, that I never come across you again, or I'll be on trial for murder."

Three days ago at the end of the trial, the prosecutor, a young black woman with the fire of justice burning in her belly, had given a powerful summation. Women on the jury cried when she held up photos of the little girl, their tears quickly subsumed by sobs of grief from the family.

Juror Number Seven never looked at the pictures. He had no need. Instead, he focused his attention on Booger Dave, seated next to his attorney, head bent, scribbling on a note pad, as the prosecutor summoned every ounce of emotion in her plea for justice. Below his bald pate, one of Booger Dave's eyes bulged and he worked his mouth, twisting it from a grin to a silent laugh, back and forth, finally tilting a lump of battered flesh that served as his left ear and fixing an evil smirk on his face. When the young prosecutor reminded the jury how the little girl must have felt in her final moments of agony, before the defendant tightened the garrote around her neck for the last time, Booger Dave took the eraser nub of his pencil and stuck it into his nostril and rooted around. Taking the pencil back out, he rubbed the mucous covered tip along the table top. All the while Juror Number Seven watched him with a blank expression.

Three nights later, the young thin man with the indented cheek stood outside Booger Dave's apartment building.

Around eleven, the freak emerged just as he did the previous two nights. The thin young man followed him to a bar a couple of blocks away and waited outside for a couple of minutes. Entering the place, he walked to the end of the bar where the lighting was softer and he had a clear view of the entire establishment.

Booger Dave was seated in one of the booths against the wall. A brunette cocktail waitress in red short pants, push out bra and high heels had brought him a large can of Foster's beer and a glass. He said something to her as she poured the beer and she made a face and walked away. He never noticed the tall thin young man who was watching him from the end of the bar.

It was almost midnight before Booger Dave spotted his prey. She had come into the bar, just as she had the previous two nights. She always ordered a scotch and soda, drank it for a few minutes, paid and left. Booger Dave always left right behind her. The thin young man had followed them as the woman walked to a nearby apartment building. Booger Dave watched as the woman let herself in with a key. The thin young man did some checking and learned that the woman was a practical nurse, doing home care for a wealthy paraplegic. She was a widow with an eleven-year-old daughter who was home alone while the nurse did early night duty. He believed Booger Dave knew that as well. The freak would keep following the woman until he felt it was safe to strike, maybe a push in robbery, knife to the throat and force the woman up to her apartment. Then Booger Dave would do them both. The little girl for sure.

The thin young man knew as he followed them out of the bar that he couldn't wait any longer. He quickened his steps until he was only a few paces behind Booger Dave.

As they reached the alleyway by the woman's apartment building, the young man tapped him on the shoulder. Booger Dave turned and when he saw the young man a smile quickly formed on his lips. "It's you, my savior," he said. "I'd love to chat, but I'm in a bit of a hurry."

The young man unzipped his leather jacket and Booger Dave quickly stepped back. Not quickly enough as a fine mist from the aerosol can of animal tranquilizer covered his face.

When Booger Dave came around, the young man set down his drink and walked over to him and ripped the patches of thick gauze from his eyes. Booger Dave blinked and tried to rub them but felt his hands and arms secured tightly. He saw that he was tied to a straight-backed wooden chair, a wire looped around his neck and running down his back where it was secured to his feet. He attempted to yell but his mouth was sealed with silver electrical tape and the only sound he could make was a pathetic gurgle.

The young man ripped the tape off of Booger Dave's mouth and stood looking at him with a blank stare.

"What is this place?" Booger Dave asked.

"A courthouse."

Booger Dave looked around. The room was made up of four cement walls painted a dull gray and a bare small wattage light bulb hung from the ceiling. The only other furniture was a small table with a bottle and glass on it. And some odd-shaped object he couldn't fathom.

"What the fuck you talkin' about? This ain't no courthouse."

"You're in my jurisdiction, now."

"You're no judge."

"You're wrong. Dead wrong."

"Fuck you. You're fuckin' crazy."

The young man went back to his drink and took a sip. It was overproof bourbon, strong and good, with a smoky and simultaneously spicy taste on the palate. He swallowed and set the glass back down on the table. "If you keep talking like that, I'm going to have to hold you in contempt of court."

Booger Dave glared at the young man, his mouth twisted with hate. "You better let me out of here, now."

The young man again sipped his whisky and said nothing.

"Just let me out of here and we can forget this whole thing."

The young man ignored him. "The beautiful thing about this country is that everyone gets a trial, even sick bastards like you," he said.

"I already had a trial," Booger Dave sneered.

"I've reconvened the proceedings."

"How's that?"

"The jury's going to take another vote."

"What? What jury?"

"You're looking at him."

"You're crazy."

"But first we need a little more evidence. Remember you haven't testified yet. Do you swear to tell the truth, the whole truth and nothing but the truth?"

"Testimony? I don't have to testify, it's my right."

The young man walked back over to the table and picked up the odd-shaped object. It was a long thin scabbard made of leather and brass-tipped at the end. Pulling on it, he withdrew what appeared to be a long knife.

"An antique Afghan Khyber short sword," he said. "Isn't it beautiful?"

The blade was long for a knife, over twenty-two inches, and had been crafted for close quarter mountain fighting. He had brought it back as a souvenir when his tour of duty ended. His uncle, who had been a Marine in the Pacific during World War Two and an avid deer hunter, showed him how the short sword could also be used for hunting, gutting and skinning wild game. He admired the carved horn handle and its brass fitting with its intricately patterned inlay. Even in the squalid gloom of the lone light bulb, he could sense its beauty and it made him sad.

He walked over to the chair. Suddenly, his hand slashed down with the knife. Once. Twice. Blood poured from both sides of Booger Dave's face. "Remember the whole truth."

The freak started screaming and the young man sealed his mouth once again with the electrical tape. Going back to the table, he set the knife down and freshened up his drink and sipped it. After several minutes, the screams had been reduced to muted whimpering sounds

When the screaming finally ended, the young man ripped the tape back off. Booger Dave vomited on the floor, filling the room with the sour stench of fear mingling with pure evil. The young man was unfazed. He had seen and smelled worse.

"Unfortunately, you won't be able to raise your hand and swear on the Bible, but I can take your word that you'll be truthful, correct?"

"Yeah, okay. I'll tell the truth."

"So help you God?"

Booger Dave bobbed his head, splashing thin drops of blood on the front of his shirt.

"Good, then we'll take your testimony. How many more little girls were you planning to kill?" the young man asked gently.

"I don't have to answer that. I have Fifth Amendment rights."

"The Fifth Amendment doesn't apply in this jurisdiction," the young man said, picking up the Khyber short sword. "You have to answer all questions, the penalties for refusing can be severe." He prodded Booger Dave's groin with the point of the sword.

"My ears, you cut them. They're bleeding too much, you've got to stop it . . ."

The thin young man picked up a backpack that was resting in a corner and took out a small towel. Walking over to the table, he poured some of the overproof liquor out of the bottle onto the towel. Then he dabbed the towel against the sides of Booger Dave's head. The sicko didn't even flinch and saw the surprise in the young man's eyes.

"My old lady did worse than that to me, many times," he said.

"Is that how your ear became mangled?"

Booger Dave laughed. "The old bitch would get drunk and hit me with her fist, a lamp, the iron, anything she could get her hands on. But I deserved it, not minding her, not taking care of my little sister when she went out."

"So that's why you hate her?"

"Who, the little girl?"

"No, your mother."

"I loved my mother, she only wanted the best for me, that's why she had to punish me. I was bad and I made her drink too much."

The thin young man nodded, he had heard enough about Booger Dave's childhood. "I'll ask you again. Where were you going tonight?"

"I was just going home."

"So why were you were following that woman?"

Booger Dave shrugged his shoulders. "I see her around the neighborhood, I thought maybe I could talk to her, get to know her."

"And get to know her daughter too?"

Booger Dave shrugged again. "I saw the little tease prancing around the supermarket once. She wants it more than her mother."

"You're a real expert on women, huh?"

Booger Dave smirked. "I know what they all want, just like my little sister, the cockteaser, leading me on, then trying to fight me. But in the end they always give it up."

"And if they don't?"

"Then they have to be punished. When you're bad you have to be punished."

"Anything else you want to add in your defense?"

Booger Dave leaned forward. "I'm having trouble hearing you," he said. "My ears are ringing."

"The jury will now deliberate."

The thin young man finished his drink and put on a long plastic raincoat. Then he opened his backpack and took out a pair of heavy duty leather field gloves and put them on.

"What's going to happen now?" Booger Dave asked.

"This is the death penalty phase of the trial," the young man said, walking over to the chair and starting to work.

The police administrative aide dropped the small gift-wrapped box on the florid faced detective's desk.

"What's this?" he said.

The aide shrugged her shoulders. "Beats me. Delivery boy said it was for you. Make sure you got it. Right away."

"Delivery boy?"

"Yeah. A young thin guy with a scar on his left cheek and wearing a leather jacket. Funny, the scar looked like an old bullet wound."

The detective blinked but said nothing. After the aide left, he opened the box and saw a photo of a face so mangled and mauled that it was unrecognizable. The photo rested on top of a thick wad of gauze. The detective turned the box upside down and shook it. The gauze fell out on the desk. He picked it up and felt something hard inside. Unwrapping the gauze, he saw the misshapen mass of flesh and cartilage that he had seen too many times before.

The package was in the mail box when the little girl's father went outside. He brought it in with the mail and set it on the kitchen table. Then he took the mail into the bedroom where his wife was resting. He set the mail on the bed, kissed her forehead and went back into the kitchen. Taking a bottle of overproof bourbon down from the cabinet, he dropped a couple of ice cubes into a glass and poured a long shot on top of them.

The old man took a drink and then slowly unwrapped the gauze until he saw what he had expected. A right ear caked with dried blood.

He smiled a grim smile. He had taught his nephew well.

Breinigsville, PA USA
23 August 2009
222818BV00003B/11/P